Echoes of Home

Nordun's Way Book Three

Elles Lohuis

Also By Elles Lohuis

The Horse Master's Daughter (*Nordun's Way* Book One)

A Pilgrim's Heart (*Nordun's Way* Book Two)

Download your copy of the hand-drawn map of Nordun's travels, specially commissioned for the *Nordun's Way* series books One, Two and Three at www.elleslohuis.com or scan the QR Code.

Echoes Of Home

Nordun's Way Book Three

ELLES LOHUIS

Black Peony Press

First published by Black Peony Press in 2023
ISBN 9789083240886 (Paperback)
ISBN 9789083240893 (Hardback)
ISBN 9789083240879 (E-book)

In loving memory of my parents
Geerhard and Annie Lohuis

Contents

One

Tibet, Eastern Kham
The Year of The Wood Rooster
1412 (1285 AD)

Dawn has broken. She basks the kitchen in pale hues of purple and pink, the stove murmurs a mellow good morning. It's my first time waking at home after a long and eventful pilgrimage to Lhasa. All went well, and all should be well on this fine fall morning—except it isn't.

"Let me get this right." Father's voice sounds eerily calm as he takes his seat opposite Karma. "You left my daughter in Lhasa without a word, disappeared for many moons on all of us, and now you're back, asking my permission to take her to the jaws of hell?"

My empty stomach clenches. That subtle dark tinge in Father's voice—it's the reaction I expected. He's my father, so it goes unsaid. Besides, the facts are not in Karma's favor, and Father got them all right—except for one.

My heart goes out to Karma, sitting opposite Father, his head bent, his hands on his knees. I knew he would leave me in Lhasa. After all, I let him hear his mother's voice, her desperate call for her long-lost son to come home to her. How could he not give in to his mother's plea?

"Yes, Palden-la." Karma's manner mirrors Father's calm. "I am asking you for your permission." He looks up. A faint ray of morning sun catches his eyes and reveals the rich shade of emerald in them.

Karma, my love.

We'd gotten so close on our journey to Lhasa, but I had to let him go. Little did I know our parting would hurt so much. His absence ripped right through the tender hollows of my heart, leaving it raw and exposed. I would do it all again—even though I didn't expect him to come back to me.

"I made a grave mistake by leaving." He straightens his shoulders. "I betrayed your trust, the family's trust, but most of all, I betrayed Nordun." His eyes search and find mine as I sit at his side. "I shouldn't have left like you like that, my love."

I wring my hands around my cup and nod. "You're here now." My heart is his, no matter what happened, and he knows it.

"I'm sorry for all the grief I caused." He puts his hands on the table and faces Father. "I'm willing to do whatever it takes to set this straight, Palden-la."

Father's eyes narrow on Karma in a harsh stare, and I bite my lip. This is not looking good. Father shakes his head.

"I trusted you with my daughter." A sharp edge rims his voice. "Abandoning her like that. What the hell were you thinking?" Bitter blame soars over the table at Karma, and I cringe. Father's going to fly off the handle any moment—for sure, he will.

Heavy boots resound in the hallway, rapid thumps paired with a few rough huffs. A sharp outcry roars from the doorway. "He wasn't thinking, the idiot!"

My spirit lifts—it's Dendup, my trusted family elder who came with us to Lhasa. With his shirt wide open, and his chuba slung across his chest, he lurches into the kitchen in his typical boisterous way.

"You fool!" He charges at Karma and takes him in a mean hold, saving us all from Father's expected show-down. "Disappearing on us in the middle of the night," Dendup croaks.

For a moment it looks like he's going to wrestle Karma, but then his face bursts into a rowdy laugh. "At least you've got the decency to come back." He throws a cheeky smile my way. "Knowing we're going to give you hell, right, sister?"

A fierce heat flushes my cheeks, flaring all the way up to my temples. Dendup teased me all the way to Lhasa and back, and I'll never get used to it—silly me.

Dendup squeezes himself on the other side of Karma and gives Father a curt nod. I tear myself away from the looming silence and hasten to pour the men tea.

"What were you thinking, taking off like that?" Dendup slurps his tea with delight while our cups stand untouched. He's a master in savoring the pleasant in a tense situation like this.

"You've been trying to hide it on me, but I know you've been wanting to search for your blood relatives for a long time—why now?" Dendup's cup lands with a bang on the low table.

Blood relatives. The sheer contempt with which he utters that word makes me shudder.

Karma shrugs, and I wring a cloth between my hands. How to explain?

"It's me." My voice is thin, but the words grab everybody's attention. "I told him to go look for them."

Karma's eyes flash at me and Dendup jumps in his seat. Father doesn't even blink. I wish he would.

"You?" Dendup snorts over his tea. "Why?" Foam sprays from his mouth, and I bow my head.

Dendup's been nothing but good to me, and I never told him, not once. So many times, he comforted me on our way home, thinking Karma had left me for no reason. My fingers fray the fringe of the rag. What must he think of me now?

"It came to me that Karma's mother is still alive." The words slip from my lips, but I don't know how to tell them more. For sure they would not understand? Only Karma does, for we share our dreams, he and I. We're bound by them, but how to explain?

"I told him that night in Lhasa." I fling the cloth next to the stove and sink down at Father's side. "So you see, he had to go."

Karma's hand moves across the table and his eyes lock mine in a tender hold.

"I took off too hastily," he says. His restless gaze darts from me to Father and Dendup. "But I didn't want to burden any of you with my obscure past—or my uncertain future." His fingertips brush against mine.

"Uncertain it is, as these kinfolk of yours are brutes." Dendup's face twists in a grimace. "We've all heard the stories, butchering everybody who stands in their way."

Karma's jaw sets, and I slide my hands over his. Dendup speaks the truth. Karma's kinfolk came from the North over our mountains, and established a truce with our tribes a long time ago. Seems we have been fortunate though, as the tales of their conquests in other lands speak of a cruelty that can only be whispered. Ruthless plunder and vicious slaughter of boys and men alike, of young girls and women violated and enslaved until death, and of entire settlements and even monasteries burned down to the ground. These men have no mercy, it seems. Still, it has no bearing on my love, as he grew up on Grandfather's side of our family, and has only known of our way.

"But surely, their Khan has turned to Buddhism now?" I try, but Dendup's scornful laugh swipes my argument right off the table.

"Buddhist or not, their ways are barbaric." Dendup's smug tone says it all.

Of course, he's right, but how conveniently he seems to forget the reason he and Karma went to Lhasa. They didn't go on pilgrimage. No, they went to hunt down and kill my father's brother—on orders from the family to avenge my mother's death. Luckily, they didn't succeed—but they sure came close.

I rest my head against the wall. He seems so calm, so quiet, my love, but only I see him for real. Regret and restiveness cloud in the far yonder of his eyes. How my heart longs to hold him close.

"Dammit, Karma, I've cursed you all the way from Lhasa to here." Dendup sighs and rubs his bushy brows. "Hell, I even cursed you getting up this morning for pulling a stunt like that."

I can't help the brief smile peeping through my lips. He sure did curse Karma—all the way.

"But I've known you since you came to the family, being no taller than my knee's high." A grave shadow falls over his face. "We've been on the road together a long time and you've proven to be a real brother—more than that. You've proven your loyalty to the family over and over again." My ribs tighten and my mouth goes dry.

Loyalty to the family. How neatly Dendup places these tricky words. Karma never mentioned it, but Lanying, my sister from the Han side of the mountains, explained it to me. Loyalty to the family means executing the family's orders, and Karma's done more honor killings than anybody ever had to.

"I can't stop you from venturing out there, you're too damn stubborn, like me." Dendup's sneer is snarky, that's for sure, but there's an airy undertone sounding through.

"I guess the only way to make sure you return safe is to come with you on the search for those kinfolk of yours." His arm slides over Karma's shoulder. "Besides, it's time we conquer that side of the mountains once again in favor of the family's trade."

Karma shoots up, and my heart skips a beat. Father still doesn't move.

"You are?" Karma's voice soars with surprise, and I don't know whether that's good or bad. All I'm thinking about is how Dendup's company will strengthen my case for going too.

"I am." Dendup's tone is persistent. "But first we prepare." He slaps Karma's shoulder and hands me his empty cup, with a shifty smile.

I gather the other cups, still full with lukewarm tea. It's a done deal for Dendup—but for me? If only Father would say something, anything. I don't dare to look.

"Winter's coming and the mountains won't let us pass." Dendup's all reasoning now. "We'll leave some time after Losar."

Father sips the cup I poured. Still, there's not a word from his lips.

"That's great." Karma beams a smile at Dendup. "But I'm not leaving without my love." He bows his head to Father, but there's still no reaction from his side.

"I'll wait for you." I swing the kettle. Steam hisses as tea slushes on the scorching stove.

"I'm not leaving without Nordun." Karma lifts his chin and looks Father straight in the eye. "Tell me what it will take to get your permission, Palden-la."

I have to give it these two, the two men I love most—they're quite a match. I hold my breath as the stony silence between the two of them submerges the kitchen in a suffocating solidity.

With reluctance, Father shifts in his seat.

"I'll think about it." His response releases my trapped breath and I gasp for air. He'll think about it. *This is good.*

"Nordun and I will go to the ngakpa this morning." Father sits back. "He deserves to know what happened to his wife in Lhasa firsthand." He rests his hands on his knees.

The ngakpa. An iron fist locks around my heart. It was the ngakpa's wife who provided my father's brother with the snake spell that killed my mother. The two of them fled to Lhasa when their devious play came to light this summer. Now Father wants me to tell the ngakpa how Karma and Dendup hunted them down. *This is not good.*

"We'll be back by midday." Father gets up. "We'll talk after that." He moves out of the kitchen without saying another word.

"I'm sorry, love." Karma jumps up, and I freeze.

I don't want to go. His hands hold mine.

"All of it?" I blink and he nods. Of course, all of it. It's all or nothing for us now.

My feet stumble through the hallway. My mind cries out. *What a fool I've been.*

For only a fool would expect Father to be satisfied with the vague account I gave him of our Lhasa adventure yesterday.

Just as only a fool would expect him to let me go with Karma in search of his mother and kinsfolk.

After all, what father *would* let his daughter go off with her lover to the far grasslands of Mongolia like that?

Two

A crisp breeze sweeps around the courtyard. Winter will come any day.

"We'll walk," Father says. So we walk—out of the gate, along the lane where the tall trees sway their barren branches and the hardy grass retreats. From the corner of my eye, I watch Father stride on and my heart expands at his sight. His shoulders squared, his chin held high—he's looking better than ever. Now that Uncle and his sons have left the stables, Father's the master, a force to be reckoned with once again.

"I never got the chance to tell you how proud I am." Father's arm pulls me in and I flinch at my own secretive scheming. Here I am, with Father expressing his truth to me, when all I think about is masking the terrible facts.

"Making that arduous journey to do all that merit." He looks at me, his eyes radiant and clear. "And protecting my only brother from a certain death; you amaze me again and again, my child."

He knows! Gravel crunches under my heels. Father knows I had a hand in Uncle's rescue. How? My mind twists and turns. I'm not good at hiding and he knows me well, even though we spent almost my entire childhood apart. Maybe he's just guessing. My shoulders sag. I glance aside.

"I am right, am I not?" The sharp tone he carried in our earlier conversation has faded and a warm smile breaks on his lips.

"Want to tell me what happened before we get to the ngakpa?" His hand squeezes my shoulder. "It won't change the facts or the outcome." His gentle gaze catches mine. "Nor will it ever change my love for you."

Shame blurs my vision. No, it won't change the outcome, not for Uncle, and not for me. Father's love knows no boundaries, nor does it set any conditions, and my heart understands that by now. Still, it might change the outcome for Karma if Father knows the details. *My love.* Do I really need to tell it all? I take in a sharp breath.

"Karma and Dendup, they took real good care of me along the way." My voice wavers. Where to begin? "When we came to Lhasa, they got me a safe place to stay at a nuns' monastery."

Father's hand still rests on my shoulder. He will not let this go. I better not mention that Karma tried everything in his power to keep me at the monastery, including bribing the guard. He worried for my safety, I understand, but Father might take it all wrong.

"And there was a woman from the other side of the mountains in our caravan," I say. "We became good friends, and she helped me." I won't tell him of Lanying's flamboyant ways, but I'll have to mention her part in it all.

"Helped you with what?" Father's hand slides off my shoulder. We've come to the higher grassland surrounding the village.

"She found out where Uncle and Khandro were staying." I heave. The truth weights heavy when climbing a hill. "We went to see them with two of her guards, hoping they would flee if they knew Dendup and Karma had come." Well, that was what

I had in mind, but Lanying thought they needed a bit more convincing. That's why she brought the guards, which turned out to be a good thing.

"When we arrived, Karma and Sonam were already there." My thoughts scramble over to that frightful night when Father's best friend Sonam turned up too.

"Of course they were, they had to act fast." Father tips back his head. "And Dendup stayed at the inn, keeping the company of his trusted chang, I guess."

I nod and halt as we reach the top. "So then we made this plan that I would go in and talk to Karma and Sonam, distracting them so Lanying and her men could get Uncle out." I turn to face Father. He shakes his head.

"Talk." He anchors his hands at his hips. "To Karma and Sonam?"

I shrug. "It was the only thing I could think of." I stare into the distance. *Talk.* How silly I must sound right now.

"But things got a little confused as I went in." My fingertips swipe the last of the long grass as we make our way to the village ahead. *Confused.* That's quite an understatement.

"Khandro tried to flee with the spell." A flash of sharp silver slices in front of me. I blink. *Karma's blade.* "But I threw it into the fire," I add in one breath—there's no way I'm ever going to tell how I hurled myself in front of that knife.

"The spell, it burst into flames." My voice lowers. "It spread so fast." I shudder as Uncle's twisted, blackened face flashes through in my mind.

"Fortunately, Lanying's men got us out before everything came crashing down." My heels dig into the soft earth. The sweet stench of Uncle's scorched flesh fills my nose again. Bile rises against my throat. I swallow hard. *What a night.*

"And these men brought you to safety." Father's voice sounds far away.

"Yes, me and Uncle." I clear my throat. "To Palmo's monastery." Cold sweat trickles down my neck. Here it comes.

"And where was Karma?" His quiet question says it all. Father's already made up his mind about Karma, and it's not good.

"I have no idea." My hesitation is too loud. "I passed out after Lanying's guard carried me out of the building." That's the truth. Karma never told me, and I never asked.

"I see." It's all Father says, but his disappointment pulses in the fragile space between us, crushing my hope—Karma wasn't there for me and Father won't be as forgiving as I have been. My heart sinks in my boots.

"So you don't know what happened to Khandro either?" Father chooses his words with care as we approach at the ngakpa's, the first house on the left in the village.

"My sister told me," I whisper. The ngakpa's already at the gate, his lanky figure standing tall.

"Tell him, for he can take it," Father says. "Nothing's worse than dwelling in the dark." His hand rests on my shoulder as a heartening reassurance. He too lost his loved one through tragedy when I was only a little girl.

For too long Father suffered, thinking it was his horse that killed Mother. It drove him to a certain madness. He even abandoned me, his only child, and left me at my grandmother's monastery, not knowing how to carry his enormous burden. For so long we were apart. This spring we got to know the terrible truth of Mother's passing, and it brought us back to where we belong—together at our home.

So yes, I get what Father's saying—the ngakpa deserves to know what happened; he deserves to know it all.

And I'm the only one who can tell him—the truth about his wife's gruesome fate.

Three

Swirls of weisang curl up to the morning sky and white silk flows around my neck—the ngakpa welcomes us with an auspicious offering of gratitude and appreciation. My fingers fumble with the frayed ends of the khata, and my heart goes into hiding. Never have I been the bearer of bitter news like this.

"So good to see you all again." The ngakpa's slender hands urge us into the house, down the hallway into his room where the golden sun sprinkles her delicate dust all over the richly hued carpets, and the zest of pine and cedar ambles on a fleeting draft from the open window pane.

Blood rushes to my head as I lower myself three times in front of the small shrine, curated with care. My temples throb, and my mind stirs in all directions. Even the ever-loving gaze of the Buddha can't put my restless self at ease.

"Sit, sit." The ngakpa takes his place left of the shrine. The tower of darkened braids on his head sways from left to right as his hands drape the long scarf around with care.

A twinge of relief settles within me. His elongated face is still thin, but his tawny cheeks have filled. A healthy blush has replaced the hollow shadows, and a vivid spark graces his deep amber eyes. He looks so much better since the last time we met, that day when he asked Father and me to retrieve the snake spell from his wife.

The snake spell. I rest my trembling hands on the low table between us. *His wife.* Oh, how I failed. I open my mouth, but the words stick to the back of my throat. My eyes shoot to Father, his solid frame beside me.

He nods. "Just start at the beginning."

So I do.

"I'm so sorry I failed you, gen-la." The first words tumble from my lips. I meet the ngakpa's eyes and a blur of gentle golden floods my mind. I swallow hard to summon the courage hidden in the hollows of my heart. It helps. The truth about that fatal night in Lhasa releases itself, and this time I tell all.

"Khandro tried to escape with the spell when we came, and I could not get away." I rub my hands as I recall the woman's long fingernails drawing my blood in our vicious struggle. "So I threw the spell in the fire, where it burst into a terrible hell." My voice trails off as my eyes flit from the ngakpa to Father and back. Both men sit in the hesitant hush my wary words have woven between us.

"Uncle got burned, almost beyond recognition." My voice breaks, even though the inevitable has not been said yet. "He's taken care of by the nuns in Lhasa now."

The ngakpa's eyes flicker. "He's alive then." A slight smile cracks around his lips.

"He is." I take in a sharp breath. "As is Khandro." My hands clench to fists, and I squint as the fiery flavor of incense scorches the rims of my eyes.

"I didn't see her, but I've been told." I pause and my fingers reach for the red string around my wrist—the blessing cord my sisters tied for me. How to tell?

"They sold her—into slavery." The words of damnation flare from my lips and I'm left with nothing but a gaping hollow in my heart, for not a trace of hope has remained. My fingernails scratch the rough timber side of the table. Shame and sorrow crash down on me from the restless reticence my truth created. *Slavery.* I shudder and meet the ngakpa's motionless, yet gentle gaze. His demeanor is so serene, and most of all so full of love—it should not surprise me, for this is the way of the advanced practitioner, after all.

"You didn't fail, Nordun." His raspy voice cracks in the brittle air. "You rescued two precious human lives." The bone beads around his wrist rattle as his hands draw over the table. "And you did right not to take the spell back here as it is comes with evil, and with death."

By now I've lost the battle, and heated tears streak my face. A sob escapes from the sorrow inside of me. How I wish I were not here.

"I know you wanted a different outcome, my child, but that is not up to us." The ngakpa leans back and folds his hands in his lap. "We don't know what karma they've collected over their past lifetimes, nor do we know what karma will come into fruition in this life." He pauses. The bones click under his thumb. "All we can do is focus on the truth of our actions itself—and in that you did well, very well."

I cast my eyes down and the red string blots on my wrist. "Thank you, gen-la." I think this is what I needed to hear.

"And now you're preparing to venture out even further." The ngakpa's words soar straight to my heart.

He knows. The ngakpa understands my calling to go with my love in search of his mother. Father's quiet presence shifts beside me, and I recoil. He hasn't spoken of his permission, and I doubt if he will.

"Palden-la." The ngakpa whispers Father's name, and the warm breath of the sun gusts through the room. "You want her to stay, but she has much more to learn." He leans in and speaks to Father, looking him straight in the eye. "It was the lord Buddha himself who taught us that if we want to do the actual practice of the dharma, we must go into the world and wander where we have never been."

Father clears his throat. "I understand, gen-la." He bows his head.

"The winter is long, Palden-la, and she will learn the way of Mo." The ngakpa turns to me. "It will be an excellent way to prepare as it allows you to see what might come." He rests his hands on the book at the side of the table.

My eyes widen. *The way of Mo.* The ngakpa wants to teach me the practice of divination. He mentioned it before, when I was about to leave for Lhasa. Now he speaks of it again. My breath shallows. This is an advanced practice, and I'm only a beginner on the path.

"Used with the right intention, it will be of benefit for all in this worldly existence, helping them to overcome the obstacles that might be." He waves his hand, and I can't but stare at the crimson-clad book on the edge of the table.

"You will come and learn, and of course copy the text," he says, and his eyes gleam a soft determination that's hard to deny. "This is a good time."

My mind wavers, but the ngakpa is sure, so who am I to refuse?

"Thank you, gen-la." Father speaks at last. "That is most generous of you." His voice is steady as ever, yet I detect the subtle resignation it carries. I don't dare to glance at him, but my heart jumps with joy. *This is good.* Father has agreed for me to learn the practice of Mo. Who knows what else he might agree to?

"You will come tomorrow then." The ngakpa stretches his hands to us in a blessing, and Father and I bow our heads. It is our sign to leave.

"Mongolia." Father draws his hat over his eyes. I shield my head with my scarf. The midday sun is at her highest and despite the late season, she's burning bright.

"It's a long and arduous journey." Father marches us out of the village. "You're sure about Karma?" He sets an impossible pace.

"You told me yourself, it's the heart that knows." I heave as my breath has a tough time keeping up with his stride. "Like when you met Mother, your hearts knew you were meant for each other, even though Mother was promised to your best friend."

She was—she was promised to marry Sonam, father's best friend. But my father followed his heart anyway, and he married her, the love of his life.

"Even though I've left the monastery, I still want my life to be of benefit for all sentient beings. That has not changed." My eyes go over the rolling grasslands, down where the stables nestle in the brown leaved bushes and are crowned by stalky frames of the almost barren trees.

"I thought the monastery was my place to practice the dharma, that it was my home to live in this life, but my heart knows it isn't, not truly." I turn to Father. "My heart has found its home with Karma."

Father's jaw sets in a hard line under his drawn hat.

"I heard his mother's call, and I have to answer." I twist the ends of my scarf between my fingers. Father widens his stance.

"Karma disappointed me." He tips back his hat. "And to be honest, I doubt if he'll come back once he finds his blood relatives." The restless gloom of worry stirs in his eyes.

A trickle of sweat runs down my neck. Father speaks of what I have been afraid of but won't admit to myself. *Not now.* I turn my thoughts away.

"I want you to be able to make your own decisions, my child, any time you wish to do so without needing Karma's approval." He shakes his head. "He has not shown that he respects your choices, so I want you to stay free."

I stare at him. *Free*. What does he mean?

"You can go with Karma in search of his kin, but he has to bring you home to me after your journey, home right here at the stables." His fingers dig into my shoulders, the caring grip of a father hesitating to let his only daughter go. "And if it is still your wish to be with him, then you have my permission to be his wife, but only then. Understood?"

Father. I nod, as the lump in my throat won't let my words of gratitude pass. Despite all that happened between us, he respects my wishes, even if it is to follow my love to the ends of the world. Letting me be a free woman, enabling me to make my own decisions—how lucky am I with a father like this?

"In the meantime, I hope we can have some time together." Father wraps his arm around my shoulder as we walk on. "It would be good to get to know each other again, so stay for the winter, stay at the stables with Sangmo and me." I raise my eyebrows and glance aside.

"Of course," I say and laugh. "Where else would I stay?"

Father pulls his hat over his eyes again. "Well, the family's camp is not too far these days." His arm gestures over to the right. I crane my neck.

That's true, I forgot. The family moves their tents and livestock to lower pastures before the cold arrives. I visited my grandfather's camp for the first time this spring. My eyes scout the mountain ridge afar. They were way out then, but it will be so much easier to call around in winter.

"Karma's welcome to spend his time with us." Father mumbles now. "Anytime—I'll let him know."

"Thank you, Father," I say, and my heart delights, for he just gave me the greatest gift any father can give to his daughter—his trust and his belief in me.

Four

"Karma's back!" Sangmo jumps from her seat near the stove, and despite her protruding belly, she's mighty quick. A wide smile creases on her face from eye to eye, and my heart lifts in my chest.

My dear Sangmo, how distraught she was yesterday when Dendup and I returned from Lhasa without Karma. Even though they're not related by blood, her brother is everything to her.

"Come, sit." She fusses over Father. A hearty thukpa releases its rich, meaty flavor and my stomach grumbles in anticipation as if I denied it breakfast this morning.

Father ignores Sangmo's plea. "Where's Karma?" He scouts around the otherwise empty kitchen.

"At the horses—where else?" Sangmo hauls the cauldron to serve, but Father boots out to the corridor.

I sag in my seat. I know what Father's up to, and I don't need to be part of it now. My eyes close for a moment. *Om Tare.* Let him go easy on my love.

Metal clatters on the wooden floor and I veer up.

"Let me." I shoot to Sangmo, who is sinking on her knees to retrieve the lid fallen from the cauldron.

"No way." She fences me off. "I'm pregnant, not sick." Her hands tug at the hem of her chuba, the weave of the wool stretched tight. No, she sure doesn't look sick—bright eyes, a healthy flush on her face—she looks gorgeous. Being pregnant suits her, and it's obvious she's found her home here at the stables for now.

"Here." She hands me a bowl filled to the rim. "Careful, hot." Our eyes meet and I can't help but smirk. The fragrance of fresh cut grass and bits of sticky green that used to surround her have made way for the fatty smell of fried bread. A dusty veil of ground tsampa pales her raven locks. What a change from the Sangmo I first met this spring at the family's camp.

"What?" She plants her hands on her side.

I steady the bowl between my hands and shake my head. "It's nothing."

Her face makes a grimace. "Oh, I know what you're thinking." She sucks in her cheeks. "You just wait until this little one has arrived." Her hands pat her plump belly. "I'll be out of the kitchen, riding the fields in no time again." Her longing gaze goes over to the window.

"As long as it's not twins." Her big brown eyes widen. "I mean, I'm getting huge and I still have many moons to go." She tosses her hands, and I burst out in a laughter.

"Don't worry, you can fit two little ones in the saddle." She can, she's a terrific rider.

Twins. My thoughts drift back to Pema and Tsomo, my beloved sisters at the monastery, far away. They're in retreat now, advancing their practice on the Buddhist path. Even though our paths diverged, and there are many mountains between us, they're always looking after me. Their red protection cord on my wrist holds me strong.

"Who would have thought we would both be here now, at the stables?" Sangmo sinks beside me and blows the steam off her thukpa.

I glance at her as she wipes the small trickle of broth from her chin. Yes, who would have thought—Sangmo, the family's wild child now living at my childhood home, carrying the child of Sonam, my father's best friend, and me, leaving the monastery to rid the stables from my uncle's dark presence, and then riding all the way to Lhasa on pilgrimage to save his life—who would have thought?

Lhasa. If only things had turned out differently.

"At least you ended up well." There's a tinge of melancholy in her voice. "And you're going to be Karma's." Her warm hand slides over mine.

"Oh, sis." I lean into her. "You and the little one are home here, with us."

My hands squeeze hers. She's made it very clear she doesn't want to be Sonam's second wife. To be honest, I think she's doing them both a big favor. She's one of those free spirits that needs to roam.

"And you won't trail off again?" Her thumb scoops the last of the thukpa out of the bowl. "You've got everything you need right here." She gestures at the window, with the stables and its inviting buzz going around in full view.

"Besides, Palden's thrilled to have you back." She tilts her head, and I cast down my eyes before they meet hers.

"I know." A sigh floats from my lips. *If only.* A big yawn follows. The long days in the saddle, the many sleepless nights under the stars, Karma's return at dawn—it's all catching up on me.

"Let's get some fresh air." Sangmo slaps my knee. "This little one's getting restless." Her arm hooks in mine.

"It won't be long before I need to drag you up like this." I jump and pull her up, ducking at the same time as a filthy rag skims close to my head.

"Out with you!" Her feet stumble behind me as I flee from the kitchen.

"Too hot for this time of year." Sangmo's hand shields her eyes as we step into the courtyard where the afternoon sun welcomes us with her warming orange blush.

Fresh white stucco covers the walls, rich autumnal colors bedeck the landscaped flower beds, and fresh bales of hay line the sides, ready to be taken in for winter. Rows of heavy carpets and woolen blankets have been taken out to soak in the last bit of sun before winter's cold will creep between their weave. The place looks immaculate.

"You've worked wonders here." I pinch her arm. "I mean, for a girl who declared she would never live under a solid roof—only lay her head in a tent."

Sangmo's smile widens. "It's not about a house or a tent." Her feet pause, her hand points ahead. "It's about the freedom to move around, like they do."

Father hangs over the beams of the pen. Karma stands in the center, his loose shirt billowing in the breeze as he reigns a dashing horse on a long leash. My heartbeat speeds up that bit faster at the sight of my love and his quiet confidence. The way he handles that stallion—his intense focus, that unmistakable energy oscillating between the two. It's fascinating.

"Please, sister, don't go." Sangmo's hands press my middle. "Make him stay, he'll listen to you."

Her eyes plead and my heart hurts. I loosen her grip, but slowly. He's her only brother, and he's all she has.

"Why go?" She raises her chin. "They abandoned him, a small boy, left him to die." A cold glow hardens her eyes. She's raising her walls.

No, we didn't. A shiver runs down my spine. There it is again—the voice crying out to my heart. *No, we didn't.* The desperate call I heard in Lhasa. The one only I seem to hear.

"And now he wants to go find them?" A sharp sneer curls around Sangmo's lips. "He should be nothing but grateful for Grandfather, who saved him." Her hands clench into fists.

I blink as the voice fades in my mind. "Sangmo." I take her clawed fingers and spread them in mine.

"Maybe they didn't," I whisper. "Maybe something else happened, and they didn't leave him, but lost him. We don't know." My eyes meet her opposing stare, ready to battle me. *No use.* I take a sharp breath and let the air flow right to my heart.

"You'll always be his sister." My words of honesty smother her seething insecurity in a loving embrace. "That won't change, no matter what." A cool breeze caresses my face, and I tuck a strand of her loose hair behind her ear.

How swift we humans are to question a love that's already proved itself to be sincere for so long. Or is it we distrust our own ability to love without setting conditions, to love beyond the borders of our heart?

Sangmo averts her reddened face and slides her sleeve across her cheek. *Tears.*

"Look what pregnancy's doing to me." She stares at the ground.

"I know." My hands cradle her belly. "It's all this little one's fault."

She looks up and a faint sparkle breaks through the saddened haze in her eyes.

"I'm sorry." My voice falters. "He has to go, or it will haunt him, forever unsettling his heart." How to explain? "We won't leave until this baby is born." I take her hand, warm and wet.

"You better not." The hesitant spark in her eyes ignites to a glowing grin, and with that she sweeps off the last bit of rumbling disquiet her insecurity placed between us.

"Now come on." My heels turn in the gravel. "Let's see if these two over there have established some sort of truce."

Om Tare. Let's hope so.

My lips make a rapid, yet urgent plea once again—for with two headstrong men like Father and Karma, divine mediation is more than welcome, that's for sure.

Five

The evening settles into a quiet night with rays of rich ruby fading into a deep sapphire sky. A persistent nippy breeze slips through the cracks of the tiny window. Finally, we are alone.

"Your father's quite a remarkable man." Karma slides his arm around my waist. "Wanting you to stay a free woman until we return."

I lean in and lay my head against his chest. The sweet scent of mountains and meadows, and of the churned earth in the summer sun, floats around me. *My love.* His fingers caress my cheek. How I yearned for this moment, just the two of us after a day that's been too long.

He and Father settled into a truce, and Father even asked him to stay after we said goodbye to Dendup this late afternoon. *Dendup.* My dear elder. His lively laughter echoes from afar. I'll miss having him around.

I offered to ride with him to the family camp, to face the council of elders. After all, it's through my doing that he and Karma failed to execute the revenge killing the family ordered. He just waved his hand at my suggestion.

"Karma's beat us to that," he said, and slapped Karma on the shoulder. Both men seemed unfazed, but I wonder if there will be any consequences for them, especially for my love. I look up and let my fingertips wander in the crook of his neck.

"I'll respect your father's wish." Karma twists his fingers through my hair. "As long as it is your wish too."

"It is." My thumb skims along the hard ridge of his collar bone and he pulls me closer.

His lips press the top of my head. "You've gone so thin, my love."

What can I say? How do I tell him I've been living in the hollow he left at his parting?

It was my choice, and the right decision to let him go, but it feels my life has been suspended since that night, our first—and only—night coming together in Lhasa. I've been holding my breath ever since, and I'm still waiting to exhale.

That night I opened to a love so immense, a love I never knew could exist. He moved within me, in all my senses, and left me awakened, feeling alive, and wanting for so much more. My fingers search for the edge of his shirt. The thin cotton crumples under my touch.

"I'm so sorry." His breath drifts along the rim of my ear. "I should have known better than to leave you like that for you and me, we are kindred spirits." His hands draw down my back. My shoulders raise and our breath falls into sync.

"The further away I traveled from you, the colder my heart turned." His voice wavers, yet his chest rises and falls with a sure and calming rhythm. "The memory of you, of us, sharing our dreams and desires, our most intimate knowing, only burned brighter. It scorched my inner being, branding the mark of belonging in the depths of my soul."

My fingertips melt into the heat of his bare skin. I close my eyes to his pulse, throbbing under my touch.

"I never knew my true home, but it's you to whom I belong." His voice is urgent now. His arms cross, closing me in. "And it's you who belongs to me."

A sob escapes from my chest, as if it were waiting for these words to set it free. *This man, these words.* So true to me, so true to him.

"You're here," I whisper. "That's all that matters."

His intense grip muffles my voice.

"I am." His lips search for mine. "And this time I'm here to stay."

As our breath meets, and his hands prepare my body to be his once more with that most tender of touch, I'm amazed all over again. How well he knows me, and how well I know him too. My love, his beautiful mind, and his wild, beating heart—becoming mine all over again.

And although his last words rush a shiver of doubt through my mind, I push it away. *Not now.* I've waited long enough.

This time we come together, not at the desperate call for an unknown truth as we did that fateful first night in Lhasa, too long ago. This time we come together from the deepest desires of our hearts, as lovers intending to spend a lifetime together.

Six

Winter moves in without warning. Overnight she flings her frosty veil of silver and gray over the mountains with a vengeance, as if to say, "I've arrived."

It's still a struggle to me, settling into lay life at my childhood home. I'd only left the monastery this past early spring, and I've been on the road ever since. First, I chased a wild horse in the Four Sisters Mountains, then rode to Lhasa on pilgrimage. The community of monastic life, the daily routine of prayer, and my study and work too have fallen away. It's up to me now to forge my own way in this mundane world, with my Buddhist practice at the core.

My body eases into the idle rhythm of lay life, taking no objections to naps in the afternoon, or lazing about at the horses. It takes all my strength to not let my mind fall into the same pattern, but I keep my prayer and meditation at the opening and closing of the day. It's good for me and my peace of mind to go to the ngakpa in the afternoon. With his profound wisdom and pure devotion to the path, he's a sure beacon to guide me in my quest. For one thing hasn't changed: my most heartfelt desire—to serve all sentient beings in this samsara as best as I can.

He was already waiting for me, that first afternoon. Wrapped in thick white wool, his tall figure stood erect at the gate.

"Glad you're ready to learn the practice of Mo." His tawny hands rested on the top of my head for a while. "You will be of benefit to all."

He had already prepared, as a second low table was set in the prayer room, right next to his seat—a blank stack of beige pothi pages, ink in a vast array of colors, a few pens on the side. My heart expanded at the sight of his faith in my being.

"First tea." A youngish lad came scuffling in at a shrill ring from the ngakpa's bell. His lanky arms balanced a full tray.

"My sister's eldest has joined me." The ngakpa gestured at the shy youngster. "He's interested in the dharma." His voice had sounded proud when he spoke of his nephew. "And a decent enough cook." His mouth eased into a smile as the boy skirted away.

He's actually a wonderful cook, now that I think of it. The creamy tea and warming thukpa tasted delicious on those laborious afternoons when my breath steamed on my frozen fingertips. It would have been warmer in the kitchen, but the practice of Mo is sacred, not to be brought into a place of filth and dirt.

What a delight it was, curling my fingers along the length of a pen, and letting the ink flow on the page in swirls of black and dark brown again. How fortunate I am, being able to read and write. The boy's prying eyes made me aware of that privilege, every afternoon again. I couldn't wait to start on the book, even though I wasn't ready that first afternoon. I had to receive and master the preliminaries first—the meditation to Manjushri, the Bodhisattva of wisdom, and the recitation of all the mantras by heart.

"Your grandmother has taught you well." The ngakpa seemed content at our first sitting. "A proper understanding of emptiness and the interdepend origination, very good." He had mentioned that to me before, and now that I've ventured out in this world, I sure understand. My grandmother taught me well, and all that I'm lacking is on my account.

"How is your meditation practice these days?" His beady eyes searched mine for an answer. "I remember it used to be firm." My cheeks had flushed with shame—they must have been crimson red. *My meditation.* How I've been slacking, keeping too much time in pleasant company instead of spending it in my own unruly mind.

"I understand, there can be some tension, having an intense worldly love while still standing in the shallow of your practice." He leaned in and a glimmer tuned in those dark eyes. My hands fumbled with my beads. "But then again, having the right partner can strengthen our practice too, as it brings forth obstacles to further our practice much more swiftly."

I'd wanted to ask him how to make worldly love and spiritual practice work side by side. But my heart had sunk at the little quiver in his voice. *The right partner.* Khandro—how could she betray him like that? I let it rest, but the question is still on my mind. I guess it's a matter of discipline, but even that's lacking for now.

"Don't worry, winter's the time to rest and prepare," Sangmo said, as I stumbled into the kitchen one of those first mornings, scolding myself for sleeping late again. *Rest and prepare.* Well, I've left most of the preparations up to the men. Beside my daily visits to the ngakpa, I'm working my days around the stables, getting to know Father again, while we take our orders from Sangmo.

Being pregnant, Sangmo's settled into a surprising new role—that is, surprising to all of us who knew her as the wild child she used to be. She's assigned herself as the vigilant keeper of our home and hearth, assuming her responsibilities with the same passion as she used to ride the rolling hills.

With Karma spending most of his time at the stables, I've started to learn the Han language from him. He's a willing teacher, my love. As he helps me wrap my head around the right pronunciation, we're even fitting in a bit of his mother tongue, the Mongolian language. He says he only remembers a little, but he must be fluent. He won't admit it, though—especially to himself, for it's the tongue of his mother, of his kinfolk, and it's seeded deep inside of him. It spread its roots firm within him before they casted him aside—a little boy, only a knee high. I can see how it's taken him, for there's a vibrancy shining through in his emerald eyes whenever his throat releases these snakelike sounds with such ease. It's in those moments something stirs in my mind, that sliver of doubt, that makes me wonder, reluctantly: *My love, will you come back with me?*

He's assured me, "You're my home now."

He's told me more than once, reaffirming it in his most tender ways. It's what I want to believe as I already put my heart on the line—many moons ago. That beautiful summer day at the Karub ruins stands out my mind. The first time he ever shared with me—or anybody—his loss and longing for home. I tied him a necklace with five beads after that—three clay beads we found on the road together, and two jade beads I took off my mother's mala. It's a reminder from me to him, letting him know that his heart is free to go wherever it needs to be; no matter what happens between us—he'll always have a home to return to, he'll always be home with me.

Three beads for the wide open road to roam, and two for me, coming home—in hindsight, I might have balanced them better. I've gotten to understand the call of the captivating strength of the mountains with their promise of freedom as his favorite place to be. Having gone all the way to Lhasa myself, the excitement of discovering foreign places, meeting new people, hearing different tongues—I get it, it's a distant, yet alluring call from afar that keeps drawing him in. And if I'm honest to myself, it's appealing to me as well.

I've always felt content at the monastery, wanting no more than living my life for the benefit of all through study and prayer. But ever since I rode down that remote mountain, something's changed. Or maybe nothing's changed and it was always within me hibernating—that curiosity for what lays beyond. Maybe it was always waiting to be awoken at the brink of spring from its deep winter sleep.

As the turning of the moon slips through my fingers, my fidgety doubt about Karma finds its place of hiding, nestling itself in the furthest crevasse of my mind. I will not battle it, nor will I give it anymore of my attention. That which we attend to will grow, so I'm best off letting it be. It will rear its ugly head again at some point. I'll deal with it when time comes.

Being with him, here at my childhood home...it's such a joy for me to discover our love strengthening even more. It's growing, expanding to something beyond my wildest imagination, right at the touch of our hands. He's a patient man, my love, as I'm relishing him with all my senses, exploring all we have in common and all we differ to be. We're sharing the matters of our mind at the brief light of day, and the most intimate of our bodies during the long winter nights—until his duty to attend the family calls again, helping Dendup to prepare.

Seven

Grandfather's family has decided on a trading expedition as soon as the mountains allow us to pass. Grandfather's brother found Karma somewhere along the road from Ya'an to Chengdu, a well-known route for traders to travel, so that's where we'll go. It's safest to join a caravan heading that way, and knowing the family by now, they'll never miss an opportunity to profit from trade.

I'm not sure what it all involves. When we went out to Lhasa, Dendup and Karma also brought a few horses packed. I never got to see what was in those bags. I guess they'll be sending tea back from Ya'an, but what will they bring? Usually it's horses that are traded to the east, but I can't imagine us driving up a herd. Could be deer musk, wool, or yak hides—I have no idea.

I asked Father when we shuffled the snow of our roof, one clear winter morning. He told me not to worry about it, anyway.

"Your Grandfather's family is always up to something," he said. "Just make sure you stay with Dendup and Karma and keep safe." He had peered at the gray mass that came moving with the speed of a gale over the barren mountain range. "Let's get inside, snow's coming again."

He was right.

Snow came and covered our world in heavy blankets, blinding us with her shades of crystal white and pearly blue.

"Too much this year," Sangmo had grumbled as we stamped the slush from our boots in the hallway. "Too cold for too long." But Father just smiled, and I knew why. It meant the day of my departure was still far away.

The night after even more snow, Sangmo's baby girl was born. She came with such speed—I was almost late catching her. I'd been sleeping next to Sangmo in her quarters while Karma was at the family's camp.

"Sister, I think she's coming." Sangmo's hand had gripped my arm. "Please hurry." Her palm left a stain—she was drowning in sweat.

As I rushed to the kitchen, the memory of Yeshe's delivery and her beautiful baby boy flashed before my eyes. Death and despair had paid Sonam's family the cruelest visit that night. *Om Tare, please not this time!*

Buckets clattered, steam rose, feet waded through snow, knee deep. I was back with the boiling water just in time to catch the little one from Sangmo's hands.

I will always remember the baby's first cry—vehement and ear-piercing—and the tears of sheer relief that streaked my cheeks. *She's here, and she's fine.* I didn't think I'd been worrying this much.

"Am I not supposed to be the one crying?" Sangmo said, the jokester as always. Her tears came later, after the initial shock, when she held the little bundle in her arms.

"Well, at least it's clear who her father is," Sangmo said as she stroked the baby's head.

I hadn't even noticed, being too relieved at the swift and fortunate birth. As she pulled the blanket back a bit, the resemblance was striking. Sticky black curls crowned the little girl's head, thick dark lashes rimmed her eyes, and her wide nose set a brooding frown—she's the spitting image of Sonam, no doubt about that.

"It's a good thing newborns look like their father." Sangmo let out a sigh, and I glanced at her. *What?* It was only when she gave me that cheeky smile of hers that it dawned on me. She'd always proclaimed Sonam was the father, but she had her doubts about that herself, the wild girl that she is.

Father sent word and the next day Karma came riding, delighted with his first little niece. He brought Sonam with him. Turns out he's joining our traveling party after the winter and was helping at the family camp with the preparations for our journey ahead. I should have known—Sonam's always looking for a good deal and for adventure. He's got that free spirit too. I'm more than sure Father's delighted he'll keep us company—his closest friend and another pair of trustworthy eyes to look after me.

Sonam offered Sangmo a place at his homestead in Dawu as his second wife, next to the family at the nomad camp up North. She refused, more than once and adamantly, to nobody's surprise. It seemed to relieve Sonam, but then again, you can never tell. He's coming around a lot more than one expects of him, and she's in a great mood whenever he's around. Sometimes the desires of our heart remain hidden, cloaked under the perceptions our mind has made up, of what we think is best for us, and for the better of all.

With the celebrations of Losar behind us, bits of young green pop their budding heads through the last shreds of crusty snow on the lower grasslands. We'll be leaving within three days—the ngakpa's done the divination for the date.

I could not be more indebted to him, my generous teacher. His constant encouragement in carving out my lay routine on the Buddhist path has been invaluable to me. I've finished copying the book, but more important to me, under his guidance I've learned the correct way to serve sentient beings with the practice of Mo. Today's the last day. My afternoons of writing and studying with him have come to an end.

"I'm very pleased with your progress," the ngakpa says as I clean the pens. All is done, the last dice is thrown.

"Now you have your book." His slender hands unfold, and two bone cubes roll over the table. "And your dice to go with it." I blink as their translucent pearly sides gleam before my eyes.

"When you return, you'll learn the rituals." His hand gestures at the side of his table. His spell book's there, clothed in red and gold. "It will be of benefit to all."

I bow my head. The tips of my ears burn. *My very own dice.*

"Thank you, gen-la." I say, but my words fall short of my feelings of gratitude. How he trusts my faith and ability to do right.

I take a deep breath. "It's just..." *Betrayal.* The ngakpa's voice rings in my ears. "The divination." I rest my hands on the edge of the table. A heavy weight sits in my heart. *Betrayal.* It was foreseen even twice.

"Yes, the divination." The ngakpa stays unmoved. "The divination was clear."

I close my eyes, for I don't want it to be. I want it to be undone.

The ngakpa and I, we did the divination for Karma's journey to come, and the gods answered us both, loud and clear.

"What was once lost, will be found." The bones around the ngakpa's wrist rattle an ominous echo. "That is said to come." He shifts in his seat.

"And there will be betrayal." My voice sounds from afar. I open my eyes. My feverish breath clouds in air.

"Yes, there will be betrayal from ones that are near." The ngakpa affirms what has been a constant sorrow on my mind. "That too is what the gods have foreseen on your path." His quiet answer seems to offer no hope.

"But remember, Nordun, an obstacle is only one if we make it to be, for nothing in this world is ever truly what we humans perceive it to be." His hands roll the dice in a strip of thin leather, but his eyes are on me. "The path is always clear for those who practice patience and the wisdom to discern whatever may come."

Courage, discernment—if only I had a little of the virtues the ngakpa's talking about. My shoulders sag. As soon as my mind releases my doubt, I feel his eyes burning on me.

"We are never ready, nor are we meant to be, Nordun." His long locks coil over the table as he leans in. "We are always meant to go beyond than we believe we can be—that is, if we want to go further on the path and serve unselfishly, with all our being."

His voice resounds a discreet truth between us. My heart quivers. No matter how much I'm looking forward to going on this journey, there's also doubt and fear stirring in the depth of my mind.

"We must be willing to move beyond the word we already know." He hands me the leather package and sits back. "And you, my child, you are destined to journey far from this place, as a real bodhisattva is to be."

I swallow hard. This truth tastes sweet, but the aftertaste is bitter. Only a little but enough to sting. My heart knows and never left me astray. It's the right way to go with my love, but it's far from anything I've ever known. It scares me, and I'm not afraid to admit it.

"Yes, gen-la." I fold my hands to my chest. "And with your most generous support, I'm as prepared as can be."

My knees shake as I bid the two of them goodbye; my trusted teacher and his nephew, receiving me with warmth in their own way—every afternoon as the winter passed.

Iron clangs, and the gate falls in its lock. I draw my scarf around my neck. My hands seek their shelter in the furry lining of my sleeves. A pair of open arms hauls me in. It's Karma. He's been waiting to walk me home.

"We're set to go then?" His hands find mine in my sleeves.

"We are," I say. How I love the tenderness of his cold cheek against mine.

Slush crumples under our boots as we stroll back. The sky flames with an orange sun that sinks behind the charred mountain ridge. Dusk will arrive soon, but Karma seems in no hurry. His fingers fumble with mine, and his pace hesitates. I glance aside. *Something's up.* A cold gush grates my cheeks.

The divination. I never told him, but that doesn't mean he doesn't know. Karma's got "the gift" as Sangmo calls it, the gift to see things that are lay hidden in other minds.

I tilt my head, and meet his eyes, where a bleak gray clouds the usual vivid green. What does he see?

"I made your father a promise," he says. "Well, several, as you know." His tone lowers. This must be serious. A pale shadow darkens his face.

"I need your help in this." His gaze moves over to where the lower valley hides the stables, the home I've just gotten to know again. "For there's one promise that's proven hard for me to keep."

One promise. His words stop me in my track. Which promise is too hard to keep?

My ribs tighten. The promise of home. *No, not that one, please!*

"I promised your father I would bring you back safe." He lets go of my fingers. "But after all that happened between us, I'm not so sure." His hand picks a loose strand of my hair and nuzzles it behind my ear.

No! My heart's missing a beat. *Please don't say it.* Please don't talk of it, not anymore.

"Not sure about what?" I wring the mangled words from my throat. My fingernails dig into the flesh of my hand.

"You see, my love, it is hard for me." He pauses. His fingertips stroke along the rim of my ear. "I can't keep my promise if you keep sneaking out in the middle of the night behind my back, and throw yourself in front of my knife again, like you did that night in Lhasa." A slow, playful smile cracks through his serious facade.

What?! I gasp and recoil as his eyes ebb from ashen to a brilliant green.

His laughter bursts through the valley. How can he joke about something like that?

I freeze, and he shoots away, the tails of his chuba flying behind him.

He's already too far out with that lean and strong physique of his, but I try to speed up. The icy air bursts in my lungs. I heave and stumble behind.

It's useless, I'll never catch up, but there's no stopping me now, for I'm set on chasing him—all the way home.

Eight

Frost crunches beneath our horses' hooves, white clouds steam from their breath. The clear indigo night sky fades into a light blue dawn. Patches of bronze and orange haze through the courtyard—it's the promise of a glorious day.

"Too early," Father had said, when the throw of the ngakpa's dice had sealed our day of departure. "Better wait a few more days."

Still, we're going, for the word is, the mountains will let us pass.

A baby's cry sounds from the outbuildings. Sangmo's coming to see us off.

"Please, stay with Karma," she said. We talked until late last night, the two of us. "Whatever happens, don't leave his side." Her eyes bore an unusual anxiety, nothing like the usual carefree Sangmo at all. "You're all he's got out there." Her hands had cradled her little one tight.

I frowned. "But Dendup and Sonam..."

She'd shook her head. "They mean well, I think." She swiped a loose lock from her forehead. "But they don't care for him, not like you do." She sucked in her cheeks and flung her gaze in the distance.

"Promise me you won't leave him." Her fingernails dug into my forearm. "No matter what they say about him, no matter what they do." My stomach clenched. Her eyes clung to me in a desperate plea.

"Sangmo." I leaned in, not knowing what to say. This was not the ever-optimistic Sangmo I knew.

"I promise." I swung my arms around her rigid body. Becoming a mother has made her heart fragile. She sobbed until we both fell asleep.

Morning came soon—too soon, as Father would say. The vague fatigue of the restless night still dwells in my bones, but not for long, as sheer excitement surges in my veins.

A thick column of weisang curls up from the main gate—my nostrils sting with its powerful scent. The eager bray of my stallion echoes through the courtyard. His long manes rise and fall in a slow motion with the twirling of his ears.

"Time to go." Father ties the last khatas at the bridles. Karma's horse prances beside me. It's only now that I notice him. My mind's been too occupied with Sangmo's worry and Father's last words of caution to me.

"You're ready?" Karma reaches over, a playful brush on my cheek.

I nod. "Ready as can be."

With Dendup in front, we ride through the main gate, along the swaying skeletons of the trees in winter. A biting breeze swipes along. I slide my hood over my head. It won't be long before the sun will tempt the buds of green to crown the barren branches. I won't be here.

I blink and turn.

Father stands tall at the gate. A last wave after so many goodbyes. All the family visited over the past days, all but my grandmother. I haven't seen her since I left for Lhasa.

She sent word before the new year—she's gone into retreat and established a last new rule as the parting abbess of the monastery. When in retreat, there will be no receiving of visitors. Same for my dear sisters, Pema and Tsomo. A sharp yearning gushes through the hollows of my heart. I guess she has her reasons. Still, it's been too long.

Dendup's cry roars over the rolling hills. We're on our way.

"The winter's been too long, sister." He turns with the biggest smirk. "Let's go!"

His horse speeds off, his two packhorses follow in the throw up of slush and sleet.

I can't help but smile. I met his wives. They couldn't wait for his departure either.

"We'll let Dendup lead for a while." Karma steers his horse beside me.

"Seems like he needs it." My words won't reach over the fast canter.

"Oh, more than we'll ever know." He leans in. I always forget how agile his body is—even on the horse. "Or that he will ever admit." He throws me a wink.

"First stop Dawu, you know the way." His stallion bolts ahead.

"Woah!" My hands grip the reigns as my horse leaps to compete for lead position with Karma's. My eyes set on the hilltops. Yes, I've been to Dawu, to Sonam's homestead, on my way to get the wild horse. It's a two-day ride, and it seems like ages ago. It's hardly been a full year.

From there on we'll go to Dartsedo, last stop before we are leaving our mountains. Then to Ya'an and onto the road to Chengdu, where Grandfather's brother found Karma.

I glance sideways at my love. The mellow morning sun envelops him in a moment of golden, and my heart misses a beat. How I long to be with his man, no matter where it will take us.

If we're lucky, we don't need to ride to the far planes of Mongolia. A lot of the Mongols have settled along the trade roads, maybe Karma's kin too. The only tangible lead we have is the marking on his forearm, a tiny deer's head tattooed in fine black lines, most likely by his next of kin. I made a precise copy of it and stuck it between the pages of my book.

Grandfather's uncle also remembers two tiger bells, the bells of a shaman sown into Karma's shirt, but these somehow got lost over time. I guess we'll just have to follow his mother's call from Chengdu on.

We ride for most of the day, only taking brief breaks along the creeks to let the horses rest and refresh. I have to admit, Dendup's not the only one who loves being back in the saddle. The sun on my face, the wide-open planes in front of me, and my mind settling in a silent prayer on the cadence of our horses—oh, how I relish this first day riding with my love at my side.

Now and again his eyes search for mine, a tender nudge to let me know he hears. Yes, he hears my prayers as I let them drift on the stream of my thoughts. He's the only one who hears, like I'm the only one who hears his dreams when our breath and heartbeat fall into synch. Dreams of eagles' wings soaring and deer hooves clapping, and his mother's call crying on the wind. I heard it all this winter, every night when he lay his body next to mine. It's a call that only gets louder, a call that won't be ignored.

The sun bathes the lower grasslands in ochre and orange as we come into Dawu on our second day. The days are still short but will lengthen soon.

My eyes scoot up the road. There it is, the biggest homestead in this abundant valley. Huge timber beams frame an impressive gate. It's already open—Sonam's expecting us.

I pat my stallion on his neck as we enter the courtyard. We've done well our first few days after winter. My stiff legs won't let me slide off as easily as yesterday—my body takes its time to settle in the saddle again. A servant hurries up to take the reins.

"Finally!" Sonam's voice spurts from the doorway. "What took you so long?" Open arms press me in a broad chest.

My breath stalls as my gaze meets his. *Yellow.* His entire face, even his otherwise ruddy nose, it's all tinged with yellow. Dark-hued shadows rim his eyes. Sonam's not well, that's obvious. I vein a quick smile. What to say?

"Ah, these men." I turn on my heels and wave my hand at my two companions. "Slowing me down—all the way."

The stomping of boots resounds in the hallway. A head of boisterous curls peeps up next to Sonam.

Norbu! It's Sonam's eldest son jumping right here in front of me.

Gentle Norbu. Radiant speckles of gold shimmer at me as the last light of the day captures his deep brown eyes, just like that day in the pen. My mouth opens, but the words won't come out. So many times I thought of the kindness he showed me. I never got the chance to thank him, and now he's here.

My cheeks flush with what I'm sure must be the brightest of red, and my feet feel like they're nailed to the ground.

"Nordun." He steps out. "So good to see you again." His smile reaches the corners of his eyes. "And there he is, the wild one you tamed." His hand brushes mine ever so slightly as he steps past me. A tingle shoots up my arm.

His eyes go over my stallion. "He's gorgeous, I knew you would do well."

"You always believed in me," I say. My hands hide in my sleeves.

A brisk breeze billows through the courtyard. A steady arm draws me in.

"You were the only one who doubted yourself," Karma says. "We always knew you would come through." His firm fingers fold around my waist. "Right, Norbu?"

A trickle of sweat runs down my temples. *What's this?*

Karma's voice carries a subtle yet sharpened edge. It's one I haven't heard before, and one I don't like.

"That's right." Norbu nods. A light amber swirls in his eyes. He steps aside as Dendup saunters our way and holds his gentle gaze steady on me.

"Come on in, you must be thirsty—all of you." Norbu points his chin at the door.

I stay put. My feet won't move. My toes curl in my boots.

"That sounds more like it." Dendup marches right past us. Sonam and Norbu follow in his trail.

"I'll be right in." Karma's voice urges in my ear. "Just checking our horses." His hand slides down my hip.

I watch his tall shadow stride to the back of the courtyard.

Dusk has fallen in dim shreds of purple and blue. A nippy gust of late winter's frost breezes by. I draw my scarf. A weary sigh escapes from my chest.

Somehow it feels like the end of a day, but knowing my companions, there's still a long night to come.

Nine

As usual, Sonam has spared no expenses for our welcoming. The spicy aromas of seasoned meat and sweetened fruit draw me straight to the formal room. Copious, mouth-watering dishes pile on lacquered low tables. Chang's already overflowing from the cups. Sonam and Dendup have wasted no time—they're already toasting to good fortune.

"Tea for you, right?" Norbu's smile hasn't left since we met at the doorway.

My body plunges into the plush seat opposite him. "Tea would be great." I bow at the servant.

Within no time, my parched palate soaks up the rich refreshment. My teeth sink into a chunk of buttered bread, it's salty savor bringing a new zest into my weary bones. This food is superb. My eyes go over the table. The best of everything—like at home.

I never realized how fortunate, how prosperous our families are. Spending most of my childhood at the monastery, I took it all for granted. Until I got to travel last year and witnessed the men and women, and children too, on the fields, breaking their backs to feed their families from sunup to sundown; their tiny dwellings housing too many people under one dilapidated roof.

The stink of stale sweat hits my nostrils as my mind wanders back to the exhausted beasts of burden in the caravans to Lhasa. The yaks and mules, even humans—toiling several times their own weight on their back over the mighty mountains, scraping a meager living together. *Privileged.*

My fingertip draws over the rim of my cup. My mind sinks to the bottom of the nourishing brew. Sure, somehow, I've always known, but never saw—or wanted to see—how the suffering of others provides for my cup of tea.

Privileged. I've never had to work, being able to study and pray for all sentient beings, supported in everything I've done. I look up and my heart cracks open at Norbu's gentle gaze.

"I haven't thanked you enough." My small voice doesn't do justice to the rush of gratitude gushing through. "Your encouragement and patience in the pen—I would never have been able to tame the stallion without you."

He leans in. "It was my pleasure." He cocks his head to the side. "Besides, you're a natural with the horses, you owe it all to yourself."

I blush at the sincerity of his words—yet again.

"You mean I'm a natural in hitting the muck with a certain grace," I say. "That I remember." My body sags back in the seat as we both laugh at the recollection of me tumbling in the dirt while training a horse.

"You made a mean landing there, I have to admit." He pours me another tea and slides me a plate of dark sugared plums. "Here, so good." He takes one too.

"I had hoped to see you sooner." He pops the whole plum in his mouth. "Especially when I heard you hadn't returned to the monastery." His jaw chews with vigor, never letting go of his smile.

He means when he heard I'm not a nun anymore. I take a small bite and suck the sweet juice trickling down the corner of my lip. Yes, so good.

"Well." My voice wavers. "After I came back, I went on a pilgrimage." My tongue pokes at the sugary bits between my teeth. "I guess your father told you all about that too."

My eyes dart over to Sonam, who is raising another cup with Dendup. His hollow eyes, his ghostlike complexion—such a contrast with his lively manner and rowdy laughter.

"I know, he doesn't look good." A tightness sets around Norbu's mouth as I face him again. "He's the reason I'm here." His fingers spread on the table.

"I see." I glance over at Sonam again. It surprised me to find Norbu here at the homestead. Being the eldest, he takes care of the family with Zinzin, his mother, up North. He's the acting head of the family there, as Sonam's always away, doing trade.

"This place doesn't hold the best of memories for me." Norbu gulps the rest of his tea in one go. "But Mother asked me to." His sleeve draws over his mouth to wipe away a dribble of liquid.

I nod. Zinzin told me the story about her first years of marriage here at Sonam's homestead on the lower grassland. How her wild heart had longed to roam where the eternal peaks reach into the blue yonder, and the winds of freedom sweep their sweet fragrance over meadows in full bloom, and where she had laid her head to rest under the infinite splendor of the star-struck sky at night in her younger years. The yearning for the higher mountains had brought an illness to her body and her mind. She had even lost her precious newborns to the calling of her home.

Sonam had understood Zinzin would whither away at his homestead, so he let her go back with their children to the mountains, where she belonged. They both made their homes, and with unconditional love as their common ground, they found their own way of being with each other, even though it means a lot of times they're living apart.

My eyes narrow on Sonam's lackluster complexion and I wonder what ails him these days. Sangmo mentioned to me Sonam had stomach problems when he last visited her and the baby. She thought it was the heavy drinking he's taken to, but he didn't appear as sick as he does now.

"Not sure what's wrong with my father." Norbu rolls an orange between the palms of his hands. "He thinks that woman jinxed him." A tangy zest drifts between us as he slices the peel with precision.

"Woman?" My breath slows and my mind jumps ahead. "What woman?" *No way!* It can't be.

"The one that was with your uncle in Lhasa." Norbu frowns, and the juicy fruit reveals its ruby core under his fingers. "The one with the spell." He shrugs. "But I don't know."

Khandro! A nauseating crimson flashes before me—Khandro's fingernails drawing my blood that fateful night in Lhasa.

"It can't be." My mouth opens, but Lanying's voice shrieking in my head silences my words. *This place, it's everything she deserves.* It was Lanying who sold Khandro into slavery—she told me so herself. If it was Lanying, then why would Khandro curse Sonam?

I blink. It makes no sense.

"What can't be?" A crisp breeze drafts in, and Karma slides beside me. A light haze rises from his breath, and the scent of hay and something sweetened, rich and heavy—musk, maybe—clings around. His eyes question mine, and I slip a wedge of the bittersweet between my lips. *This is not the time to ask.*

"What took you so long?" Sonam's yell thunders over the table. With his cup raised, I notice his hand trembles ever so slightly. A servant speeds to pour more for all.

"You've got some magnificent horses out there in the stables." Karma's hand lifts his cup to Sonam in approval, but his eyes flit over the room, avoiding Sonam's question.

My fingers pick at the plate of fruit before me. I sit back, but my mind won't let it rest. Thoughts keep spiraling—what did Sonam have to do with Khandro's ill fate? The tangy fruit lingers a sour savoriness in my mouth. My eyes go over my company. What do they know that I don't?

"You're good?" Karma's arm slides behind me. A relaxed air graces his face.

"A bit tired," I say. And I am—my misplaced mistrust is draining me. *Leave it.* I swallow hard as a sour flitter of orange seed sticks itself at the back of my throat.

More freshly prepared dishes steam up the room, and the flow of chang picks up with the conversation. As usual, I'm the only one left drinking tea. My body tells me it's time to go.

"Don't wait up for me," Karma says under his breath as I excuse myself. "I'll wake you, anyway." His hands trail over my ankle as I pass.

That man! I'm not looking back as I dart out of the room—my shy reply won't be a match for his cheeky grin, I know that by now.

The night turns out to be a long one—for the men, that is, not for me. When Karma's hungry touch wakes me from a deep, dreamless sleep, the blue hue of twilight caresses our skin. It won't be long before dawn arrives, still, neither of us is in a hurry. We savor this quiet time before daybreak, letting our breath and bodies rise and fall as one before slipping back into a soothing snooze.

Despite the enticing, warming hollow of Karma's body in which I'm nestled to sleep, I can't resist the call of the first pearly sparks of morning sun hitting the window ledge. Feet first, I slip out of bed and tiptoe my way to the prayer room. Our journey's long and not without danger—we need all the help we can get.

The door creaks and my feet sink into the woven woolen. The burning butter lamps blaze their instant warm welcome on my cheeks. Brocade and silk hangings cascade in vibrant hues from the raised ceiling. Intricate thangka's, depicting every deity and protector desirable clad the towering walls. The giant gilded statues that adorn the lavish shrine would not be out of place in a grand monastery temple. This prayer room is like everything else in Sonam's house—large and embellished, with no expenses spared. Spanning the entire top floor, this shrine room is exactly what Sonam intended it to be—the crowning glory of a prosperous man and his homestead.

I settled in the center and close my eyes to the bedazzlement of it all. My fingers slide my beads and my mind turns to prayer. *Om Tare.* Mother of all Buddha's, guide us on our journey, remove all obstacles on our way. Help me see with clarity and may all that we do be in the best interest of all. *Om Tare.*

As prayer fills my being, the doubts of the early dawn fade away. They're always there upon awakening, as their vague sense of anxiety and fear seeds in my bones. By now I know well how to be with them—soothing them with my prayer. I trust that someday they'll leave to never haunt me again in the desolate dawn of morning.

That day is not today, and I'm fine with that.

Stillness surrounds me, and all is good. It's not until a soft breeze settles beside me I open my eyes again. Norbu's gentle smile brings a blush to my face.

"Thought I might find you here," he says and leans in. "The place you feel most at home."

I smile and pull up my knees. The prayer room has always been my refuge—how right he is.

"This is a gorgeous room." I wrap my arms around my knees, and I let my gaze wander around to avoid his. There's something in his truth that nags at me, and I don't want him to notice.

"Tea's ready," he says and jumps to his feet. "I'm going to see about our horses. We'll be leaving soon." His hand reaches out.

"You're coming?" My hand grabs his in surprise. My breath gets caught as he pulls me up.

"I am." His smile widens and my mouth falls open.

He sprints off before I get the chance to react.

A little dazed, I step into the hallway. *Norbu's coming.* That's a pleasant surprise.

Dendup's sawing snore resounds from the formal room as I pass. *Good.* That will give me the chance to ask Sonam.

I hasten to the kitchen but halt at the threshold. It's in this kitchen I took off my red robes and changed into lay clothes. It's been only a year, but it feels like a lifetime ago. I didn't want to change, for my robes made me a nun, but Sonam persisted. "Safe and convenient to travel," he said. At the time I told myself it was only a temporary change. Was I that naïve, or was I just too ashamed to admit it to myself, thinking a nun was all I wanted to be?

"Hey." A tired smirk draws on Sonam's face. Ducked next to the stove, he's wrapped in a heavy blanket. The blend of the copious intake of chang last night and whatever ails him turns out to be quite a recipe for disaster this morning.

"Good morning." My voice pitches as I try to sound too cheerful. "What's that I hear—you're not coming?"

My eyes scout the colossal kitchen. A dedicated servant scoots to serve breakfast. A few more are working away in the back. I'm dying to ask him about Khandro, but there's too many around.

"I'm not feeling the best." A rough cough rattles in Sonam's chest. "It's a long journey, so Karma suggested for Norbu to come."

Karma? I sink in the seat opposite Sonam. That is unexpected, and interesting, for sure.

"I don't want to miss the opportunity now that you're all heading East." He flicks his hand at the steaming delicacies covering the table, and I don't have to think twice. The spiced aroma of the broiled meat is simply too much to resist.

"Besides, it's time for Norbu to get out there." Sonam blows the steam of his mug. Seems he's keeping his intake to liquids this morning.

I nod and lick the fat from my fingers. I get it. As the eldest of his children, Norbu's set to follow in Sonam's footsteps, running the trading after him. But until now, he's always been at the family camp, and he's been more than content with that.

"And it's time for you to stay home for a while." Norbu's fiery voice sears from the doorway. He's standing there, arms crossed, legs wide apart.

My hand stalls halfway between the dish and my mouth. Juice drips from my fingers. The stubborn stance, the harsh look in his eyes—that's not the Norbu I know.

Sonam clenches his fist and Norbu steps in. I cast my eyes down as a troublesome tension soars between father and son.

My body shifts to the back of the seat. Somehow the servants have all gone, and there's just the three of us, and a menacing restraint that has descended on the kitchen. My thoughts run at full speed. *This is not good.* I don't know what has happened between them, but it can't be just about Sonam being away all the time. There's more to it—Norbu's silence reproaches rage through the air. The stove hisses, and I flinch.

"And a good morning to you all." Dendup's croaky greeting tumbles into the doorway before he even steps in. He slumps on the seat nearest to the stove and throws around the silliest smirk. "And let me point out, how I just saved us from the most stormy start of the day."

For a moment, we all hold our breath—only to burst out in a relieved laughter, for Dendup's done it again. He's a master in pacifying a touchy situation by barging in with the most unlikely response, and I love him for that.

"Now sister, seeing our brothers here chased away their good servants with their despicable behavior, would you be so kind to serve your wiser elder a decent cup of tea?" He addresses his words to me, but his narrow stare is on father and son, now seated beside one another.

I shoot up with relief, more than happy to move away.

"Yeah, yeah, brother." Sonam snorts as I fill the cups. "We got the message by now." He slaps Norbu on the back. "Well, at least he's not as tame anymore as he used to be." Norbu looks away.

Men. My hands wring the handle of the kettle. Why do they always feel the need to trump each other? The Norbu I know is anything but tame. Gentle and kind in his manners, yes, but not tame.

"Well, that's a good thing since tame won't do any good where we're going." Dendup slurps his tea with contentment as I wait to pour him some more. "But not to worry, you'll keep a close eye on him—won't you, sister?" Dendup's eyes beam with the boldest grin intended for me.

My heels dig in the hardwood, and the kettle lands with a bang on the stove. We haven't even hit the road yet, and Dendup's already making insinuations. My chest tightens. I don't know why.

I sure don't like it from my elder. He wouldn't have done it if Karma were near. I'll let it pass for now—setting off on a friendly note this morning is more important, and there's already been tension. I wipe my sweaty palms on my skirt and stride out of the door. No need to reply.

He'll outsmart me with his wicked words anyway, but I'll keep his advice in mind.

I will keep a close eye, like he says—I will keep a close eye on him.

Ten

The sun's already well on her way to the highest peak when we mount our horses in the courtyard. Sonam wouldn't let us leave without what he called "a decent breakfast" and an elaborate toast to good fortune and prosperous trade. Of course, Dendup agreed—as always if there's chang involved. Since he's our elder, no one can refuse.

With the men inside, I use the time to burn the weisang and settle my nerves. With all that tension between us, the morning didn't start off as it should have. *Om Mani.* We better appease the gods, for we have a long way to go.

By the time we ride out of the gate, the cleansing aroma of smoldering cypress and pine envelops us. Clouds of thick smoke rise in a straight white column to the heavens—an auspicious sign of a blessed journey ahead. *Good.* My body relaxes in the saddle as my stallion's hooves kick up the dust on the road. All will be well. We've been granted safe passage today.

Before Sonam's house is out of sight, we fall into our familiar pattern. Karma's stallion leads the way, my horse follows in his trail, and Dendup's closes the ranks. By now my stallion knows his position, making no attempt to challenge Karma's horse anymore, the undisputed leader of our pack. It doesn't keep him from putting Norbu's horse in place, though, allowing him to pace between mine and Dendup's—and so we ride as one to Dartsedo, at least a good five to six days ahead.

As the sun gains strength, it's a treat to take our midday rest in the grasslands along the winding creeks. While our horses dash the stream and graze the lush embankment, Norbu makes a fire at Dendup's command.

Dendup's been asserting his position as elder ever since we hit the road together, bullying Norbu around every chance he gets. Norbu doesn't seem to mind; he carries out all orders with a smile and a spring in his step. Still, that brute tone of Dendup's—it's unnecessary and I cringe every time he barks another demand in Norbu's way.

"Seems like our respected elder found himself a new personal servant then," Karma says, as Norbu gets the chance to sit with us for lunch at last. "To obey and serve him at all times, like he tried with me when we first hit the road together." His manner's quiet as always, but there's a strained tinge in his voice—something's brooding, something's stirring underneath.

My gaze shoots toward Dendup, slouching opposite us in the shade of a swaying pine. He draws on his elbows and faces the sun. With a growl he bares his teeth, and his tongue pushes the thin twig he's been chewing aside. A substantial spittle splatters from his mouth and lands all the way over at Karma's feet.

I sigh. *Here we go again.*

"Ah, that didn't last long though, did it?" He lets out a vast belch. "You tell them, or will I?" A roaring laugh follows. He extends his cup to me and I jump up with relief, for underneath that dark frown of his flickers an amusing spark.

"Well, I think it was two days of you bullying me around." Karma slurps his tea with content. "Then I had enough of it and put it to an end." His jesting glance meets Dendup's over the rim of his cup.

"Two?" Dendup shoots up. "It wasn't even a day before you let that vicious creature loose on me!" His hands fly in the air.

"You what?" Norbu and I both turn to Karma at the same time. The kettle thumps in the soggy grass.

"Come on now." Karma's eyebrows draw up. "The poor critter was a pup, no more than a knee high." He's not even trying to convince us, for the grin that graces his face is too bold.

"This one here." Dendup jabs a finger in Karma's direction. "He unleashed a huge haunt on me while stirring up the monster with a big stick." Our elder scratches the back of his neck and shakes his head. "And the foul language he uttered while doing so, I tell you, brother and sister—no respect, no respect."

I suppress a chuckle, considering the unpredictability of Dendup's temperament. Norbu, on the other hand, bears no reserves and slaps his knees in laughter.

"Now, now, brother." Karma tips his hat back at Dendup. "I don't remember any foul language at all."

He turns to Norbu and me, a veined apology donning his face. "I only told our respected elder that if he needed a dog to bark at, I'd find him a fine specimen to do so." He shrugs. "That's all, I swear." With a casual swig, he gulps down his tea.

Karma's got all of us in stitches, including Dendup, who beckons me for another fill of his cup.

"And that's only one of the many stunts that young man pulled on me," Dendup says as I try to steady the kettle while pouring.

Karma answers Dendup's grumble with a respectful yet gleeful nod. "And still we travel on together, elder brother."

Dendup raises his cup in a pleased agreement. "Until the road reaches its end, younger brother, until the road reaches its end." With those words, Dendup guzzles down his tea and draws himself back in the shade for his midday nap.

With a loose swing, I turn the kettle to release the last of the tea and nudge at Karma, who is lifting his cup.

They're good, these two, whatever happens between them—they're good.

As I empty the kettle, Karma's hand catches my sleeve and pulls me near.

"I think that will do the trick." He speaks ever so quietly, his words only meant for me.

"Thank you," I say and sink into his lap for a moment. "Now, did you really?" My fingers fold around the back of his collar.

"I did." His lips brush the tip of my ear. "I had to as I was only half his size." His hand trails down my spine and rests on my hip. From the corner of my eye, I see Norbu rushing off to gather our rowdy horses frolicking in the stream while Dendup's sawing wood in deep sleep. *Men.* At least that's settled—for now.

As warm as the days turn out to be, dusk arrives early, heralded by a strong wind with a chill to the bone. Fortunately, we're taking a road well traveled, and there's plenty of inns and family houses to spend the nights. Dendup and Karma are picky though—like it was on our way to Lhasa, we only stay in smaller lodgings they seem to know.

Well fed and rested during the nights, we set out with the early morning with the frost crunching beneath our horses' hooves. We've found our familiar rhythm on the road again—now with the four of us—and I'll soon lose count of the days.

"What's that?" I veer up and crane my neck. Sharp spikes of dark silver and bluish gray rise among the budding green, piercing through the rolling grassland like the jagged back of a fierce dragon, one I've never seen, but heard of many times.

"Stones." Norbu speeds up his horse to ride beside me. "Rows and rows of rocks and boulders." His eyes skim over the vast landscape into the cloudless blue sky. "Nothing special." He catches my gaze with his wide-open smile, and as always he warms my heart.

He might be right about the stones, but I'm not convinced. I lean into the saddle to get a better look at these strange, somehow captivating crags in the distance.

"Oh, come on then," Karma says as he sees me twisting and turning. "I'll take you." He halts and gestures at Dendup. "You guys go ahead, we'll catch up."

With a chuckle, he rides with me down the towering sarsens, standing in pride together like a stone forest, adorning the vastness of the verdant fields with their contrasting colors of shimmering pearl and paled ink.

"There's a warmth in them." I rest my hand on the rugged surfaces. A faint but definite pulse radiates under my palms. "It's like they're alive." My gaze runs up to the uneven edges ascending right out of the soggy grasslands. What a wonder, this splendor of nature.

"It's good to see you marvel like this." Karma leans into a mighty boulder. "You had me worried there for a while, you know."

I raise my eyebrows. "Worried?" I join his side and tilt my head to see what he's on about.

"The winter was long." He smiles, but only barely. "I saw how much you relished the company of your father and Sango at home." His gaze settles in the distance. "And those afternoons at the ngakpa, studying and advancing your practice." His fingers lock with mine and my mind wanders back home for a moment.

He's right. I savored my time at the stables—getting to know Father again, the birth of my precious little niece, and yes, developing my lay practice—all of it has been of immense benefit to me. My eyes meet his, and their light shade of green makes a perfect match with the tinges of beryl that stretch in the creases of these rugged crags.

"For a while I thought you wouldn't come with me." His lips press a tender kiss in the palm of my hand. "That you wanted to stay, I really did." His words bring a blush to my face.

"You never told me." My hands slip, my fingers hook at the belt of his chuba.

"Nope." His smile deepens. "Like I never told you how I love you, all of you." His arms wrap around me and his hand presses my cheek against his chest.

"No need," I mumble, before his breath takes mine away. He calls me his love, and we're kindred spirits, bound by so much more than mere words can express.

"Still." His firm grip relaxes around me. "Some things need to be said—if only now and again." His lips leave a balmy trace on my forehead.

This man, this candor. Somehow his confession surprises me, while it shouldn't—my heart already knew. I squeeze his hand and we stroll around the mighty sarsens, at ease with each other once again.

"Karma." My voice wavers. Now's the time, if there ever is one, to bring it up. "Did Sonam tell you what ails him?" I shouldn't, but my mind won't leave it to rest.

My words tiptoe in the tranquil space between us. All winter we remained silent. Never did we mention that fateful night in Lhasa again, not after Father asked. We let deceit come between us. Knowingly, as we both agreed. Karma told me he didn't know where Khandro had gone, while he knew Lanying sold her into slavery. I told him I trusted his truth, while I went out searching to find another one.

"What is it you really want to ask me?" he says, and he grins. Sangmo's right—somehow Karma always knows.

"Why would Sonam think Khandro jinxed him?" My breath stalls and Karma's hand drops to his side.

"I don't know, love." His eyes narrow as his gaze lingers over my shoulder. "That night, Sonam and I got separated in the chaos of it all." His voice sounds casual, but he chooses his words with care. "He told me he got to her first and handed her to Lanying." He shrugs and still looks away. "Lanying was adamant about it."

My mouth turns dry. My mind spins. That's true—Lanying was set on getting even with Khandro. She made that clear, more than once.

"And Sonam didn't have the guts to kill the woman, of course." Karma's voice rims with rejection. "He should have, though." His jaw sets.

My knees buckle. My hands search for something, anything to steady on.

"She's a dangerous woman, that one." Karma's eyes glow a mean green. "She's been the ngakpa's wife for many years, so who knows what other spells she has taken to benefit her own evil ways."

My fingernails scrape the porous surface. Their shrieking scratches send a shudder up my spine. "Any idea where Khandro might be?"

"Nope." His answer is definite. He pauses. "But I pity the fool who assumes himself her master." His teeth grind a sprig of green. "Lanying should have done what I would have—what any sound man would have done."

My eyes shoot up at him. "What do you mean?"

The moment I ask, I'm sorry.

He looks away again, and my heart shrinks at the understanding of the frightening fact. He would have killed her—for sure. I swallow hard. Oh, how that hurt.

"Come, my love." His determined arm draws me in. "Let's not dwell on what's behind us."

With a convincing stride he leads me back to our horses, grazing the tender young foliage budding between the sage winter green with content.

"A few more days and we'll hit Dartsedo." Karma's hands grip around my waist and land me with a smooth swing in my saddle. "You'll love it, you wait and see."

He slides the reins over, and I nod. He's right, I do love it—the new and undoubtably thrilling unknown. But the exciting prospect can't chase away that vague, unnerving feeling of past things left undone.

My eyes trace the disappearing dots on the horizon; Dendup and Norbu are making their way in a slow pace.

There's time. My heels spur on my stallion, as if he needs it. My hands grip his manes as he bounces on Karma's trail.

There's time, and that's a good thing as I'll need it to mend what once was undone.

Eleven

The sun sinks in a flaming auburn behind the mighty Gongga Mountain, barely lighting our way as we enter the deep gorge where the roar of the raging Zheduo river leads us right into the heart of Dartsedo. We just about made it as the night beats the day, bruising the thin haze of smoldering orange into shrouded shades of blackened beryl and blue at the bat of an eye.

"At last, my favorite village," Dendup says, with excitement. He's quick to take the lead and commands us through winding back alleys to his preferred inn. This place's familiar ground to him and Karma; it's the gateway to the world outside our mountains, where traders from all four winds meet to exchange their goods. We'll only be staying the night, though, heading straight to Ya'an from here, so no trading tomorrow, I guess.

I still have no clue what's in the bags they loaded on the six packhorses. Father told me to leave it to the family when I asked him.

"Their business," he said. "Your only concern is to return home, safe and sound." So, I'll leave it—for now.

As our horses' hooves clatter through the gate, the lady of the inn rushes out, welcoming us—well, Dendup really—with open arms and a smile that lights up the dim courtyard.

"Is it too late?" I'm off my horse with a swift slide and turn to Karma, still on his stallion. The shadows have blended, and the darkness will soon be complete.

"Never," he says and bends forward. He waves at Norbu whose secure arms lift me in one go on the back of Karma's stallion.

"I'll take care of them." Norbu reigns in our horses. Dendup's already disappeared inside—no doubt in close company of the lovely lady of the inn.

"Thanks." With a curt nod, Karma turns his stallion and we're off into the maze of narrow backstreets towards the outskirts of town.

A biting breeze sweeps through my scarf, and I bury my face in the dense weave of his chuba.

"It's close." He points up. His stallion mounts the steep hillside with surprising ease; it's been a long day, after all.

Night has fallen as we arrive, but the golden blaze of butter lamps guides our way to the entry. The intense essence of charred spices and herbs dispels the bitter cold from the air. A bolted gate greets us with a deep creak, but only after Karma's shoulder forces it with great determination. We enter in silence, leaving our boots at the door.

I stretch my body onto the floor. My hands slide across the rough timber. My heart breathes a sigh of relief as I feel it descending upon us—the benevolent smile of the Buddha, the most gracious blessing of all.

As Karma stacks up an offering of tea, butter, and dried fruit from his bag, I turn my mind to prayer, releasing some of the lonesome burden I've carried since we left. I haven't told him about the betrayal my divination revealed—not yet. Maybe I don't have to. His solemn silence tells me he feels it too—we need all the help we can get.

I would love to stay longer—all night if I had my way—but the remains of the day leave their weary traces on us. No doubt my eyes don the same faded shadows as the ones that rim Karma's eyes. As silently as we came, we make our way back to where the invigorating smell of boiled meat and lively chatter of our slightly intoxicated companions awaits us at the inn.

The matron slips beside me with a cordial squeeze on my forearm. "Nordun, right?" With a solid swing, a full jug hits our table.

I nod and delight in her hearty home-made brew.

"Your sister mentioned you might be in the company of Karma," she says, and smiles as I look up.

"My sister?" I raise my eyebrows. *My sister.* My heart skips a beat. Pema or Tsomo maybe? My mind jumps ahead. My dear twin sisters have left me messages from afar before. This time too?

"Yes, your sister Lanying." The matron glances over at Karma. "I think you both know her well." The corners of her mouth reveal a cheeky grin, and I blush. Lanying. *She knows.*

My eyes scoot to Karma. Then again, who doesn't know about Lanying and Karma being lovers? Former lovers, that is. And whenever her name gets mentioned, no matter how indistinct, Dendup's attention is caught. Yes, there he is, already eyeing me up.

"Your sister left a message for you." The matron's words address me, but her eyes go over to Dendup and Karma. She's got their full attention by now, even over the chang running rich in their cups.

"Lanying will wait for you in Chengdu, and she's delighted to receive you at her home." She shoots aside. "She'll send an escort once you've reached near." A rag flies over the table and the cups, empty and plenty, stack in her hands.

"Oh, and your brothers are welcome too, she told me." With a soft chuckle, she scurries away, as if she's expecting the outburst that follows from the table.

A fist pounds and cups clatter. "The hell we are!" Dendup's holler rolls over the table. "That damned woman, she's nothing but trouble." His words drown in the flow of his beloved liquor, but he grumbles on.

I sigh. *Not again*. Dendup's not fond of Lanying and vice versa, and that's an understatement. We traveled in the same caravan to Lhasa. The two of them were at each other's throats whenever the occasion called for it. The very mention of her name combined with the copious amount of chang he's already consumed—and still consuming—seems to set him off in a frenzy.

Karma slurps the last of his thukpa with an eerie calm, pretending not to have heard a word anyone has said. Norbu slouches back in his seat with a lopsided frown. By now he knows when not to speak.

I push my bowl across the table. Lanying's been nothing but good to me, and my heart expands at the thought of seeing her again. She's a true sister in every way. I miss her, although Dendup has a point. Death follows her wherever she goes. My eyes search for a safe haven. I suspect the sudden calm after Dendup's minor storm won't last too long.

"Who's Lanying?" Norbu squints as he faces me. Poor boy. Dendup's drinking tactics have gotten the better of him, and he speaks anyway.

So Sonam didn't tell him anything. My tongue rounds up the last bit of thukpa stuck on my gums. My mind pokes at all corners to find the right answer. I wonder what he told Norbu about our adventure in Lhasa, or why he went there in the first place. What to say?

"Oh, you'll soon find out." Dendup's sharp sneer cuts through the edgy disquiet between us. "She'll devour you with skins and bones, that one." His face gloats with disdain. "Especially a youngster like you." He snorts. "She's always on the prowl for fresh meat." His eyes go over at Karma, and I hold my breath.

Karma looks up. "We'll see if we'll make use of her invitation." He sounds unfazed, but somehow, I don't buy it. "We're not even near yet." He looks around.

There it is. I catch his glance. There's a subtle shift of gloomy green in the depth of his eyes. My love, he's good at shielding his genuine feelings, but not good enough. I've gotten to know him by now.

"Nope, we're not even near," Dendup says and slaps Karma on the shoulder. "We still have a long way to go, brother."

Karma shakes his head, and I repress a snicker. With the speed Dendup's goggling down the drink, he'll be going nowhere, at least not tomorrow. Norbu's body slumps back into his seat altogether. His mild snore confirms my suspicion—he's no match for Dendup and his drinking rate.

"Going beyond here, I don't like it." Dendup's slur moves to a mumble again. "And it's not like we haven't traveled that way before." His hand hangs off Karma's shoulder. His head drops down, and down.

With an abrupt jerk, he opens his eyes in a stare of bewilderment. "I know you've been asking around on our past travels." His voice pitches as he lurches at Karma, who shoves him back in his seat.

My ribs tighten. *What's this?* Karma never told me he searched for his kinfolk. My hands diddle with the empty cups on the table. Nor did he tell Dendup, as it seems.

"But now we're with you." Dendup's voice eases out. "And that's a good thing, for who knows what they want from you once we'll find them, those bloody relatives of yours." His lips curl at the vicious undertone in his voice.

If he's trying to provoke Karma, it's not working. Quiet as ever, Karma pulls back in his seat.

"You ask me, it's a long shot." Dendup's hands wield into nowhere. "Your mother being alive after all that time."

She is. My mind screams in a silenced solitude. I'm sure she is, for I hear her voice, these nights louder than ever before.

"After all, your father isn't." Dendup blurts out his words with a solid determination.

Karma and I both shoot up. *What?*

"What do you know that I don't?" Karma's hand grips Dendup's wrist. My hands rescue the jug from tumbling down our table.

"Well, that's obvious." Dendup's face takes on a glaring look. "He would have come for you, his son, for sure." He wrestles his hand free. "Like I would search the ends of this world for any of my daughters—and you." His body falls back, his face still a gloat.

Dendup's blessed with a large brood of daughters—none of his wives ever gave him a son. I guess Karma's the closest to a son he ever had.

"And besides, you were the only one they found alive." Dendup raises his cup, but Karma's sturdy grip slides over my hand, pinning the jug on the table.

"What do you mean?" Karma's fingers crush between mine. "I was alone when they found me."

I bite my lip as I drag my hand from underneath his.

"Well, yeah, I guess." Dendup's eyes narrow under his furrowed brow. His gaze shifts from the bottle to Karma and back.

"Or is there something you know I don't?" Karma's hand lifts in an endless slow motion.

Dendup growls, and I recoil.

"I wasn't there, was I?" Dendup snatches the jar. "But at the time, I heard the elders talk of another man." His hand trembles and liquor spills. "Must have been a dead man, for they floated him in the river."

My mind boggles at the conversation, or rather confrontation, in front of me. My body heavy, I fall back in my seat.

"What other man?" Karma leans in at the edge of the table.

"I don't know." Dendup's voice takes on a whining tone which doesn't suit him or the situation.

Annoyance stirs my stomach, and a vague sense of unease nestles itself between my ribs. I breathe in deep, but the unsettled feeling won't leave.

"I wasn't to sit with the elders yet." Dendup's shoulders hunch. "But I saw the horse they brought you on—and it wasn't one of ours." He rubs his forehead. "The man in the river, I overheard it once. That's it." His gaze drowns in his drink.

"You never told me." Karma's voice urges a calm consent. As if he understands—the family, they've never been easy on either of them.

"I thought Grandfather told you." Dendup raises his chin, an unusually coy look in his eyes. "Now that you got the family's permission and all." He sighs, almost apologetic.

"He didn't." With those words Karma ends the conversation and pours himself and Dendup another drink.

"More tea?" He turns to me.

I twist my cup. "No, thanks, I'm off."

His longing eyes meet me in a tender embrace. "I'll be up soon." His hand tangles in my loose tresses for a moment.

My fingertips slide along his shoulder as I pass. My heart hurts for him, my love—and the loneliness of him—in all of this.

That night, I surrender my worries and weary thoughts to Tara, my refuge in these challenging times. There can be no room for doubts in my heart, for I've seen the doubts he carries in the depth of his. How he needs me; how he needs us.

Om Tare. Please guide my way.

Twelve

The dense fog at the early morning dawn cannot hide the onslaught of last night's liquor on my companions. Backs stooped and holding on to the pommels, Dendup and Norbu hobble on their horses like a pair of wounded warriors returning from the battlefield.

Karma seems fine. He prompts his stallion in a fast trot, leading us out of the gate onto the main road. I didn't hear him come to bed; I found myself folded deep in the tender hollow of him when his fingertips awoke me, brushing a quiet "good morning" onto my skin.

Karma's stallion shoots ahead, showing no mercy on the slumping pair behind us, a swift shadow fading fast into the surrounding fog. Frost bites my fingers, stiff leather creaks under my rigid grip. With only the dull echo of hooves scrambling on the path to guide us, my stallion frolics in his trail with ease. We reach the outskirts of town in no time, where ghostly silhouettes of men and beast flock together, shrouded in the milky haze of their own breezeless breaths. Dull cracks of whips and muffled cries of horsemen urge through the leaden air—the caravan's lining up to take the road.

We're joining the convoy to secure a safe passage now that we travel beyond our own mountains. Karma's stallion scurries beside mine. "Just making sure we're not late." With a tease in his tone, he turns in the saddle. "I knew you'd keep up—unlike some others."

I crane my neck. The swaying shades of Norbu and Dendup come wading through shreds of bleak pink and ivory hues. The caravan sets itself in motion with a mighty groan; we're right on time.

Karma's fast to steer our party to the front—his favorite position when riding in a caravan. I shift into my saddle. It's onto Ya'an where "great opportunities await" according to my companions. I overheard them discuss prices and permissions with other horsemen a few days ago. I'm sure they'll send some tea home from Ya'an. Not all are allowed to trade in tea—there're special permissions granted by officials, costly clearances which I'm sure neither Grandfather's family nor Sonam possess.

A pale sun peeps through the sluggish sky. My eyes glide over the six packed horses, rimy bags piled up, and swinging on all sides. No way my traveling companions possess the pass for the trade they're doing. Why else would Karma negotiate these with shady characters if our family had the consent required? I shiver and seek my position in the saddle. And if Sonam was in the possession of the right papers, how come they charged him with smuggling a few moons ago?

My fingers loop the leather, now supple in the warmth of my palms. I'm still not sure how they go about it; they're wary of disclosing the details of their dealings on the road with me. My mind stirs up a restless disquiet in the morning calm. Seems after last night's surprising revelations, Dendup and Karma are even reluctant to share their ways amongst themselves.

I soothed my troubling thoughts last night, but they bottle back up with a vengeance this morning. A dull throb settles in my temples. Why did Dendup not tell Karma about the dead man in the water before? And why was Karma silent about the fact he's been looking for his kinfolk before? I've been the one encouraging him to search for his mother; I'm the one who let him hear her plea. My heart quivers ever so slightly, and I draw my scarf near.

I rest my gaze on the back of him, moving so still in front of me. But my mind turns a nasty corner. *What are you hiding from me, my love?*

Troubling thoughts fill the anxious void of not knowing, trying franticly to figure it all out while tightening my chest. *Secrets.* My stallion brays from afar. I take a sharp breath to lift my weighted heart. He's not the only one, as I still haven't told him about the divination. *Om Tare.* My fingers slide under my scarf, in a search for the jade beads underneath. *Suspicions.* My mind ripples with aimless assumptions; my thoughts drift on bothered beliefs. This morning's tea is churning with a nauseating twirl in my stomach. *Om Tare.* This is not how I want to be with my love.

I clasp the reigns—too tight. My stallion snorts and shakes his head in a wheezy protest. "Sorry." I lean back. *No use.* I turn my face to the creamy, clotted sky. The frigid air bites my nostrils; a sharp knowing bursts through my heart. It's no use getting caught up in this whirlwind of foolish thoughts. A hot burn floods around the rims of my eyes. Strange how our mind always spins treads of assumptions and misbeliefs, weaving a blanket of false reassurance for us to cushion the daunting space of the unknown. It does that every time we're unable to figure things out.

Another neigh sounds in the distance. My fingers fumble with the beads, going round and round my neck. "Best to step away and observe," Dechen used to say as she taught us about our mind's contentious chatter. "Then you see, most of your thoughts are like a current passing through the empty space of your mind. You let them slip in as you didn't guard the door with discipline and dedication. There's nothing to them—you can just as easily let them out."

Right. My lips pinch and my thoughts turn to my grandmother, my dearest teacher. *Discipline and dedication.* Good thing she can't see me struggling now. My breath grates along my ribs. A familiar ache of longing stretches across my chest. How I miss them, my dear sisters. It's been over a year now. How I miss them all.

Hooves scramble, a sudden scrape along the sparse gravel. As if he senses my surging disquiet, Norbu drives his horse beside mine.

"You're good?" His voice lingers in the bleached brume between us. His hand tips the rim of his hat.

"Better than you, I think." I cock my head aside, expecting anything but the lively spark of golden amber that meets me amidst the slivers of mist.

"Ah, I'm fine," he says. "But I sure hope I didn't make a fool of myself last night." A coy grin folds in the corners of his mouth.

I shake my head. "You didn't," I say. "Even your snoring was utterly polite." A chuckle slips from my lips.

He sags back in the saddle. "Good." The genuine relief on his face lifts my heart.

"I would hate to think I'm anything like my father." He draws his hat further over his eyes.

My eyebrows raise. “Why?” My stallion slows his pace. “I think the world of your father.” I slide back my scarf. “We all do.” My fingernail catches a loose thread on the frayed hem.

Norbu stares in the distance. For a moment he wavers, but he keeps his thoughts to himself.

I let it rest; I get what keeps them apart. Not too long ago, the same vast ocean of estrangement existed between my own father and me. We stood on shores of shifting sands and let ourselves be moved by the tides of senseless emotions—mine of blame and his of shame. Yet we were able to navigate through this void of confusion, and despite all the missteps and misunderstandings, we found each other right in the messy middle of this human life.

I glance aside, and my heart surges open at the sight of my lonely companion. It takes courage, but most of all humility, to cross the wide space of not knowing, not understanding each other. Not easy for us humans, for we tend to be proud, stubborn beings—but so worth it. How I wish that for Norbu and Sonam too.

“Will the two of you ever move on?” Dendup’s holler rolls from behind. I duck and Norbu waves his hand.

“I get it by now, he’s all bark and no bite.” An honest smile broadens from under Norbu’s drawn hat.

“For sure,” I say, and spur on my stallion. “But he’s also our respected elder, so we better do what we’re told.” Norbu’s horse follows in an easy trot.

“I’m better off putting some of our elder’s good-willed orders aside.” Norbu straightens his back. “This headache’s the worst ever.” He shakes himself; his horse brays.

“You sure don’t show it,” I say.

A snicker sounds from my side. “I guess I do look like my dad after all—if only a little.” His words carry a slight hesitation.

I nod and meet his smile halfway. If only he knew. There's nothing brass or bold about Norbu, but he's got a heart as vast as the sky that stretches above us, just like his father—and they both wear their hearts on their sleeves—of that I'm sure.

I relax in the saddle and let the reins lose. My body breaths a sigh of relief. My heart has settled without me noticing. Gravel grinds, muck gets churned, our horses' hooves clap and fall into a comfortable sync.

So we ride on to Ya'an, while the short days lengthen, and the mighty peaks smoothen their jagged edges. A warming sun seeps through the milky swirls that curl along the foothills, but she loses the battle higher up along the crests, waning into a fog that never seems to end. A clammy vent nudges the crisp chill from the air with a musty, muggy breath. The weather is turning like the landscape, soft and mushy. Little beads of sweat pearl on my neck.

"I told you so." Dendup lets out one of his famed grumbles as the mist mellows into fine sprays of rain, sneaking its way into our bones. "I can't remember ever riding to Ya'an without that damn drizzle on the way." He swipes his nose with his sleeve.

I shrug. Yes, he told us, many times, about the perpetual rain and all the other things that are not to his taste. Like the food being too spicy, the tea too bitter, the milk too watery, and the women too scrawny. His face had twisted in a cheeky grin when he uttered that last remark, and for once I wasn't the one that blushed. Norbu did; his face flashed a bright red as Dendup's hand hit his shoulder.

Dendup has made it quite clear, he's taken a liking to Norbu and has decided to let him in all the "tricks of the trade," the same way he did with Karma, as he put it so finely. I have no doubt he will.

The mist hasn't cleared as we ride on our seventh day, but the sun seems to regain her strength over the winter, pushing the pearly crusts of snow back to where bursts of youthful green salute the everlasting blue yonder. Fresh verdant hedges loop in parallel pathways over the rolling hills from top to bottom, carrying a crop I've never seen before.

"It's tea." Norbu's arm stretches over the wide plain before us. "Tea trees, with the tops ready to be plucked for the first time." His horse scampers beside mine. "Father told me all about it." His eyes scout the endless rows of fertile shoots. "One of these must be famed Mount Mending, it's kind of a holy mountain."

We both halt for a moment. A sacred mountain—that's not something to be passing without paying respect. Ahead of us, Karma turns and Norbu tips his head. We're fine, but Karma's horse is already sprinting our way.

"Mount Mending?" He raises his chin. "Up there, we're getting close." His gaze sweeps ahead as his stallion smoothly slices his way between Norbu's horse and mine. "It's where men grew the first tea a long time ago, so for some it's holy ground."

My eyes follow his gaze towards where the sun greets the ribbons of thin threaded silver, floating along the foot of the mountain famed for its tea.

"It's rated as the finest tea, and very pricy." Karma turns. "A bit too light to my taste." His fingertips skim my leg as his horse pushes mine aside.

"Never mind your taste, brother," Dendup says, a rebuke from the back. "It's all to our liking when there's good profit to be gained."

A greedy guffaw follows, and Dendup's horse skits ahead.

My hand slides over Karma's, resting on my knee with the usual ease. His fingers spread and interlock with mine in a silent understanding. We're in no hurry.

Though maybe we should be. After all, what brings us here is so much more valuable than prized tea from a holy mountain, or any other material revenue to be gained.

Thirteen

The door groans from afar. Tiny tiptoes draw in a dim thud over the timber. The sweet smell of something powdery, like apple blossom with a trace of lemon, skims around the edges of my mat. A dull ache throbs in my temples as a whisper of silk settles beside me.

"Sister." Someone's calling, but I dread opening my eyes, for the room will spin as it did at the first light of dawn, when bitter bile awoke me and lashed against the back of my throat. I just about made it to the back of the courtyard in time.

"I told you so," Dendup said, and Karma held me when my legs wouldn't anymore. "It's the food, too spicy—and this damn weather." Both had rushed after me, and for once I was grateful for the thick fog surrounding us as my stomach rose and emptied itself—several times.

"Sister." A small hand presses on my shoulder, encouraging me to open my eyes. A rich reflection of plum and purple drifts before me. My eyes rise with the pattern of little lotus leaves twining up and fading into a folded collar of meshed golden thread.

"Sister, come, sit up." Her voice is fragile, and she calls me sister, but she's no child, nor is she my kinfolk. Eyes shaped like almonds set in a delicate, pale-pasted face, glossy black hair pinned back in an elaborate bun—she's from here.

I haul myself up. My cracked lips move, but utter no sound.

"Drink." A woody, tangy scent steams from the cup she holds. "She told me you're sick, so I got you some medicine."

I frown. She must mean the lady of the inn who came to check on me a few times this morning. Karma asked her to, but only after I begged him to join Dendup and Norbu for the trade in town.

"I'm Xia." She steadies my trembling hand. "I've come to get you for tea but first we must clean you up."

Xia. The pungent liquid hits my throat. She slides back my tangled hair and I cringe. My cheeks flush. *I must look a mess.*

"Never mind." Her petite fingers glide along my sleeve. "Any sister of Lanying is a sister of mine."

I jolt my head and gulp a big breath. *Lanying?* A placid smile meets my wide eyes.

"How?" I don't recognize the croaky sound coming from my mouth. A driblet of the spicy concoction spills from my chin.

"Laying told me you would be here." She sits herself near. "Your kinfolk, they always stay here when in town." A slight disdain draws around her mouth as her gaze sweeps across the bare room. "Too predictable for their own good." She sighs and straightens her back.

"But they've gone for the day, and there's no need for you to stay in." Her thin eyebrows arch, and her face turns into an almost mischievous smile. "Some pleasant company and decent tea will do you a world of good." Her nose twitches. "And with tea I don't mean the crude brew your people drink."

I blink and slide my feet over. My toes probe the rough wood underneath. Solid ground, all is well. I take my time to sip the last of my drink. Whatever she gave me, it's working—fast.

"You speak my language." I clear my throat and wipe my mouth.

"Only so-so." She bops her head. "My mother's mother came from your side of the mountains, but sister told me you might be speaking my language by now." Her eyes twinkle with a curious charm. "She remembers you were very keen on learning."

I stare at the bottom of the empty cup. *Please love, stay in until I'm back.* Karma's voice presses in my ear. *Promise me.* His cool hand had drawn across my clammy forehead, an unusual worry in his eyes. He knew I wasn't capable of going anywhere this morning. Yet, he made me promise, and I did.

My thumb rims my cup, and I glance aside. Xia's eyes narrow to half moons, pensive, yet a bold tinge of challenge shines through.

"Sister said they would keep you under their guard." She tips her head. "But they can't object to you having a cup of tea and some refreshments in good company." Her mouth, buffed with a rosy shine, pouts ever so slightly. "And this place could do with some fresh air." She hops off the matt and pulls at the shutter. Beams of bright yellow pour in.

"Woah." I shield my eyes and take her hand. My body sways, but only for a moment. A cleansing breeze fills my lungs. *Om Tare.* I'm fine.

Within no time she has me scrubbed and "presentable," fussing about me like a mother hen picking at her young.

"Come, come." She flurries across the courtyard, gesturing at the broad-shouldered guard to open the gate.

"There we go." Her hand on my elbow, we step out into the street and I come to a standstill.

For days we've been riding in a drizzle of mist and grayish sludge. We arrived late last night, entering the town as it was already shrouded in shadows and twilight. Somehow my mind still dwells in the darkened hues surrounding us all those yesterdays. I catch my breath in delight.

The sun has come in rich colors of amber and orange; like honey, her rays drip in golden all over the town. A warming wind sweeps along, and vines of young green rustle against grayish plaster. Burst of blossoms drape along white pillars and balconies, reaching all the way up to curvy, slated roofs, where bronzed clay tiles meet a stark cerulean sky. Hooves prance and clap on cobbles, carrying a rush of robes in the brightest of dyes coming through.

"Watch it." A hand hauls me aside and Xia's chuckle sounds in my ear. "Better stay close." Her arm hooks in mine.

My mind dazzles. Different tongues drift by. Something stirs deep inside of me, a thrill of the unknown. I squeeze Xia's hand on my arm—how exciting all of this is.

"Over here." She leads me past the row of stalls and their loud proprietors. The entire side of the road is packed with goods decked out on wooden boards and coarse woven blankets, large vessels and ripped baskets line on the side. There are herbs I recognize, their scent mixed in a sweet and peppery bouquet. There are fleshy vegetables in odd shapes and sizes, and strips of dried meat and skin, and bits of bleached bones and fatty marrow, strings of nuts and seeds, heaps of colored pastes and powders, and large chunks of what looks like a soft stone, and oh, there's so much more—things I've never seen. My eyes dash from left to right, prying at the curious commodities. My feet can't keep up with Xia's pace.

"In here, in here." She waves her hand in dismissal and skirts into an alley, pulling me at her side. Two giant lions, their seated pose chiseled in stone, guard a narrow entrance. A whitewashed courtyard lays behind. A rose bush is budding in the corner; tiny bells tingle as we pass.

"Good to be home." Xia slides her jacket into the hands of a servant appearing out of nowhere. She smoothens her hair, but there's not a loose strand in sight. I gather my bag close.

We sit in silence at the lacquered table. Trays are brought, with cups and boiling water, and a dish with finely ground leaves. She speaks softly, directing the servants, and I listen. Her voice pitches in an unfamiliar pronunciation, yet there are many words I understand.

She smiles as she lowers her head. "Different accents, but we're all the same." Her hands reach out for the cups. "All looking to come home, aren't we?" A gleam of burnished brown flashes from under her silver caked eyelids.

"Lanying told you then?" I choose my words with care. My eyes glide to my bag, the drawing I made of his tattoo stuck between the pages inside. I vowed I wouldn't mention the purpose of our journey to anyone.

"Mind you, I think he's better off staying far away." She doesn't mention his name, but there's an unnerving familiarity in her words. "If he is of Mongolian blood, nobody escapes their army, sister, especially not a man skilled with the blade like he is."

She knows him, and not only of him. A stone pits in my stomach. *Focus.* My eyes set at the cups. A warm tingle shoots right through my chest. These cups, fine and white, almost sugary with a hint of blue shining on them. They're like the porcelain cups my mother kept in our formal room. She never used them but took them out of the cupboard now and again.

"Only look, Nordun, don't touch," she would say, and she was right. They would have been no match for my grubby little fingers. I draw my hands in my sleeves.

"They're not an amiable people, the Mongols." Xia slides the dish with tea leaves in front of her. "Take my word for it, for I'm married to one."

I lean back. "You are?" My gaze meets hers. Her hands stall. A shadow draws over her face.

"Yes, but I'm lucky. He let me return to my family after our son was old enough to join the army." Her voice is a whisper. "His father's in the Kheshig, so my son is destined too." Fine lines surface in the thin veneer around her eyes.

Her sadness drifts between us, like a distant memory desperately wanting to fade, yet is engraved in the heart, bound to bleed into a forever. *Om Tare.* The sorrow we women must bear in this life.

Her fingertip strokes the bristles of a small brush beside the dish. "I guess I served my purpose." She lifts her chin, and a steady voice follows. "And now I serve here—the finest of tea, the first pick of the year." A serene smile, an acceptance passes as she pours the scalding water over the ground leaves. "Unlike other tea, this pick from Mending is warming, and takes care of disease."

A refreshing clean scent rises as she stirs the tea with the brush. "A woman has to know her tea if she wants to be in this trade." She tilts her head to the side. The water tints a tender green. "Like you have to know your horses if you want to make a profit."

My mouth runs dry. I shake my scarf off my shoulders. Too hot. Is there anything this woman doesn't know about me?

"But let me not tire you with trade, today is for rest." She pours all her attention on the cups. "This tea will restore your life force and you'll need it as you have a long way to go."

I lean in. The tea is so clear I can see right to the bottom. I put the cup to my lips, careful not to spill. She nods and I take a sip, only a small one. My palate is parched, but to gulp it down would be out of place. So I take another small sip, and another one, and as the liquid wraps its warmth around me, it smoothens the last bit of unease from my body. A murmur of ease settles within.

"Lanying has her sources." Xia pours and stirs and pours again, filling the cups with utmost precision. "She knows where whomever you are looking for can be found." She stresses her words with a resolute tone.

My gaze darts over my bag again, with my book and the minute drawing folded inside. Somehow Karma won't let me help him out here, but who can blame him? I hardly speak the language, and can't do anything but follow his mother's voice I hear in the night. *Om Tare.* Where will this take us?

Xia's eyes pry at my beads around my wrist, but only a little. "Put your trust in her, and you'll understand what to do—and what not to." Her face sets in a serene smile, radiating the certainty of understanding, the unwavering faith I'm so familiar with and so envy. My grandmother Dechen has it, and many of my dear sisters have too, but me? The beads slip, my palm clammy. For sure, I have not.

Xia turns her head and directs my gaze at a scroll hanging of an intricate landscape I didn't notice before. "It's the Dao, the Way that teaches us that when nothing is done, nothing is left undone."

My eyes take in the painting, now prominent on the wall beside us. Round rocks and straight, stalky trees, dabbed in blues and greens, and a tiny figure, seated on a leopard skin, hiding inside. There's writing on the left side, and red marks that I can't read. It doesn't matter, for the serene scene brushed on the silk with the most subdued of strokes speaks for itself. There's an unmistaken stillness exuding from the painting that surges straight through my being, conveying a mystifying, yet certain solace that all will be well.

"You see, Nordun, like in nature, everything in our life has its course and not all is gained by interfering." Xia's hands slide over a few small dishes.

I look at her. A profound knowing meets my eyes.

"Rather than struggling against the conditions we encounter; we can allow things to take their natural course." She sits back in a sigh of silk and brocade. "If you don't know what to do, do nothing, and let matters unfold for they are meant to."

She raises her hand and spreads her fingers in a graceful fan across her chest. "And if you know, then take your action, but only if you genuinely know, deep down here."

My breath stalls. My hands clasp the edge of the table. Her voice clear, her words sure, I want to hold this moment and never let it go. I want to wrap my whole being around it and let it into me, becoming with it until I'm one and whole with her truth.

She leans in, and I breathe out. I lower my eyes and the bluish glaze on the fine white blurs, swallowing the green within it.

"Now let's enjoy our tea, as it will quench our thirst, calm our mind, and eliminate all distractions." She pours more tea and I swipe my sleeve across my eyes. "And like the challenge of anything in life, let's give it the attention it deserves." She picks up her cup. Her chin points at my bag. "So let's drink our tea with our whole being, undivided."

A brilliant golden amber twinkles between us as her eyes meet mine over her cup. A warm glow spreads over my cheeks. *This woman.* Polished, refined, peaceful, and wise beyond what I'll ever be—yet there's a daring edge to her, just like Lanying. There's something unnerving and at the same time exhilarating about being in her company.

A sliver of doubt crosses my mind, but I sip my tea and let it pass. Her truth is mine.

I've come on this journey with my best intentions and willing to accept whatever happens. Me being here right now, that is more than enough.

Fourteen

"When you're back from your adventure, I'll have the papers done." Xia's lips curl, and a complacent smile peeps through. "We'll do some profitable trading together, nothing like the dubious deals your kinfolk is involved in."

She opens her arms in a heartfelt embrace. "And don't you dare pass by, sister, I'll find you, wherever you are." Her tight hug enforces her promise, but I had no doubt about that, anyway.

This afternoon turned out to be most enlightening. Xia told me all about trade, including the real reason her Mongolian husband sent her back to her family who's been in the tea trade for many generations. And now they're doing so well because Xia's husband, as a royal guard, had the standing to enlist his in-laws in the Ortogh, the merchant association that allows its member to do legal trade and profit from tax exemptions. To guarantee his share of the profits, he sent his wife home to take care of it all.

Xia's arm hooks in mine and we stroll across the courtyard. I glance aside. She nods at the guard to follow.

Of course Lanying had told her of Father's stables, and Xia disclosed all doings about trade to me in great detail. How strictly it's controlled, especially the tea trade, and the risks people take by "running goods the back ways," as she so finely put it. She spoke about the ins and outs, and with such a confidence—how unusual for a woman.

She snickered at me when I asked her if it didn't hinder her being a woman in trade.

"On the contrary." Her eyebrows arched, and that audacious spark gleamed her eyes to a burnished brown again. "We women have a natural talent for engaging in many partnerships, combining profit with pleasure—be it with the utmost discretion, of course."

My toes had curled in my boots, and I wanted to cringe. Silly me, I should have known—she's a sister of Lanying after all. Well, whatever her ways are, they're hers to walk. I bet there's nothing that goes on in this town without her knowing.

With her guards making way, we dash across the stalls and skirt along the lengthy shadows, drawn by a tangerine sun. Where did the day go?

"Here you are." Xia stops at a narrow gate, thrown wide open and inviting. The faint hum of prayer dwells in the yard, a pair of red robes wander inside. It's the perfect place for me to end this most interesting day.

"I'll see you soon, sister." Xia's head bends in a subdued goodbye.

I lower my head and fold my hands. Gratitude flushes my heart.

"I'll leave my guard; you'll get home safe." Xia waves at our rugged escort, taking his position with discretion at the gate.

"That won't be necessary." A familiar voice sounds from behind and spins my heels.

Norbu! A cheerful smile beams from under his hat. An enormous bag dangles over his shoulder.

"I figured I would find you here." He points his chin at the gate.

Silk swishes in a mild breeze. I turn and crane my neck. Too late—Xia's already gone.

"They sent me ahead." Norbu tips his hat. I peer over his shoulder. "They'll be home soon." The bag plops with a dry thud at his feet. He rubs his hands.

"Everything went well?" I tilt my head. His smile's still there.

"We did a few good deals—I think." He shrugs. "You know how it is when those two are together." His foot probes the bag. "All they let me do is handle the bags, but I'm sure they take good care of my father's part in it all."

"So they wouldn't let you help them either?" I shake my head. *Those two.*

"Nope, it will a long time before they'll let me be their partner in trade." He squares his shoulders. We both laugh.

Partners in crime. The words are there, but I won't let them roll off the tip of my tongue. I don't need to—I'm sure he knows exactly what's going on with those two.

With a swing, he hoists the bag around the corner. "Let's go for kora."

I slide my prayer beads from my neck and trail behind him.

The rattle of prayer wheels spins through the haze of the smoldering butter lamps. I lower my body in front of the mighty Buddha. My heart delights as his compassionate gaze descends upon my being. My mind empties, and the day is far gone.

Many times we go around, joined by pilgrims and travelers alike. Norbu stacks a few offerings on the side. I take a seat in the furthest corner. The timber floor resonates the unwavering devotion of tired feet shuffling along.

My eyes close for a moment. *This feeling.* And just like that, I am home. *Home.* Not at the stables, but at the monastery. A burning rim draws around my eyes. It's been a year since I left my dearest sisters. My heart quivers. I made my choice.

Norbu settles beside me, his gentle touch on my arm. "You're good?"

My hand crosses his. "I'm fine." And I am. My choice was the right one for me.

"You miss them, your sisters?" He nods at the red robes drifting by.

"Now and again," I say. My fingers search for the crimson string on my wrist. "But they're never far away." I keep them close to my heart.

His hand reaches out. I take it and he pulls me up. Three more prostrations and we're ready to go.

"You know, Nordun." He hauls the bag on his shoulder. "You surprised me." He hops and straightens his back.

I frown. "How so?" I guess he expected me to take my vows, as most did who knew me back then.

"Well." He hesitates. "I never thought you would be with Karma." His eyes narrow. A bitter breeze sweeps through the courtyard.

I pull my scarf close. The sun's sinking fast. A restless chill stirs the air.

"I mean, Karma's so different from you." He sounds almost apologetic.

"That he is." I laugh. "I'm very fond of home, while he can't resist the call of the mountains." My breath shallows as I meet Norbu's stare, void of the usual sparkle. Instead, there's caution and concern coming through in the honeyed hazel in his eyes.

"Yes, that too, but..." His voice drops. His feet scuffle. "You do realize he's the one the family calls upon, don't you?" He stalls and averts his gaze.

The last light of the day dwindles into shreds of purple and blue. The lone chuckle of a cuckoo calls out in the distance.

"He's ruthless." His words, ever so quiet, spatter on the beaten earth, right before my feet. I recoil. "Everybody knows."

I jerk back my scarf. "That's the past." My mind seeks for shelter. *I don't want to hear this.* My hands twist the wool. A slow ache throbs in my temples.

"You think so?" A sad smile reaches out to me. "Did you ever wonder why your cousins didn't come to their father's aid in Lhasa—or why they still haven't come to take care of him after all this time?" An eerie silence thunders between us.

Cold sweat breaks on my forehead. My mind crashes into an abyss of denial. Father received word from Palmo at Losar. It's true—Tennah's still in her monastery, and his sons never came.

"He wouldn't do that." I want to shout, but there's only a whisper. "He would have told me." My eyes search for Norbu's, and the truth he bears inside of them. Both are hiding on me. It's no use.

"Word is he took care of the last one this winter." Norbu shakes his head. "Orders of the family."

This winter. I close my eyes.

All winter, Karma's been with me. Sure, he had to go a few times, but not for long. Making arrangements with Dendup, that's what he told me. Preparing for the long journey ahead. *Focus.* An icy calm rushes through my veins.

"I'm sorry, I shouldn't have brought it up, but it bothers me," Norbu says. "And I care for you, Nordun, I do."

Slowly, I open my eyes to the truth standing before me. It's too much. *Focus.* A sharp breath surges in my lungs.

"I know." I bite my lip. My hand reaches out to hold his—if only for a moment. Sadness resides in the honesty between us. A little crack bursts the thin walls of my heart.

The wind picks up. "We'd better go." My voice is still a whisper.

Norbu hauls his bag over his shoulder, and I draw my shawl over my head.

We walk home together and let a world of shadows pass between us.

Some thoughts are better left unsaid, kept in the heart and carried through a lifetime. And some truths are meant to fade in the passing into forever. But that's not how we humans understand it to be.

"What took you so long?" Dendup roars from the back of the kitchen. Servants swing by, bowls filled to the brim fly from their hands, feeding an unruly, hungry crowd. Mouths slurp, cups bang on the tables. I wade through, fending off a hand creeping up where it shouldn't be.

"We visited the temple." Norbu lets me pass.

Karma's arm pulls around me. "Looking much better than this morning." He shifts me beside him. "The day of rest did you good then?" His hand weights down on my knee.

Dishes are tossed at our table. Steam rises, and I dig in. No need to mention my visit with Xia—for now.

"Things went well?" I glance away. The soup scorches its path down my throat. Tears sting my eyes and I gulp.

"We made a nice profit." Dendup belches and slides his cup over at Norbu to pour him another drink.

"And otherwise?" My fingers intertwine with the ones on my knee. I dare to look. A muted green greets me in the middle.

"Not here." Karma leans in. "Once we're in Chengdu, we'll know more." His thumb strokes the palm of my hand. "We leave early tomorrow, same caravan." He directs his words at our companions.

"I'll make sure our horses are ready." Norbu grins. "Can't guarantee our respected elder will be." He pats Dendup on the shoulder and receives a cordial poke in return.

It took some time, but look at these two now—my younger brother and our elder joking around. I sink back. The warmth of the soup settles within me.

"Let's go." Karma's voice prompts me. I peer up, a little dazed.

He gobbles down the last of the brew and we're off to our mats.

"A friend of Lanying visited this morning." I press my cheek in the folds of his chuba. "She brought me medicine and took me for tea." Soft fur surrounds me. "But you already knew."

His lips plant a kiss on the top of my head. "Oh love, you're simply not capable of hiding anything, especially from me." He rests his cheek against my forehead, and he sighs, almost inaudible. Even now, in the darkest of night, the subtle scent of the sun in summer, and the mountains with meadows in full bloom linger around.

"Let me guess, you met Xia." His fingers tangle my loose tresses.

"I did," I say. His arms lock me in.

"She's an interesting woman." His calm note sparks a disquiet within me. His balmy breath skims my ear.

"She invited me for tea and told me about the Dao of not doing." My fingers hook the sides of his belt. "And about the trade." A sharp edge of leather scrapes my thumbs. *Nobody escapes the army, sister.* Disquiet stretches across my heart.

“Did she now?” He pulls back a bit. “I didn’t know you had an interest in the Dao, or in tea trade, my love.” A shimmer of gray shifts in his eyes and ebbs into a soft shade of tender green. He lets down his guard and I breathe.

“Oh, I have many interests.” I raise my chin and pinch my lips but can’t suppress a smile breaking through.

“Why don’t you tell me all about it—tomorrow.” His hand folds around the nape of my neck. “For now, I need to feel if you’re still interested in me.” He tastes so sweet.

That night his dreams are fierce, and more vivid than ever. Dreams of horse's hooves thundering over desolate plains, and eagles’ wings slicing through a crystal clear blue. When he wakes, all drenched in sweat, he lets me hold him and that’s enough for now.

I’m called and my heart is moved.

We’re on the right path, getting closer.

Fifteen

A watery sun sets on our back as we ride to the outskirts of town. The road is lined with scores of bodies, moving through the feeble morning mist. Heavy coughs rattle in their chest. Most of them spend the night in the open courtyards, a flimsy coat as their blanket, a worn hide underneath. Packed to the hilt, they stumble into the new day on thin straw sandals, a few leather straps wrapped around their ankles and feet. They're heading to the massive mountain peaks, the ones we left behind.

My eyes lower. My hand slides over my stallion's neck; he's prancing all the way. *Privileged.* My stomach churns with this morning's tea. All those years in the monastery—studying and praying with the desire to serve all sentient beings. *Om Mani.* How little I knew.

My teeth grind a shaving of dried root to a pulp, and a woody sweetness steeps my throat. Xia was right—it takes the edge off the nausea. A big yawn escapes from my chest.

"Looks like somebody didn't get their sleep last night." Dendup's snicker sounds from my side. I raise my eyebrows. He seems bright for this time of day. How unusual.

"Well brother, I hate to admit it, but you're right." I flash my most modest smile at him. "And I'm sorry to tell you, but since you mention it—it was your snoring that left me with little sleep."

A loud roar rolls from under his hat. "Now, now, sister, a little respect for your elder, please." His stallion bumps into mine. "Time has worn these bones of mine thin, and the countless nights spent underneath the stars haven't been kind to me either." He straightens his back.

"I'm sorry, brother." I slip back my scarf. Two twinkle lights spark from under his hat. I know he's pretending, yet there's a tiny truth in his words. The long days in the saddle are not easy on the body, even though we're the fortunate ones spending most nights at an inn. I glance aside again. He draws his hat further down.

"Be careful now, don't let the weather here fool you," he grumbles. "It's deceiving—this muggy wind carries all kinds of disease." He snorts. "I'll take our crisp and clean mountain peaks over this sodden soil anytime."

Gravel crunches. His stallion speeds ahead, and Dendup calls over his shoulder. "Come on sister, don't be slowing us down now." His typical chuckle follows, and my heart delights. That's my elder alright.

Slope rocks replace loose pebbles and churned muck as we leave the town of Ya'an behind us. Large stone strips guide our path onto tranquil ridges decked with fresh foliage. Hooves dash with vigor, leaves rustle, and budding sprouts swish as we pass by. We're keeping a gentle pace, riding in our usual line. Stillness descends all around, bringing a light drizzle. My mind calls to prayer. *Om Tare.* Rain again.

Karma turns in the saddle and catches my gaze. An understanding passes between us—he hears my silent chant. I nod. I'm fine, my stomach has settled. A few more days, and my body will be used to the spicy food, and the clammy weather, and all that's strange to me here.

A lightness opens within me. *A few more days.*

Another yawn slips away. A few more days and we'll most likely be at my sister's house. I shift in my saddle. Patience is hard to find on this path.

A long day stretches before us as we ride through lush green and persistent drizzle. We have better luck the next day. We arrive in Qionglai as dusk sets in a cloudless ocher and orange, with our clothes and horses dry for once.

"At least they serve a decent thukpa here." Karma's strong arm hauls me in. "You go ahead, we'll take care of the rest." He waves at Norbu.

Dendup has already jumped inside, hunting down the best seats in the kitchen. I let go of the reins and give in—my stomach aches for familiar food.

Dendup's head pops up from the far back of the kitchen. "Over here."

With a servant at his side, and cups on the table, a satisfied smirk sets beneath his mustache. He has no intentions of moving again for the night, that's obvious. My body sinks into the seat beside him. I'm with him, for once. It's more than comfy up here.

My gaze glides over the kitchen. There's a good crowd already, and more are arriving, all hungry, searching a roof for the night. Most are travelers like us, or merchants as Dendup calls us, but there are also a few stately figures dressed in pressed silk and furred feathers.

"They're lost, that's for sure." Dendup's hand draws around his cup, his eyes narrow. He sips his drink.

I don't ask what he means.

Blazing bowls slide over our table. The food's hearty and filling and nothing much is said until chang flows over my companion's cups. I rest my head against Karma's shoulder. His hand finds mine, a little squeeze. It's been a good day.

"So, what's the story about this place you were on about today?" Norbu pours another round and Dendup veers up.

"Let me tell you, younger brother," he says, his voice filled with verve.

Karma sighs. "Here we go again, another tale of adventure." A mumble sounds from under his breath and I laugh.

"You will find this one particular interesting, sister." Dendup's lips curl. "For this one is a tale about a woman's undying love." He jabs a finger my way.

"A woman's love." I veer up, but Karma's arm hauls me back in.

"Yes, and it happened right here in Qionglai, a long time ago." Dendup points at the jug on the table. "To a young woman named Zhuo." He empties his cup in one swag and leans in.

"She was beautiful, and educated, and very wealthy, of course." His face rests in a complacent smirk. "But very unlucky as her husband died young, and she had to return to her parents. It was there that she met her true love, a poet called Sima, who was as poor as can be." His hand signs at Norbu. Another drink finds its way to him.

"But you know women, they fall for the most unlikely ones." A swift wink flies from the corners of his eyes across the table. A slow burn creeps up my face. "When everybody was asleep and the moon nowhere to be found, the two of them ran away." He leans in even further. Karma's fingers trail down the rear of my neck.

"Needless to say, Zhuo's father was furious and withdrew his support. Now who could blame him, right?" Dendup rubs his mustache and takes a moment before he proceeds.

"But Zhuo, stubborn as she was, she wouldn't give in. She sold everything she owned and started a wine shop right here in Qionglai." His hand folds around his cup. "Smart woman, if you ask me."

Karma shakes his head. "If I didn't know any better, you could be talking about one of your daughters, brother." He raises his cup and Dendup meets him halfway for a toast.

"But something tells me you don't let your women off that easy." Norbu delivers his words with an unease. A hesitant smile follows.

I bite my lip. Norbu's right. I saw Dendup chase and catch his youngest wife at Losar, after she wouldn't give in to one of his whims.

Dendup bares his teeth. "Damn if I would, brother."

Cups clang in agreement across the table, and another round gets poured.

I wiggle in my seat. Surely this can't be the end of the story?

"So?" I tilt my head and meet Dendup's watery eyes.

"So then, sister, the Emperor noticed Sima's poetic talent and offered him a job at his court in Chang'an." His furry eyebrows draw over his eyes, veining a serious look. I try not to laugh but I can't help it, it's too much.

"Of course Sima went, and he got all famous and desired another wife." His eyes narrow. "As all men do after a while, right?" He leers across the table, seeking out my companions.

Karma's muscles harden under his grip, still firm around me. Norbu seeks the bottom of his cup. *Good.* Dendup finds no support.

"Anyway," Dendup says and snorts. "Sima writes to Zhuo, who's still in Qionglai, and she pens him back an elaborate poem, declaring she's not having any of it." He squares his shoulders and takes a sharp breath. I hold mine.

Where's this story going?

"It must have been some verse, I'll tell you." Dendup's voice raises, and a dismissive edge drifts along the high-pitched tones. "Because Sima came running straight back to Zhuo and took her to Chang'an where they lived happily ever after." He turns to me in a slow motion, and a stifled silence wraps the two of us tight.

"Now tell me, sister, wasn't that a tale of your liking?" His eyes pry into mine; a cagey glimpse passes by.

"For sure." I shift in my seat and avert my gaze. Something's off. My fingers pick a loose thread at the hem of my sleeve. Norbu's eyes fix on the table. Karma's calm hand slides down my back. I lean in; his quietude smolders a gentle heat behind me.

Still, my body tenses and I glance aside. Knowing my elder—there's bound to be more coming my way.

Dendup sinks in his seat with a sure but wistful sigh. "Well, that's the only elopement story I know to have a happy ending."

There it is. Sweat trickles down the back of my neck.

"Let's not go there again, brother," Karma says, but it's as though Dendup whacks his words right off the table.

"You know sister, when Rapten found out Dechen was pregnant, he reached out to her family, trying to make amends." His gloomy stare angles around, hooking me in. "But her brothers moved in the dark of the night to slash his throat, like only cowards do." His hands draw over the table.

"The filthy dogs!" His fist bangs, cups clatter, and Norbu ducks to catch a jug rolling around.

"That's enough now." Karma lashes out, and his hand seizes round Dendup's. More cups shatter. My ribs smash into the rounded edge of the table. I gasp. A stale mixture of sweat and chang stifles the air.

"Enough." Karma cautions and Dendup recoils. His body slouches back in his seat.

A dull throb sets in my temples. *What's wrong with him?*

Spit spatters on the earth beaten floor beside us. Seems Dendup's having another go.

"It's a sheer miracle Dechen survived that family, and the way they treated her." His words are steeped in liquor, but he delivers them with a dogged determination.

"The woman's a true saint, and smart as hell." His tone mellows. "The way she turned that dilapidated hermitage into a mighty monastery with Ghedun." His voice trails off to an inaudible grumble.

A moment passes, and a slight reprieve unfolds between the four of us.

Norbu slides a cup of water my way.

Karma's hand skims along my ribs. "Sorry, love."

I shrug. "It's fine." It's nothing I haven't heard before. Dechen's brothers got away with murder, and it's still a mystery to me why my grandfather's family didn't seek their revenge.

"Nothing to be sorry for, brother." Dendup hauls himself up from his seat. "Things all turned out better than we could ever have imagined." A satisfied grin flashes our way. "And we have you to thank for it."

Karma's arm freezes around me. I catch his gaze. An icy green frost shifts in his eyes, fast as lightening. *What's this?* I shiver and turn to Dendup.

"How?" I hesitate. A wary calm stirs within me.

Dendup points his chin at his cup for another pour, but Norbu's not moving.

Do I really want to know? Seems I don't have a choice.

"Ah, sister." Dendup's face is all innocence, but his nostrils flare. "What better revenge than having you, their only granddaughter, being a wife in our family?"

His truth slices right through me, like the sharpest blade.

My stomach hardens. *Ouch.* That hurts.

"And you, my brother, you didn't even have to snatch her." His hands clasp together, his knuckles crackle. "It took you some time, but she came running right at you." He flashes a satisfied grin Karma's way.

"Well done, you've always proven to be our best man for revenge, but you're the only one who could pull this stunt off with that Mongol blood of yours." Dendup raises his empty cup to an unnerving silence. No one moves. I close my eyes.

Those words. Karma's pulse throbs through the thin cotton between us. *Focus.* My mind's taking a dangerous turn.

"I'm off to bed." My knees wobble, but I make it to the door.

The room is dark. A shadow moves. Karma's arm hurdles around me.

Those words. My heart weeps. Tears streak my face.

"Love, don't even go there." A feverish cheek scorches mine. "You know better than that." His fingers twist in my hair, and desperation mingles with a restrained calm.

"I do know better." I choke. My mind stalls in the corner. *Focus.* Which way to go?

"But the family…" Too late, my thoughts slip away. "You always…" I bite my tongue. I can't say it, but I'm no fool. Not anymore.

My fingers find the edge of his shirt. My face folds in his collar.

His lips press on the top of my head. His thumb skims my jaw.

He clears his throat and tilts my chin. "You mean I always follow their orders." His sober stare meets mine.

My heart shrivels and hurdles itself to the deepest alcoves hidden within me.

"I know you'll don't want to hear it, my love, and you'll never understand, but for me taking a life is easy." He chooses his words with the utmost care, still they shatter the very core of my being. "It's something instilled in me, a long time ago."

My fingernails scrape his chest. "Please." *Don't say it.* I reach out. The salty savor of him stings my lips.

"We both know it's true, no need to speak of it anymore." His words seethe on his breath. "Let it rest in what's behind us." His mouth grazes the tip of my nose.

My mind surrenders. I want to. I can. I'll let it rest.

"Now loving a life, that's something that doesn't come natural to me." His fingers lock the back of my neck. "I was never taught how to, and loving you, it isn't easy." His breath leaves as his shadow shifts before me. A deep yearning lingers on.

"Loving you makes me vulnerable as you unearth the deepest and darkest of me—my dreams, and my demons." Sparks of emerald ignite in the dark, and my heart lifts herself from her sanctuary. It knows it's safe to return.

"I spent my life running, fleeing from them, but you made me see—they both dwell inside of me." His fingertips trace my collarbone to the place where he left the conch shell pendant last summer, a reminder of the Buddha's melodious call to awaken from our ignorance in this human life.

"That's a cruel truth to a man who's used to fighting only the enemy lurking on the outside, to claiming a victory that's won with ease." He tilts his head. I blink. A ghost vanishes into the shimmer of polished jade before me. "Slaying the demon inside, that's a whole different battle, one that I'm not trained for." I reach for his hand on my chest.

"It's a battle that turns into a ravaging war within the blink of an eye." I steady my voice as I still my mind. "But this too is a battle that can be won." My heart beats a steady drum underneath our palms.

"Yes, but love, your years in the monastery prepared you well." He lays my head under the soft curve beneath his shoulders. "You dare and step into the eye of the storm with the trust that victory will be yours, no matter what."

A little smile breaks on my lips. Yes, my grandmother taught me well. All the doubt and confusing remaining in me are entirely my shortcomings.

"I'm nowhere there yet, as I am only skilled in drawing my blade." His mouth whispers. "Still my love for you is stronger than ever, and I'm more than willing to learn."

A faint draft from the window brings a chill to my spine. I look up and smooth a long dark strand behind his ear. My lips pull him nearer.

"Give it time, but most of all give it your fullest attention." My teeth sink in the flesh of his lip with no intention of ever letting go.

"That's an order," I whisper. The salted aftertaste of him makes me want so much more.

His hands anchor my hips and I hold my breath. *Did I just say that?*

"Well, well, are you getting fresh with me, love?" His eyes widen. A wild spirit blazes through. "Good, it's about time."

There's no escaping the darkness as the night closes in on the two of us.

There's no need to, for it's been a good day, after all.

Sixteen

Luscious, broad-leaved trees line our path through the fertile plains of Chengdu. A few scattered homesteads hide among the burgeoning green. There's nothing particular about this stretch of our journey, yet it unsettles the two of them—Karma's eyes have combed the banks of the meandering creek ever since we left this morning; and instead of slouching in the saddle like usual, Dendup swerves around the edges.

At first, I thought Dendup's disturbing words two nights ago had caused this behavior. But all was well yesterday, so that can't be it. I'm not imagining it either—something's off with them. Norbu notices it as well.

"What's up with these two today?" he says, and steers his stallion closer to mine. "Seems like Dendup's sitting on a bag of beans instead of in the saddle." He points his chin at a tense Karma in front of us. "And Karma acts like he's expecting an attack out of nowhere any time."

We both laugh. A vague apprehension tenses my shoulders. I shrug it off, but my mind won't let go. Even I can feel it—there's something about this place, and it's not good.

When the sun shrivels our shadows to the narrowest of forms, our caravan seeks shelter in the shade of stalky thickets of bamboo that hem the inlet we've been riding along. Dendup's quick to retreat. Norbu takes care of our frolicking horses, kicking up a refreshing spray of glaring silver and azure. Karma wanders off, following down the fleeting stream, his hand trailing me along.

"It was here, somewhere along this river." His voice almost inaudible, I lean in. "That's what grandfather told me, but he wasn't sure anymore." His gaze sweeps over the water. "It was too long ago." An absent arm draws me in.

Grandfather. My thoughts are right back with the man he calls Grandfather. The man who received me with open arms at the family camp last year. Even after all that happened between our families, he never held a grudge. "This family is your sanctuary now," he told me, this gentle man with the opaque mist of advanced age in his eyes.

"Maybe Grandfather's mind is leaving him." A fresh breath settles in my chest. "He's old now, and like he said, it was long ago."

A pair of mosquitoes whizzes by on a musty breeze. A snow-white heron tiptoes on his golden slippers, splashing in the shallow waters across from us. My eyes search for something my heart already knows. There's nothing to see down here—there's nothing left of what once was.

"I don't recognize this place," Karma says in his usual calm. A muscle twitches under his skin as he holds me close—and yet he feels far away.

"How could you?" My fingers hook behind his belt. "You were only a boy."

"I was." He looks at me and his eyes burst with the darkest of green, the hue of a pine forest in the midst of winter. "But if I still carry my mother's tongue, why can't I remember this place?" A twilight sets in his face.

"Or her." His last words slip away on a deep, weighted sigh. He presses his lips on the top of my head.

His mother. He doesn't remember her or even the sound of her voice. It must be that her memory is too painful for him, for she calls me, the one who he trusts, the one who he has let into his heart.

"We've stopped here before, Dendup and me." A weary resignation dwindles his confident stance. "I've even asked around." His head points towards the nearest homestead, a simple abode nesting in the verdant fold of the hill ahead. "There weren't many around back then. Nobody recalls anything about a lost boy found here either." His foot grinds a few pebbles. A flurry of white soars over our heads—the heron decides it's time to take flight.

"Still, it makes you wonder, doesn't it?" His lips purse. His question latches like a dull lump at the back of my throat.

"Wonder what?" My mouth lets out a whisper, and my mind turns a corner. *Don't go there!*

I look up. *Too late.* In his eyes moves the gloom of doubt and distrust, and a silvery gray blends with frosty green.

My fingers flit along the fur of his lapel. A firm hand folds around.

"Tell me, love." His thumb circles my knuckles, pressing me on. "If you took a little boy lost, and left a man for dead floating in the river, would that memory ever leave you in this lifetime?"

My heart plummets and I seek refuge in the heavy weave of his coat.

"Yeah, me neither," he says.

Betrayal. A sour taste stains my mouth. My mind has taken a dangerous corner. *Focus.* I shake my head and halt my thoughts. *No use going there*. It's him and me now. My fingers lock into his and steal the steady beat flowing from underneath his skin.

The shadows lengthen before us. In no rush, the two of us make our way back to our group.

We eat in silence, the four of us, and although the tea is good, it won't wash the solid lump of Karma's words lodged in my throat. It's only when Norbu jumps up to reign in our horses that a certain sense of relief clears the air.

"Playtime's over, Chengdu's expecting our company." Norbu's genuine smile lifts my spirits.

"And I get to meet that famed friend of yours, the one you've all been talking about." He hands me the lead of my stallion and his face dons a masked grin.

"Don't you get me started, young brother," Dendup hisses, his words a warning. It doesn't work. Norbu rolls his eyes and I mount my horse as we let Dendup's grumble get lost in the clatter of hooves.

And like that we're back on the road again, with Karma leading and Dendup closing our row. We'll reach Chengdu before the sun sets on the mountains and meet Lanying—it's been too long. With the thrill of our reunion close at hand, everything in me wants to rush, yet I better prepare—for knowing my illustrious sister, our adventures have only just begun.

Seventeen

Billowing clouds of dust darken the sky, and thunder strikes the ground before us. Frightened hooves clatter, ferocious throats roar, and a frenzied tumult swells in the air. I duck and my stallion bucks on all fours. Norbu's resolute arm reigns it in.

"Get out of the way, now!" Dendup shouts his command from the back.

Our caravan sways and scrabbles to all sides. My hands dig into my horse's manes.

"Get back!" Karma drives his stallion beside mine, forcing us further into the field.

An unrelenting hurricane crashes by. Warriors on horses, decked in scaled, blackened leather, pound the earth in a ruthless valor. Tuffs of black hair crown their helmets; fur earflaps fly from underneath. A frighting void of violence obscures their faces.

Mongols. Cold sweat breaks on my forehead. Swords and shields blaze the daunting glare of dogged determination. Long black banners howl the deafening cry of carnage and dire victory over a raging gale. Never have I seen men more savage than this hoard. Dogs of war, they call them, these warriors—now I know why.

"We're good." Norbu reaches out to me, an iffy reassurance. "They're riding out to join their comrades, they're not out for us."

I turn aside and shiver. "How do you know?" The rancid stench of cruel sweat and desiccated bloodshed breathes all around. My teeth clatter. I draw my scarf close.

"The banners." He points at the searing black horse tails high in the air. "They carry these black ones on the battlefield to protect their spirits."

I heave. Time moves in a slow motion. The troop rages by in an endless blur of vicious black and bruised blue.

Gravel and dirt settle as the last of the war horses speeds away. A strange silence descends, loud and arresting. A bloated sun sinks in the hills before us. Shadows lengthen behind us, lurking like stealthy predators at our heels.

Our caravan limps back on the road, like a crippled dog cast out by his pack.

"All good?" An unfazed Karma prods his stallion in the lead position.

I nod. My shoulders sag. Norbu's horse paces beside me. Dendup closes the row with our pack horses trailing behind. All good, I guess, and so we ride on with Chengdu in our sight.

"How come I've never seen them like that?" I clear my throat and turn to Norbu. "I've seen groups of them roaming our mountains, and settling in our towns, but never so many of them riding towards battle." My tongue pokes my teeth, the aftertaste of anxiety clinging to my gums.

"You and me, and even our parents before us, we've been subject to the Mongols as long as we can remember." Norbu tips his hat. A sober look sets on his face. "These people here, they resisted for far too long, and now they're paying the price." His horse brays, and he draws in the reins.

"We're fortunate, the Mongols like our religion and our monks, so they let us have our own ruler." He turns. "You heard about Pags-pa, right?" His hand slides across his stallion's neck.

I frown. "You mean the high Sakya lama?" I've heard his name mentioned before, but I'm not sure where or why.

"Yeah. The Mongols appointed him to rule our lands for them." Norbu draws up his sleeves and tilts his face to the sun. "He died, but the Sakyas monks still hold that appointment, collecting the yearly taxes for the Mongols in our part of the mountains."

"I see." My mind searches for something familiar. Taxes, yes, Father mentioned it over the winter, but I've paid no attention to it. I guess it's time I should.

"Mind you, there're rumors of revolting, especially by the Kagyu monks." Norbu straightens his back. "They won't succeed—the Mongol Khan's too fond of the Sakya clan."

The Sakya clan. I slide back my scarf. Sweat pricks my neck. "Where did you get all this?" Somehow Norbu never ceases to surprise me.

"Well, I might not be well traveled, but I do have a keen interest in who deems himself ruler over our mountains," he says in a most serious tone.

"What?" My voice pitches—somehow, I don't buy it. "You and politics?"

I was right. His teasing chuckle meets me halfway.

"No, not really." He shakes his head, and a modest hesitation slips from his chest.

"But when Father went missing last year, I had to venture out and search for him." He draws a deep breath, and the spark of amber dulls in his eyes. "I learned how power and politics work—the hard way." His gaze sweeps back into the distance. "And it's not my thing, not at all." He draws his hat.

"I see." My thoughts bounce back to last summer. Sonam disappeared on us for a while. He got caught by officials on charge of smuggling but bought his way out—at least that's what he told me when we met in Lhasa later that year.

My eyes fix between the twirling ears of my horse. A vague unease snakes through my mind. *Not now.* I glance at Norbu. This whole thing about Sonam being ill, cursed by Khandro—somehow my mind won't leave it alone. I'm sure there's more to this story and what happened that night in Lhasa. My thoughts speed ahead. Sonam wouldn't tell, and Karma claims not to know. That leaves Lanying. I wonder...

"Nordun." A voice calls from afar, halting my ever-curious mind from wandering into nowhere.

I shift in the saddle. Speckles of gold and brown meet my eye. My heart lifts. Good—Norbu's all smiles again.

"Something tells me your sister is coming." His chin points ahead.

I crane my neck to see, and three horses with riders speed our way. Puffs of steam cloud from the horses' nostrils. Their stocky limbs move faster than I would have thought possible. Sods and shale splatter in arcing sprays from their hooves.

My heart skips a beat at the sight of the stallion at the front. His chestnut frame flies in full throttle. It carries a long crimson coat, flailing like a silken pennant in the wind. A high-pitched cry soars our way. *It's Lanying.*

"Sisterrrr!" The stallion rears at his rider's sharp shriek. His eyes wide, his ears flat back, he halts in mid-flight. It's her—no doubt about that.

"At last, we meet again." She bares her teeth in a bold grin. Her eyes flash the piercing bright blue of an infinite sky. "Great to see you, sister." She drives her stallion beside mine and reaches out.

"Lanying." I can't help but mirror her mischievous smirk. She hasn't changed one bit since I last saw her in Lhasa. My hand folds in hers; my heart delights.

"Brothers." She meets my companions with a curt, contemptuous smile.

Nothing has changed there either—Karma reacts with a stony stare; Dendup forms a perfect match with his heated huff.

"Now who's the young pup you brought along?" Lanying's stallion cavorts around Norbu. "A bit green if you ask me, but then again, most likely very easy to train."

Norbu meets Lanying's provocative stare, but the poor fellow's no match for her; his face flushes, his toes prod on his horse—too late. Lanying's stallion curls his lips and with one shallow mean swipe, Norbu's horse gets put into place.

"Let's go." She raises her hand. "We have a lot of catching up to do." Her horsemen shoot into position, flanking our sides.

I glance at Karma. His jaw sets and reluctant defeat seethes on his face.

He knows it too—any discussion would be a waste of words. His stallion strides aside.

Just like that we're off in full speed, joining Lanying on the way to her house in Chengdu.

Eighteen

At breakneck speed we reach Chengdu, where Lanying leads us through a maze of back alleys to what must be her house. A bleak, slated roof curves over a stark gray wall. A heavy, yet simple iron gate opens with a tired groan to where an empty, whitewashed courtyard awaits.

There're no welcoming blossoms cascading from balconies, no fresh vines rising on pillars, no intricate carvings adorning the woodwork—there are only lanky shadows hastening from corners to take over our horses as we dismount. As flamboyant as Lanying's appearance is, the exterior of her house seems sober to me.

"I thought for sure they wouldn't accept her invitation," Norbu says under his breath. "I mean, they're not fond of her, are they?" He hauls his bag over a shoulder. "But then again, our elder never refuses an invitation to a good meal and no doubt a generous pour of the drink." A jolly wink follows.

"That's right." I join his chuckle and take a quick peek at Dendup and Karma, directing the servants around our load. I'm sure the two of them will never admit it, but we need Lanying and her connections to get ahead with our search. My hands glide along my horse's legs—all good, no damage done. A youngster's waiting with patience to take him over.

"Sister, come." Lanying beckons me from the doorstep. With a haughty look, she turns to the men and wrinkles her nose. "You all need a wash before you join us at the table." Her eyebrows draw up. "You know the way." She adds those last words at Karma's direction.

Of course. A flush of vicarious shame sets on my cheeks. Karma's been here before—they were lovers once. I dodge my head and skip past her into the hallway.

"And you need something more." Her arm hooks in mine and directs me to the end of a long corridor.

"Wait." My hands rummage through my bag. "I've got something for you." *There it is.*

A corner of her mouth curves up. With stealth, she slips Xia's sealed letter into her sleeve.

"In here." She nods. A door opens and the fragrance of delicate flowers draws all around.

A tiny woman with the strongest of hands pulls me in. "Your bath is waiting."

I turn at the swish of silk behind me, but Lanying's already gone, the rapid rhythm of her boots a fading trail in the hallway. *That's how she disappears on me every time.*

Leaving no room for hesitation, the woman tugs at my clothes. Within no time I'm in the bath and heated water hugs every bit of my skin. Determined hands brush my back with a fruity soap, twisting and turning me at their command. A protest is futile. The sweet-scented steam smoothens the weary muscles of my being. My eyes close and my mind slips away.

I rest my head in capable hands that scrub my scalp, detangle my locks and rinse the long days past in a balmy bouquet of warm milk and rice. Distant images flee, of budding tea trees and blue-veined sarsens, and black banners soaring on the wind. A soft splash sounds from afar.

"The winter at home did you good then." Lanying's voice drifts from the water.

I open my eyes. She's slipped into the tub beside me. My heart plummets. *Those scars.* I've seen them before. Serrated lacerations cover her slender frame in a sheen of pearl and pink. *How could they?*

My eyes seek shelter from the grotesque brutality branded all over her skin. My body sinks, and a milky blur hazes by. *Om Tare.* Even the strongest of hearts get blinded when assaulted with such vicious intent, seeing no other choice than to raise their walls and strike back with violence and fear. It's no wonder she's become what she is.

"And yet here you are—together with him." A complacent glee sounds in her tone. "I figured he wouldn't let you go."

I look up and clear my throat. "Well, I'm happy to be here." What else to say?

"That makes two of us, sister." Her hand dismisses the little lady fussing around us. A door closes. She draws near.

"So, what's the plan?" Her voice sings at the prospect of another adventure.

I sigh. "You know these two—they never tell." They don't. It bothers me, but I shrug it off.

"They have no idea, do they?" A wry laughter escapes from her mouth. "Then explain to me, sister, what makes him go after his kinfolk so sudden—after all this time?" She cocks her head and catches my gaze.

My mind halts and wavers. *Secrets.* Will I tell? I take a deep breath and my heart, jaded of being cautious, meets me halfway.

"I hear her." I rest my heated cheek against the cool glazed tiles and tell her all about his dreams and his mother's voice calling him home.

"Hmmm." She shakes her hair loose, black swirls spread on a bed of cream and white. "I figured it had something to do with you."

A solaced silence floats between us. I let it soak through.

"I've inquired here and there, so has Xia—as I asked her to," she says. "She's a dear friend and has valuable contacts." A door opens. "The inking is quite distinctive, but it won't be easy to find her." She pauses. Tea is served on a tray.

"Xia thinks your best chance is the area of old Hanzhong, Xingyuan." Her lips taste the clear green liquid with an approving slurp.

"Xingyuan?" I raise my eyebrows. "Not Mongolia?" I do not know where Xingyuan is, but the name somehow doesn't sound Mongolian to me.

She shakes her head. "It's east on the route to Chang'an, where all the roads come together." She gulps her tea down and turns. "And as it happens, I've prepared my caravan, so you'll be joining me, sister." Two cobalt crescents twinkle my way.

Joining her. My heart leaps and my mind halts. "But they'll never..." My words stall at the sight of her brazen gloat. *Om Tare.* What's on her mind?

"Oh, they will, sister." Her hand orders another pour of tea. "Once they realize I've got a pass that makes the road all the more comfortable." A shameless snicker resounds over her glass. She's way ahead of me—as usual. A big smile breaks on my face. I should have known.

More tea is poured, and relief settles with a tickle of fresh green and jasmine on my tongue. I suck in my cheeks. It's different, this bittersweet, a kind of prickly zing, but certainly something I can get used to.

"It's a tricky road leading through those mountains, sister." She cocks her head. "Nowhere near the path we took to Lhasa." Her fingers rim her glass. "You're sure you're up to it?"

Her curious stare stirs a disquiet in me. My breath shallows. "Sure, why not?" A lengthy silence stretches. What does she mean?

Her eyes narrow. "Does Karma know?" Her tone's unusually soft.

My stomach pits. *Betrayal.* The divination. Is she guessing?

"What do you mean?" I try a casual tone. It doesn't work.

She points her chin at me. "That you're with child. I suppose it is his?"

No. Blood rushes through the drums of my ears and I freeze. My eyes seek solid ground, but only find hers, carrying a startling realization wrapped in rich cerulean blue.

My lips move. *No.* There's no sound. My mind stumbles into hiding.

"Xia mentioned the medicine she gave you." Her gentle voice calls me out. "How many turns of the moon—two?"

My hand folds over my stomach, the other clutches the teacup that was already there. "I... I thought it was the excitement of preparations." The words hinge on my lips. "And then the long days on the road, and the spicy food." My face blushes. *How naïve of me.* I've never missed a turn of the moon since the bleeding started, even when traveling to Lhasa and back. *Never.*

"It's still early." Lanying's hand steadies mine. "If you choose to rid yourself of it—we'll have you back in the saddle the same day." With a stealthy swipe she rescues the cup from drowning.

No. My heart quivers at the thought of losing the very thing my mind didn't want to concede.

"Don't tell." My thoughts scream, but my words are only a whisper. "Let me wait until the next turn of the moon." My numb fingers coil around hers.

"No worries, sister, I would never disclose." She reaches for another cup. "Besides, these issues often dissolve themselves, and if not, you just say the word." Her arm slips around my shoulder. "Here, drink and let's relax for a while—for I'll tell you; it's going to be a rough ride."

Nineteen

Dusk scatters in pale purple and blue through the tall windows, draining the lanky shadows from the late afternoon. A lone warbler sings the last notes of its high-flung, teetering song, and a pleasant tranquility weaves through.

The bath has worked its wonders on my body, infusing it with a refreshed vigor to face the evening ahead. My legs stride through the corridor, but my thoughts amble behind. As much as the lengthy soak smoothened my weary muscles, the conversation with Lanying frayed the edges of my already fragile mind.

Even before the door swings open, merry voices welcome me into the room. Servants swish around, decking the table with copious dishes and colorful fare. Mouthwatering aromas of sweet and sour, and savory blend in the air. Dendup clenches a glass filled to the brim. The satisfied smirk on his face says it all—my elder has made himself at home.

"Nordun." Karma's open arm pulls me next to him. His lips seek my neck. "Hmm, all clean then?" A strand of his hair tickles my nose. His warmth radiates through my skin.

"Hey, hey, first we eat." Dendup's laugh tumbles over the table. "There's plenty served here." His eyes prowl round the graceful girls presenting the plates and pouring the drinks.

"And by the looks of it, it's a tasty mix of all." A shy Norbu next to him sends a wincing look my way.

Silk rustles and a gust of the cold evening whirls from the door. Lanying dashes in, her two guards at her side. Dressed in garnet and golden, she settles at the head of the table. With a swift hand she directs the stocky men to the door.

I catch a glimpse of the guard who rescued me from the blazing fire in Lhasa. *It's him.* He casts his eyes down at my gaze. A sliver of shame tugs at my heart. He risked his life for me that dark night, and I didn't even thank him for it.

"Brothers, I might not have said it, but I'm happy to receive you at my table." Lanying raises her glass in my direction. "I see the winter has done you all well." The corners of her mouth curl up.

I blink. *That woman!* A gleam of bright white blinks my way. I meet her mischievous stare full on.

"Please eat—and drink." She clacks her tongue. "It's not the chang you're used to, but then again, variety is the spice of life, brothers." She reaches over and clangs Dendup's cup with a grin. "Now eat."

The satisfying sound of smacking lips and grumbling appreciation fills the room as we dig into the elaborate meal set before us. The delicious dishes demand our full attention, and my palate delights at the variety of foreign flavors—there's so much to savor that I've never tasted before.

More drinks get poured. I lean in and Lanying's ever watchful gaze meets mine.

Her eyebrows raise and my chin dips down.

It's time. I sit back and relax. *Here we go.*

"Brothers." Lanying veers up, sweeping her wide sleeves all around. "We all know why you're here—let's drop the facade."

Dendup's cup comes down with a bang. Karma's hand moves over my knee and Norbu withdraws to the back of his seat. My fingers roll around my beads. *Om Tare.* How will this play out?

"I've done some inquiring." She lifts her chin. "My contacts are reliable—they say your best bet is Xingyuan." Her hands settle on the table. "Now as it happens, I'm leaving for Chang'an in a few days, and I'm more than happy to offer you all a place in my caravan, a safer way to your destination."

An alarming silence plunges over our company. Even the tiptoes of servants have fled from the room. I glance around as Lanying's words leave an echo in the gaping void of sound.

There's Karma's blank stare beside me, and Dendup squints his eyes across from me, matching his brother's suspicion. I get it—they don't trust her. She sold out her entire family, and she shouldn't have, but when pushed to the edge... It's so easy to judge.

The pearly sheen of my sister's tainted skin drifts before me. They don't understand—they never experienced the vulnerability of being a woman, being under constant threat of brutality, unable to fend for yourself, betrayed by your closest of kin. They've never been there—raw and hurting. My heart sighs the smallest whisper. *And they don't believe.*

I straighten my back. My hand searches for Karma's. No, these men don't believe in the innate goodness of all beings. They don't believe that even good hearts sometimes can be led on the wrong path, trying to make all things right. I slide my fingers through Karma's and a firm hold welcomes me. For sure, it's not the past actions that define us—it's the present choices we make.

"I offered to help before, you didn't take it." Lanying's voice slices through the quiet—stealthy and swift, like the way she draws her long knife. “Don’t be a fool this time.” She tilts her head to the side. “I’ve got the papers to travel that way.”

Her eyes gleam an enticing indigo as she sets them on Dendup. “You know my way is faster, brother, and more comfortable too.” Her hands lift a jug, and she pours him another generous cup, never letting him from her sight.

Dendup chucks down the drink in one go. “The right papers.” He snorts and rubs his mustache. A leery smirk peeps from his lips. I hold my breath. He’s our elder—he decides.

“I wasn’t keen on venturing out here.” He shakes his head. “Never mind staying at your place.” His arm reaches out to Lanying, who fills his empty cup all over again.

“But I have to give it to you—you’re doing good out here.” Dendup raises his drink, and my shoulders sag. *This is going rather well.*

“We’ll never be the best of friends, that’s a fact.” Dendup’s voice pitches. “But we don’t have to be, for we all want what’s best for my brother, here.” He flicks his wrist at Karma. “So let’s find his bloody relatives and go back home—in peace.”

He aims his cup to toast, and Lanying’s cup meets him mid-air. Karma’s fingers rim around his drink. He doesn’t speak, nor does he join the toast. I guess he’s alright with what Dendup has decided for us.

“That’s good enough for me, brothers.” Lanying throws a triumphant look around. “Now let’s eat and drink and enjoy the company I’ve arrange for after our dinner.”

She waves her hand and four shapely girls swarm into the room, draping themselves around our table.

A sudden cold hits my core. I blink and draw my hands in my sleeves. Karma’s arm stiffens around my midriff. I’m stunned—and I shouldn’t be. This is Lanying’s house, and this is her way of showing hospitality—like any other excellent host would do.

"Didn't I tell you, it's a glorious mix of all?" Dendup gropes the girl at his side and slaps a flushed Norbu on the shoulder.

"Just like real men want it, right?" Lanying slings a wicked smile Norbu's way.

The poor guy ducks and drowns his eyes in his drink. I still can't move.

Karma leans back. A lovely young woman with long, luscious locks flowing like dark swirls of ink over her delicate, sheer shoulders, invites herself on his lap.

My stomach turns into a knot, and I flinch. *What will he do?*

"No, thank you." Karma voices a respectful, yet resolute reply. His arm locks around my shoulder. "I'm very well taken care of here." The girl hisses and withdraws with a pout on her rounded lips. I cast my eyes down.

"Now, now, Karma." Lanying anchors her hands on the sulking girl's hips. "I remember the times you didn't object to a crowd in your bed." She takes on a taunting tone.

"Oh, I do too." Karma puts on a smile. His tone is one of utter restraint. "But that's in the past now, for this woman is all I desire."

His fingers tangle in my locks, and his lips rest a soft kiss on my temple. The sweet scent of the sun on churned earth, and the rich bloom of the mountain meadows on a midsummer's day lifts my wary heart.

"Hmm... as you will, but why deny Nordun the pleasure?" Lanying draws out a snicker. I cringe. Will she ever let it rest?

"Oh, I'll see to my woman's pleasure myself." Karma hooks his fingers around the back of my neck. "If you can just have your guard show us our room."

Before I know it, he's got us marching through the door.

"See you tomorrow, sister." Lanying's hilarity trails behind us through the vacant corridor. *That woman.* Still, it's good to see her again.

The door slams, and I catch my breath. "You sure are in a hurry." My feet could hardly keep up with his pace.

Karma's arms haul me in and his hungry mouth melts with mine.

My hands explore the warmth under his shirt.

"Don't doubt me again." His balmy breath mingles in my ear. "That was then, and it was good because I didn't know what love was." His heartbeat pulses under my palms, rapid and relaxed. My lips relish the salt on his skin.

"Still, you have every right," I say, but his thumb swipes the words from my lips.

"That doesn't mean that I want to," he says and lays his cheek onto mine. "What is between the two of us, no other will ever be able to match." A slow smile folds against the edge of my jaw. "Besides, the thought of another man's hands on you enrages me, so why would you not feel the same?" I close my eyes and his fingers drift down the lining of my dress.

"Listen, my love." His chest swells. "I hate to tell you, but you need to hear this again." He sighs, and I look up.

"Lanying might mean well this time, and she's got good connections." He hesitates. "But the company she keeps is not trustworthy." He tilts my chin. "Be careful with her—and promise me you won't wander off on me."

Genuine concern lines around his eyes.

"I promise." I rest my head in the crook of his neck, and my heart breaks a little for this man with his quiet confidence, and his solitary soul, unable to trust.

"And love, one more thing." His fingertips peel the silk from my skin. "Don't let on that you understand the language of the Mongols."

His teeth graze my shoulder with a gentle determination. "They don't like it—she flaunts it, but don't." His words send a tingle down my spine.

"But you speak it." My mind puts up a faint protest, but my body caves in, more than willing to agree.

"Yes, but I've been here before, so please trust me on this." His lips press his request on my collarbone. "Their presence here is more demanding, and forceful." His hands slide up and cradle my face. A stormy gray spirals in the depth of his eyes.

"Our tribes have a long understanding with them." He twirls a loose lock round his finger. "Well, we had to—as you must have heard." A flicker of emerald ignites at his words.

"I did." I swallow, unwilling to focus. For sure the tales of slaughter and plunder are gruesome, but then again, what do I know? My mind turns away.

"But here, the fighting has not ceased yet." He slips a strayed strand behind my ear lobe. "So be careful and keep close to me." My dress drops with a dull thud to the floor. My body shivers. His breath fevers on my skin.

"I will," I say, more than willing. "As long as you attend to that pleasure you promised me just now."

His lips brush against mine, tracing all doubts, and erasing all hesitation. Tonight, I choose to surrender—and to allow the rise and fall of our bodies to banish the fickle days gone by from my mind.

Twenty

Fingers probe and poke, silken stretches, and needles prick in my legs. I bend my back, swing my arms left and right—but there's no escaping my predicament. Lanying's watchful eyes guard me at all sides.

"Any sister of mine travels in style," she'd said. She wouldn't budge and dragged me out of the house in the early morning to what must be the best tailor in town.

"Still got your knife?" She sifts through strips and bits of fur hanging on hooks from a rugged crossbeam.

"Don't need it," I say. It got lost in the fire in Lhasa.

She pulls out a silky pelt, black-brown with a soft silver cast, and drapes the dark sable fur along my collar. "You do where we're going."

I shake my head. *I don't want it.*

"This will do." An approving clack rolls from her tongue, and the seamstress hastens to her command.

"I'll send my men out for one." She nods at the watchmen guarding the door. "We can't be too prepared, sister." A weave of the finest silken glides through her fingers, it's close to translucent. "Here, for a shirt to wear close to the skin."

I raise my eyebrows at the fabric, looking as delicate as the wings of a butterfly. "How's this going to keep me warm?" My thumbs crease the thin cloth, challenging its strength under my hold.

"Protection." Her voice lowers. "A tight weave of silk is not only comfortable, but it will also lessen the damage to your body from an arrow or blade." Her hand draws down her collar. "When pierced through, the fabric remains intact—if you're lucky." Her fingers pluck the rose silk rim around her chest. "It makes it easier to remove the arrow and lessens the chance of poison or infection." My mouth goes dry at the thought of an arrow shot, or a blade swung in anger.

"It's a Mongol thing." Her chin points at a row of felt-lined leather boots lined up in the corner. *Mongol boots.*

"You think they wear those turned-up toes that are so damn hard to walk in just to look good?" She cocks her head. "No sister, these toes keep them tight in their horses' stir-ups so they can stand and twist to shoot their arrows at all sides." Her hands pull an imaginary bow and I blink. "And that curve traps a big air bubble right at the top to keep their toes from freezing."

She wrinkles her nose. "Those Mongol dogs are smart, so we'll better be right up there with them."

She turns on her heels and barks at the seamstress. Rolls of silk spread out in front of us. Servants swish and cloth rips. "All my men wear these, and you will too." She springs up.

"Time for some refreshments." She waves at the guards. "We'll pick up some medicine on the way as you will need it." She throws a meaningful glance at my belly.

I avert my eyes. I do need it—the mornings are hard with my stomach making cartwheels as soon as I open my eyes.

"There's still time, you know." She whispers the words I don't want to hear. "It will pass swiftly; you'll hardly notice any pain."

"I can't." My voice croaks at the idea of it. *Om Tare.* My hand searches for my beads.

"Very well." Her hand flings in the air, and the two watchmen make way. "Off to Xinxiang temple it is."

Green pines line the paved pathway to the temple grounds. Arched, slated roofs crown the towering red lacquered pillars. A pair of proud lions chiseled in white fine-lined marble stands guard at the main door.

"First, we eat." Lanying leads the way through the garden, past the scattered outhouses. "It's no secret these monks make the best noodles in town." A large pavilion comes into sight.

Benches are lined up, holding a hungry crowd. Steam rises from bowls filled to the rim. Seasonal vegetables drape in a thick and spiced broth. Puffy rolls rest in bread baskets, and cups of clear, fragrant tea sit nearby.

Servants shuffle, swift and silent, and set our place within the blink of an eye.

"I told you it's good." Lanying smacks as my teeth sink into broad ribbons of savory dough.

"It's not good, it's delicious." I wipe my mouth. Our eyes cross. My stomach settles, but my mind's gaining speed.

"Tell me," she says. "What is it you want to ask me?" My cheeks flush. She's one step ahead of me—as always.

"Do you know why Khandro would curse Sonam?" *There it is.* It's been on my mind since we met.

"I don't, sister." Her answer is immediate, and her tone crafty. "He captured her, but it was me who sold her, so why put a spell on him?" She gulps the last of her soup. "Makes no sense."

I lean back. Her eyes light up. A sharp blue pierces my way.

"I don't mind his replacement, though." She licks her lips. "That pup is cute—and a fast learner, too." Her eyes gleam with the sapphire shade of midnight.

My stomach throws up a protest. Too much food eaten too fast. My hand reaches for tea.

"What's really on your mind, sister?" She leans across the table. "You keep things hidden—from Karma." A genuine concern lines her forehead. "That's not like you." Her hands on mine touch my heart, but they can't keep her truth from hurting my very being.

That's not me. Tears rim my eyes.

"Things have come up ever since we started traveling." I want to withdraw, but my hands burn into hers. "It all felt so right at home, but now..." *Secrets.* I swallow. *Suspicions.* "There are too many misgivings coming my way." My vision clears. How to explain?

She clacks her tongue. "That's what being on the road does to us." She moves nearer. "At home, you can pretend you're secure, but here out in the unknown, you can't afford to look away." Her fingers squeeze into mine. "And most of all, you can't hide."

My gaze takes a dive in my empty bowl. *Hide.* How well she knows the road—and me.

"And besides that, this is not a pilgrimage, sister." She sits back and drags me with her. "You're treading dangerous waters here."

I look up at the jagged tone of her words and stare into the fathomless blue of the mountain lakes, and the silent shade of the sky above that tells of a thousand tales, of travelers like me and like her. It whispers she's been there too.

"But you know I'm with you in this." She rests her chin on our clenched fists. "All the way."

And my heart takes the leap.

My mouth opens and I speak of all—about the betrayal foreseen in my divination, my worries around Sonam's curse, and the rumors regarding my cousins' disappearance that Norbu threw my way. My breath falters in my chest, but I push on anyway—I even call out Dendup's nasty remarks about Karma being with me out of revenge; I've let it dwell inside of me for too long.

She listens without batting an eyelid until there's nothing left to weigh down my heart—but the one thing. *Not now.* I should tell this to Karma, but I can't. *Not yet.*

She sucks in her cheeks. "Listen, he is who he is." A small smile curls around her lips. "You knew that—you've seen him yield his sword with your own eyes." She tilts her head to the side.

Lhasa. A silver blade flashes before me. *I did.*

"If his way of dealing with the matters at hand bothers you now, well, what can I say?" She squares her shoulders. I recoil, but her hands won't set mine free.

"Let me tell you though, if the rumors are true—and I have no reason to doubt they are." Her eyebrows raise. "He's done you a big favor, and those cousins got what they deserved." The distant glower of misplaced victory draws over her face and a light breeze sweeps in, bringing sadness on its breath.

I untangle our fingers as the last bit of hope drifts away from my clasp. An awkward acceptance quivers within me. She only told me what I already knew. I bite my lip.

"You don't want him to change, trust me." She puts up her chin and leans back. "You're safe with him." She nods. Cups clatter and hurried hands clear our table.

"And as far as Dendup's concerned." Her lips curl into a grimace. "He's just jealous you've taken his place." She snorts and my eyes widen. "Let it go, sister, it's a petty man's thing."

What?

Sandals shuffle in dry sand. A few monks in muted gray flock by.

Lanying veers up; her seat tumbles from behind her.

"I've got to see somebody." She summons her watchmen. "We'll meet in the temple." Her feet fly off, her crimson coat trailing behind.

I'm left seated with the patience of a loyal man standing beside me. *It's him.* Lanying left me with the quiet guard who once saved my life.

His sturdy frame bends, and he points towards the temple.

"Yes, thank you," I say, and rise. "That is what I need."

Twenty-One

The watchman halts at the bottom of the steps. I hurry in, but his dragging footsteps go silent at the door.

Streams of mellow orange and morning yellow beam through the pillared alley, highlighting the devoid of vivid thangkas and fierce-colored banners cascading from the ceiling. Melodious chimes tinkle in the absence of buzzing prayer wheels. A light scent lingers where the heavy spices and herbs are supposed to sanctify the air.

Three times I lower myself on the smooth, slated floor. It's not the rough grated timber brown I'm used to, but a veined pattern of muted black and ivory, with an array of gray and green crawling in between.

Three times, and each prostration echoes, announcing my dedication to the Buddha, the dharma, and the sangha in this strange, deserted temple. Three times, and I am home.

The watchful gaze of the precious teacher follows me as I tiptoe around. *Om Tare.* The clicking of my beads fills a muted vent as the most exquisite statues throw their graceful shadows upon me. One by one, I bow and pay my respect, but my mind seeks for solace at the only one lacking. *Our mother of Liberation.* Where can I find her now that I need her so near?

My toes curl in the chill of the marble. A shiver runs through the soles of my feet. The barren bench in the furthest corner beckons me to sit. I fold my legs underneath in the woolen furring of my chuba. *Om Tare.* My mind rests.

A warm glow rushes as my eyes spot the ridges of a tiger claw nearby. *Jamphel Yan.* It's the Boddhisattva of Wisdom riding a ferocious blue tiger while wielding his sword. *Jamphel Yan.* My heart delights. If only I could cleave the clouds of ignorance that obscure my thinking with his flaming blade of wisdom and subdue my unruly mind in the gentle way he tames the fiercest of felines. I close my eyes, not wanting to see. *The realization of sublime wisdom.* His understanding is so far out of reach for me. If I could only convince my anxious mind to let go of the misgivings and misperceptions it holds so tight.

My hands clench, my beads snap between my fingers. I let my own foolish actions crowd my thinking—keeping secrets and judging others, fretting over the past, distressing about the future and events I can't control. Tears drip, my eyelashes tremble. I've left the door of my mind wide open without watching and now fear guides my way. A sob escapes and I press my hands to my chest.

How Lanying spoke the truth. I've raised the walls of my heart, barring my loved ones and even the one I love most.

I know Karma and all that he is. How can I love him and at the same time wish he was different? Who am I to criticize him for following orders from a family that's also mine?

I blame him for the secrets he keeps, when all the while I hide so much from him, even a part of him deep within me. How ignorant and selfish I am.

My heart shrivels with shame. All these years in the monastery, and this is who I've become. My grandmother, my dearest teacher. *What will she think of me now?* My fists sink into my lap.

"The past is gone and the future's uncertain," Dechen used to warn us junior nuns. "Our task is to remain open in the present, open to uncertainty, to the suffering in this human life."

Her stern voice surges from the bottom of my being and ripples through me like a tidal wave crashing on empty shores. "Don't try to control what is ever changing, but observe with wisdom and a compassionate heart, and let yourself unfold without bearing a fear in your heart."

I see it so clearly, my own foolish actions, and how far I've strayed from myself and my home. This is not who I want to be. *Om Tare.* This is not what I want to pass on.

My beads blur before me, and jaded green rolls over the faded red thread on my wrist. A faint pulse throbs underneath. *My sisters.* My fingers spread, and a delicate warmth emits from under my palms. The string they tied is a distant reminder of the place and time the three of us inhabited, now so far away. My insides quiver. *Yet, they're always here.*

A surge of tenderness rises in the hollows of my heart. The purest of joy lights my being. The laughter we shared, the stunts we pulled on our poor fellow sisters, the mess we got ourselves into—and out of, because Tsomo was always very resourceful—it's all coming back.

My fingers fumble. The strand of cotton is thinning. It's been a year, but their presence within me stays strong. I've wandered, but I'm always under the protection of my dearest sisters, my precious teachers, and all the Buddhas and Bodhisattva's. How could I ever doubt myself when they've put their faith in me, trusting me to do good?

A pang of remorse unfolds across my chest. *Not now.* My lungs swell. My eyes fix on the tiger in front of me, wild and vicious, yet calm and subdued.

I can do better than this. Right here, right now, as each moment brings new opportunities, wherever I am. All I need is to rekindle my intention, again and again, and prayer will strengthen my heart.

My feet land on the ground. A determined thump resounds. My body surrenders, a smooth cold slices through. The words of my grandmother resound within me. *Open heart, open mind.* I lay myself down and offer my intention. *May I be guided to where it is most beneficial to go.*

Three times I lay myself down, surrendering to the days coming, the days that are daunting me. One last prostration, and I am out of the door.

A crisp breeze brings in the fragrance of spring flowers. A bird song dances among the tinkling chimes. The trusted watchman is waiting in patience on the steps where I left him.

I bring my chin to my chest. My hands fold in front of me and in front of him. I never thanked him, and I don't know how to.

I look up. He hunches and I greet him. "Brother." He averts his eyes, but a golden sun touches the two of us, and is all around.

"There you are." Lanying's holler reaches across the yard. "Let's go." Her wide sleeves flutter around.

I glance at the watchman. "Looks like it's going to be a long day for us," I say. A coy smile comes my way.

We spend the rest of the day moving around markets and visiting back-way alleys with Lanying directing our every move. It's only when the sun deepens into a charred orange, she guides us home, to a courtyard strewn with enormous packs, bulky bags, and unrecognizable bales. Servants stumble from every nook and corner of the house.

"We're leaving tomorrow." Her arm slings around my shoulder. "No time to waste, sister." Her satisfied grin pinches my ears as she strides off.

Tomorrow. A quiet consent settles inside of me. A firm hand anchors at my hips.

"Did you have a good day?" Karma's hoarse voice pulls me in.

"I did," I say. "You?" I rest my head against his shoulder. Fine lines run from the corners of his mouth. Lanying sent the men to some office this morning to register. I think he had a long day too.

Norbu shoots by, his head ducked behind a sack on his shoulder. He disappears among the shadows. The night will fall soon.

"Dendup's not too happy, though." Karma's chin points at the far side, where Dendup slouches against a pillar. "We're riding out to where we've never been, with Lanying to guide us." He sighs. "You know how he is."

I do. He's a man, and kind of petty, as Lanying put so well. But he came with us on his own account, so I go over. He's also our elder, after all.

A sullen frown greets me. I kneel beside him.

"Karma told me of your reluctance, brother," I say. I choose my words with care here, for Dendup's all but the fool he often appears to be.

"He's got that right." Dendup puffs. "I'm not happy riding under Lanying's orders—being at her every command." His arms cross over his chest.

Of course! It dawns on me. The men had to register this morning. That's what this is all about. They had to sign up as

Lanying's workers to join the caravan. That's what bothering our elder. He's listed under a woman's command, and he can't stomach it.

"Those two over there." His grubby finger pokes at the crammed yard where Karma and Norbu haul bags and stack packs among the others. "They've already succumbed to her whims—in every way." He tucks a small flask from his pocket.

My face flushes. *In every way.*

"They've got no pride left to lose, but I do." He chugs his liquor down in one go.

I shift, putting my back to the pillar. I see his point, but can I make him see mine?

"I understand." My voice sounds humble as I intend it to be. "As our respected elder, you can say the word and we'll return home with you." I take a pause. He looks away.

"But we've come so far—together." I weigh my every word. "And we're all here for the same reason—to help Karma." My tone takes a dive to the ground. "So please brother, let us ride with him, for he needs us, as we need you, our elder."

I bow my head and rest my plea. Dendup stays silent. We sit together until the buzz in the courtyard dies down.

"You did the offerings?" Dendup clears his throat. The last of the liquor is gone.

"I did." A little hope springs from my heart.

"Good." He rises and tugs at his belt. "I trust Lanying decked you out." A long blade blinks through the crease of his coat.

"She did," I say. My hands move over to my side. A small leather shaft sits underneath.

"Then we're all set." He draws his cap and looks up. A leaden glow streaks through the twilight.

Tomorrow we ride on.

Twenty-Two

A mellow drizzle heralds the day, an auspicious sign for us travelers. Billowing clouds of clotted cream sweep among the powerful peaks on our left. High-pitched yells roar among the low hum of prayer. Musky vapors rise from the sodden bodies of men and beasts lined along the edge of the town.

With a groan, our convoy shakes its flanks and sets itself in motion, and like a mighty cobra, it snakes into the green hills ahead.

The horses and mules are strong and stout, the men guiding them bright-eyed and nimble on their feet. Even the dull weather can't dim their spirits—this caravan's in excellent shape.

"Lanying knows what she's doing." Karma's approving gaze sweeps over the unbroken row behind us. "She's gone this way many times and knows only the best of men and animals will do."

I nod. My mouth dry, my tongue turns the shavings of bitter wood, releasing their tonic as I chew them. I've kept in my bread and tea for the last few mornings, but a vague nausea plagues my stomach. Lanying said I would be fine after the next turn of the moon, and that should be soon. Still, she got me a full pouch of dried roots at the market yesterday. I tucked it down into the bottom of my bag.

"We're in for a rough ride, sister," she said. "Better stock up and say your prayers."

A rough ride. From what I've gathered, that's rather an understatement. Dendup spoke of it last night, of bridges rising all the way to heaven and rifts reaching straight down to the bottom of hell. Then again, it might have been the liquor in him talking. My hand glides along the bent neck of my stallion. A lively neigh rolls from his bulging nostrils. He's had but a day's rest, but his prancing hooves pound the stone slabs like it's the first patch of spring verdant peeping through after a long, barren winter.

"Woah!" I tighten the reins as my horse attempts his next flight to freedom. He's used to cavorting next to Norbu's stallion, which now trots in the front. We've changed positions at Lanying's request.

"Better you stay close to Nordun," she told Karma as we rode out this morning.

I get it—it's her way of looking after me, and I guess another hint at the peril ahead.

While I'm turning my mind from the menacing matters, Lanying seems to thrive at the prospect of adventure and taking high risks. Dressed in flaming crimson, she sits high on her stallion. Her coat swishes like silken flower petals that sail upon the wayward winds sweeping over our grasslands in summer. She even offered Dendup one of the best spots in her caravan this morning, all with a generous smile. Of course, he didn't take it—imagine him being put in place by a woman! Instead, he joined Norbu with a haughty mutter at the front of the line.

Hooves clap in-sync on wide and wet cobble stones. A meager sun thaws the last dew of dawn. I glance at Karma riding beside me. It's been a year since we first met, that night at the river. His quiet presence still stirs my soul. The trumpeting call of a black-necked crane thrusts above us—another favorable blessing from the gods. *Om Tare.* My fingers warm the jade beads, and my mind turns to Tara. It's a good day to ride.

With the sun at her highest, our winding path narrows and leads us into the hills with dense fir and tender shoots of shrubs reaching to tickle our horses' legs. Fleshy leaves and juicy stems throw their broad shades upon us.

Sweat pearls down my neck. I tuck my scarf under my saddle. A stale and muggy humidity closes us in.

"You go first." Karma halts his horse. The trail ahead tapers, forcing us to ride in a single line.

My horse's hooves sag in the soggy underground. A murky green growth swallows the stones.

"It's up from here." Karma points at the open slope ahead. "It will get better soon." It does. Flat rocks surface from underneath the sludge as our horses track to the top.

I rise in my stirrups. My eyes trace the line of the broadened horizon and pause on the towering mountains reaching into the infinite blue. Heavy greenery, lush and inviting, weaves over the peaks like a determined tide coming to shore. *What a beauty.* My skin tingles and my heart leaps as the wind rushes the pulse of the earth through my veins.

My gaze extends and my breath plummets. My fingers grip the reins. *Om Tare.* That can't be... Jagged edged cracks cleave the mountains before us. Vast sheets of barren rock and silted clay fracture the peaks, and clinging bushes and vines tumble into deep, spiny gorges. *No way.* A clammy breeze soaks the back of my shirt. Dendup was not joking. How do we ever get through?

As if he senses my sudden panic, Karma's steady voice reaches from behind.

"One step at the time, remember?" His horse pushes at the flanks and sneaks beside mine. "Like the many that have gone before us—look." Curved granite slabs wind down into the valley. "We're doing good today."

My mind's not moving. I drop my trembling hands along my stallion's neck. He needs no incentive though, as the rectangle carved stones pave the path as effortlessly as a wool blanket rolled out on a mat. Yet, it's steep, and moss and lichen sprawl all over, making it slippery enough to stop our horses' pace from falling into a regular rhythm.

By nightfall we reach higher grasslands where the white sheep with their golden coats roam and feed on bamboo bark and fresh fir. With the fires lit in the open, we spend our first night under the stars.

"Not to worry, sister." Lanying drops at my side. "We'll rest in more comfort tomorrow." Xia already explained that to me. Somehow Lanying also gained membership in the Ortogh, the merchant association. This means we'll be able to stay in the stations that the Mongol Khans have established for traders all along the way.

"Of course, you're more than welcome to find your own cave." Lanying tilts her head and nods at Karma, piling our bag up behind. "As we all know your odd preferences for spending the night in the open." I answer her wink with a muted giggle. Karma doesn't respond.

Sparks crackle and dance like jolly fireflies, a reassuring warmth spreads around. With the animals tied up and packs placed around, the last of the men descend into the field.

"The pup's a good worker." Lanying yawns and the corners of her mouth settle in an appreciative simper. "Most satisfying in every sense."

My gaze wanders to the rim of the darkness where Norbu stands among the others. We didn't speak since we arrived in Chengdu. He's been occupied with work, running errands and assorts. I roll my shoulders. A slight tightness weaves itself between my ribs.

"See you tomorrow, sister." Lanying jumps up. "Get a good rest." Flames flare, igniting a bright orange. She spins on her heels, and she's off.

Dendup passes his flask at Karma. "And then there were three of us," he says. He hurls his blanket over his shoulders, his chin dips on his knees. Unlike any other man I've ever seen, Dendup can sleep while staying seated, even while standing, never moving a muscle at all.

With a silent wink, Karma pulls his blanket around us and folds me in the tender hollow of him.

"Hm, in case you need a reminder," I say. "Any cave will do me fine as long as you're doing what you're doing now." My hands wiggle their way up to his chest, my fingers delighting in the touch of his skin.

"I'm going to hold you to that." His lips press on the top of my head.

The night falls around us and the fires fade. I close my eyes and the dawn comes too soon. With strong tea and a few strips of dried meat to chew on, I wake up to the day.

"Drink up, sister." Dendup pours me another cup. "You'll need it."

I frown, but then hasten to thank him. My elder serving me tea—I didn't see that coming.

With the sky blazing in pink and red, men and beast fall into formation. Our caravan sets forth on the sloped stone path it left yesterday. I slide my beads and my mind moves to prayer. My eyes settle in the distance where the massive, rugged ridge looms.

The sun rises, and an unease grows within me. The dappled shade of the woodland that seemed so inviting brings a faint yet nagging chill to my bones. My fingers fumble. The rustle of roosting birds frays my nerves. A bright glare appears up ahead.

"Time to walk." Karma's tone sounds casual, but certain. I turn around. His horse strolls on, while he slides off, like all the men before me. I glide aside and my stallion neighs. A silent weight descends upon me. My knees buckle and my mind rebels. *Something's ahead.* It doesn't feel good.

I gasp and swallow. *Focus.* A fresh breath breezes through and all halts in a slow motion. Men and beast fuse in complete calm. I crane my neck to see. *Om Tare.* We've come to the end of the mountain. A steep abyss gapes ahead.

"One step at the time, love." Karma's voice floats from the distance. My feet freeze. "I'm right behind you." My hands are numb too.

A winding bridge rises from the void below. Rough wooden beams wedge in craggy holes, cut all along the curving cliff sides. Patchy planks spread on top, forming the path to the other side of the sky.

My thoughts blank, I fix my gaze on the horsetail sweeping before me. A stilled fright rises within me. *Don't look down.* A soft nose nuzzles my backside. My stallion nudges me on, and I step ahead.

Timber creaks and moans in objection over the thud of hooves and shuffle of soles. My mind flees me, and I tread into the bardo, departing this life without knowing if there's even a next life left to go to. Suspended between a certain hell and the promise of heaven, we trudge on, silently begging the gods of these mountains for mercy with our feeble prayers. *Om Mani.* Please let us pass.

Somehow we make it across, to where all shadows flee from the blaring, bright golden sun. My knees buckle, and my hands find solid ground. My stomach tumbles right on its side.

"They say this road is harder than climbing to the heavens." Dendup roars. "You made it, sister." He hands me his flask, and for the first time ever I dare to take a swig.

A bitter burn flares in my throat. My eyes water and I swipe my mouth. *Never again.*

Karma's arm draws around me. "The first one's always the worst."

The first one. A hot burn rims my eyes. I don't dare to ask—how many more yet to go?

Twenty-Three

Another plank road hits us before the sun sets behind. It's a short one with the inn right at its end. *Almost there.*

Fires burn a bright orange in the purple and blueish sky. Crumbling walls enclose a shaded courtyard. Fields of tall grass stretch all around. The men are fast separating the beasts from their load.

A long hallway leads to the kitchen. "We'll sit here, the rest of the men will find their place in the rooms," Lanying says, putting me between the roaring stoves. Cauldrons boil over, a hefty stew brews, meat sizzles on large skewers, and the stink of charred fat chokes the air.

Dark tea is served in large bowls. I take a sip, and my mind slowly descends from the bridge behind me. *What a day.*

Boots tramp the earth-beaten floor. Foreign tongues utter brusque orders, and an occasional pleading whispers. The intense heat subsides, and the light of the eve dims to a gilded glare. A generous pour refills my cup to the brim.

I roll my head, a big yawn escapes, and my senses decide to return.

"Come, eat." Karma's hand locks around my neck. "We're all down there." I rise, and my knees wobble as I join him. The food is excellent, although Dendup judges otherwise.

"Too much water, too little meat." His fingers whisk through the bowl. "No yak either." His nose wrinkles.

"Not to worry, brother," Lanying calls from behind. "This will make up for all your hardships." Her hands slide over a huge jug.

I lean back, my bowl half empty. Karma's eyebrows draw up. Dendup slurps ahead.

"Too much tea," I say. Karma nods, but his eyes narrow; a tinge of dark green shoots through.

"I'm just tired," I say, trying again to ease his concern. His hand covers my knee.

I lean into his chest and marvel at the surrounding public. So many faces, some broad and grim, some elongated and bony—and skin as dark as a midnight sky and as creamy as the first milk from a dri. There're the familiar horsemen, their hats flipped and cotton shirts hanging loose at the collar, avoiding the men masked in dark fur and seared leather with blades that blink and tongues that bite. Strangers stroll by in robes of folded brocade and wide waistbands, fitting sleeves, and flaring skirts that hide their bulky leather boots.

Karma's fingers twirl my hair. My eyelids are heavy, yet my curiosity triumphs over my tiredness—as always. There's simply too much to see.

Servants toil from table to table. Grubby hands set another round of food before us. I peer up—a cagey look and battered lip catch my eye. The fragile girl flies off before I get the chance to thank her, her slender frame stooped, a limp in her step. *Om Tare.* My heart surges for this shattered soul and the one that enslaved it. For one human to put another in hell on this earth, that is a grave deed, and one has to answer for it in lives to come.

Strong liquor flows, and the evening lengthens. A rowdy mood falls over the crowd.

"Let's get our rest." Karma's arm stretches around me.

"I'll find the mat," I say. "You stay some more."

Dendup grins at the prospect of having a few more drinks in trusted company.

"No way." Karma's hand weighs on my shoulder.

"I don't mind." I shrug, but my argument holds no ground with him.

"Not safe," he mutters, and we make our way out of the door.

The midnight air turns its cold cheeks against mine. I shiver and draw my scarf near. Bonfires flame in the courtyard. Packs and people strew around.

"In here." Darkness surrounds me. The door closes, a tiny window gapes in a little light. Karma's arms draw me in, and deep sleep enfolds me. *What a day.* My mind surrenders, time slips away.

A shrill shriek resounds from the yard. I open my eyes, but all is silent. A trickle of sweat runs from my temples. *I must be dreaming.* Karma's steady breath brushes my ear.

Another cry, this time muffled. *A woman.* I look up. The window draws an absolute black. Shuffles echo from outside. My mind turns and blood rushes through my veins.

Before I know it, my feet hit the ground. I falter, but the door opens, and I see her—her body naked, her belly swollen. She's being dragged to the ground. A trail of crimson pales her skin.

"Stop!" I heave and the shadows are shifting. Teeth bare in a ghostly face. A sinister growl eyes me up. In a flash I see—it's human, not an animal or spirit being. It's a man, a beast of a man, and he's not alone.

My legs wobble, but my mind doesn't waver. With all my strength, I fling myself at the girl. Her body withers as I throw my scarf around her. *Om Tare.* Her muted cream pierces through me. With a dire plea, she crawls away.

A blow strikes. My chin hit the gravel. An angry iron taste chokes in my throat and I gag.

A massive boot soars above, and I dive away. My ribs crack, my ears ring. *This is not happening*. Broken glass scampers my skin. A deafening howl rolls around.

"Here!" Large hands lug at me, and I lose ground. My nails dig into rough skin, but it's no use. Two strong arms haul me in. Two others throw me over a shoulder. My vision blurs. A door opens and shuts with a bang.

My back hits the mat. The stench of fear fills the room. I pull myself up and desperation rises within me.

"What the hell were you thinking?" Karma's voice hisses. His hands grip my hair, tangled all over. An icy green flares across his eyes, and a raging anger seethes within.

"They're going to kill her." My cracked lips move. My voice breaks. It's the truth, and I can't bear it. I close my eyes. "Just let me go." My body sags, and my legs give in.

"Oh, love," he says, and lies me down. My body curls, and my heart spills over, for it's stretched too far, and it won't hold all. It pours and pours, until there's a void deep inside of me, where sadness resides and blood stains the ground.

Morning comes with streaks of raw pink and jagged white and brings Lanying barging into our room.

"You fool," she sneers, but pride glimmers within her. She washes my face with the softest of cloth. "Quite a bit of bruising, but nothing that won't fade within a few days." An ointment stings my cheeks. "At least it won't scar."

I nod. There's enough damage done.

She steers me into the kitchen and shouts an order. Hot water is served, shavings of dried root float within it. I sip the brew and she skirts away.

"I have to hand it to you, sister." Dendup shuffles beside me. "I didn't know you had that in you." He shakes his head. I glimpse at him and manage a smile.

"I didn't either," I say, but I know my words are a lie. He wasn't there, that night in Lhasa, when I threw myself in front of Karma's blade.

"Still, you could have gotten yourself killed." Dendup puts up his cup, another tea is poured. "You know better than to meddle in others' affairs."

He sighs and I straighten my back. *Ai, that hurts.* I nod and chew a sliver of bitter root. *I don't care.*

"Is Karma still angry?" I swallow. A little bile badgers the back of my throat.

"Of course, he isn't." Dendup snickers. "He's only mad you got away—again." His hand hits my shoulder. "But we all know, he's got this thing for daring women." He gulps the last of his tea. I just smile. What's there to say?

"Come on." He throws me a wink. "Let's ride together." He jumps up and slings my bag across his chest. I follow him and let his broad back shield me—for now.

"Nordun." Hastened footsteps overtake mine. A gentle hand halts me at the door. I glance up. The first light of morning streams through the doorway. It's Norbu.

"I heard." He blinks, and his worried eyes try to find me.

"It's nothing." My chin dips to my chest, and I slip through the entrance. I slide my scarf and stride across the yard. *Not now.*

They're all lined up, our men and beasts. Karma hands me the reins of my stallion. My eyes burn. *Focus.* I bite my bruised lip. My hands clench to fists.

I mount my horse, but Norbu's right beside me.

"How could you let this happen?" His words hurl a harsh accusation at Karma.

I cringe. *He didn't.* There is no answer, but a calm storm stirs from afar. Its thunder's faint yet looming. My hands reach for my beads.

"I told you, it's nothing." I spur on my horse. My gaze sets in the distance.

A high cry roars, horses bolt and my prayer gets answered. Our convoy hits the trail with no time to waste.

I tried. My thumb strokes the red faded ribbon. I failed—again—but at least I persisted. *Privileged.* That's what I am. Tears streak my face. There is nothing I can do. All that rests me now, is my humble prayer.

My hands slide my beads and my heart whispers the words—for the girl who's torment in this life has ended, and for the ones that wronged her—their suffering surely awaits.

Twenty-Four

My stallion's hooves patter like a fine drizzle on the stone slabs. It treads with care, as if it knows. I shift in the saddle, but fail to find my seat. My jaw clenches. Every move jabs a serrated blade through my chest bone. Every breath scours my ribs with a gritty wheeze. *Om Tare.*

My body hurts, and I won't wish away the pain. I'm strong enough to feel it and to endure it until time will lessen it all.

I lift my face to the sun. Her bisque beams trickle through the soggy sky, swollen with the promise of rain. I roll my shoulders. *Brave.* I've decided to be brave and let the hurt live in my heart as a poignant reminder of the young woman's agony and my own fortunate fate.

A placid neigh steams from my horse's mouth. Another steep crossing is coming up and there's nothing we can't handle after last night.

This day too brings scanty paths winding around sheer, craggy cliffs, and spanning crevasses of infinite depth and wild roaring rivers. My feet tread on patchy planks while my mind tramples the daunting fear. Karma was right—the first one's the worst. A drip of salty sweat stings my lips.

We track through the stretches of woodland where the monkeys munch on spouting treetops. Swinging themselves in a blasé way above us, their long coats shine a rich golden among the green. Clay slated roofs pop up, and a few dwellings of smeared mud on wood hurdle together. An old woman bears a toothless grin on her sunken face.

A lone musk deer twirls his white-furred ears as we reach its patch of grassland. It shoots away before any of the men can even reach for his bow. A small creek flows in a bed of moss and scattered boulders. With the sun at her strongest, a clammy veil covers my skin. Our convoy slows its trot—it's time to rest and let our animals graze.

The icy water steals the heat from my soles, palms, and cheeks. I gasp. *Cold!* Clear drops dangle from my lashes, twinkling the tiniest of rainbows from within. *This is good.* I stretch my back and roll my head. A warming wind whispers and smoothens the goosebumps on my skin.

Dendup has made his bed in the shade of the swaying white pines. Karma stays with our horses, quenching their thirst further downstream. Norbu sits next to Dendup and I know he won't let it go—ever since this morning, his eye's been on me.

I put on a smile and decide to join him. No use in avoiding him as he did me for the last few days.

"Get some rest." Dendup draws his hat above a wide yawn.

My legs buckle a bit as I sit down—my body's not eager to bend. Norbu tilts his head to me and I glance aside.

"I'm so sorry," he says. "Here." A slice of fresh bread comes my way.

"It's nothing." I try again, but he shakes his head. A ruby shade of amber deepens his eyes.

"It sure doesn't look like it's nothing, Nordun." He clears his throat. "You've been roughed up in a nasty way." His hand extends towards my cheek, and I flinch.

I shift my weight; my fingers pluck the dough. My mind searches, but there's nothing to say.

"Looks to me she's been very lucky." Dendup rolls on his side. A vexed tone rims his rumble. I rub my scraped knuckles. Out here, there's nowhere to hide.

"How can you say that?" Norbu lashes out. "She's all bruised and battered." His voice flares with anger and the brown in his eyes bursts into a charred orange at the sight of my face.

Dendup raises himself. I throw my arms around my knees and shift again.

"Well, you weren't there this time, were you, brother?" He throws a leery look at Norbu. "We were." He pauses his sneer. Norbu puts up his chin. Two heads butt in dead air with neither willing to bend.

Dry needles crack, and the wind whistles through the wavering branches, bringing Karma to us. I hold my breath. *Om Tare.* The crust crumbles under my touch.

"What's that you were saying?" Karma sits down beside me. He stretches his legs and rests his head against the scaly bark of a tree. His eyes go over to Norbu. I put a morsel of bread in my mouth. My teeth grind into it, but my throat's too dry. I can't swallow.

Norbu leans back. He clenches his fists and lets his fingers go with a slow, veined nonchalance.

"Only that I was sorry I wasn't there." His voice is too low, something brewing underneath it. "It won't happen again." He sits up and straightens his shoulders. "You can count on that." He looks straight at me; a glow of honeyed brown lightens his eyes.

"It's fine, really." I meet him half-way and let his gaze soften within me. "Thank you."

Next to me Karma grinds his teeth on a twig, and the distance between the two of us feels lonely and so out of place.

"Good, now we're all friends again." Dendup draws himself up to a sitting position. "Time you youngsters got your elder some decent tea with something to chew on the side." He smacks his lips and rubs his mustache. "It's a long ride before the sun goes down, and there are still many bridges to cross."

I rush up with relief, and a sharp pain shoots me down. Starry spots in black and gray dance in front of me. *Too fast.* Karma's chest sighs and steadies my spinning head.

"Let me." Norbu jumps on his feet. "I'll get us all some."

He strides off and is swift to return.

We eat in silence, the four of us, and ride again, until the sky streaks a bloody red and a small inn welcomes us on our way.

"Well done." I scratch my stallion behind his twirling ears and glide my hands around his legs. All good. My stiff fingers release the belt and haul the saddle. My body protest and a fierce stab punctures my lungs. The saddle slides, and I stumble.

"Come here." Karma catches me from behind. *No way.* His hands lock around my middle.

"I'm fine." With a stubborn tug, I wrestle myself from his grip. A muted huff escapes me. I lunge for the loose reins, but Norbu's ahead of me, and picks up the dragging leads.

"I'll take him." He nods at Karma. "You take care of her." He turns and is off with my horse.

My shoulders sag. My mind shuts down. I want to breathe, but I can't. My chest is weighted with the longest of days. I spread my fingers along my ribs. My eyes close.

"Let's walk it out for a while." Karma's voice sounds from the distance. "It helps, trust me, I've been where you are—too many times."

I peek up, and he takes my hand. Together we walk out in the fields where the grass waves and tickles the tops of my fingers. The blades are thick and tangled, like my horse's manes, and weave together in a coarse blanket covering the earth.

"Better?" Karma's lips press a tender kiss on my forehead.

"Better," I say, and it is.

We walk on, and the sky splashes a bittersweet orange around a bronzed sun. It's like she put her nails in a fleshy peach and ripped it open, spilling her juice and dripping it down on either side of her pitted kernel.

"I'm sorry," I say, and I don't know why.

"You've got to learn to pick your battles, love." He rests my head against his shoulder. "And I'm sorry—even I couldn't win this one for you."

I close my eyes and let his truth sit within me.

"I know," I say, and I do, but my voice sounds strange in my ear. *I would still do it again.* My heart whispers and I put my hand to my chest.

"You scared me." He swallows hard. "Like you scared me in Lhasa." His fingers brace around the back of my neck. "Promise me you won't ever do that again."

He lifts my chin and cradles my face in wait for my answer.

I can't make that promise. "I'll try." My lips tremble.

"You'll have to, love, or you'll get us all killed." His cheek presses against mine. "And I don't want it to be that time yet." His breath strokes my ear.

"Nor do I ever again want to see you get hurt like this." His lips brush a tender kiss on the side of my forehead where my brow is cracked open and scraped skin stings at every twitch of my eye.

"I know." I hide my heated face in the crook of his neck.

His fingers twist my hair, and I relish the taste of him—salty and sweet. *So good.*

His breath halts a sudden, stopping mid-air. "Don't move." His hand drops to his long blade.

"What is it?" My eyes widen, and my lips linger on.

"Turn slowly." His fingertips press the pommel of his knife. "It's at the edge of the field."

His arm slides around my midriff, and he pushes me behind him. I look over his shoulder and there it is, a wooly body hiding in the lanky stalks of bamboo. Black and white, and rounded in every way, it wiggles away.

"I've seen their hides go for decent prices at the markets, but never saw one alive." Karma's dark gaze scouts over the surroundings like a vulture soaring over his prey. "It's not fast, an easy catch." With a determined curve, he pulls out his blade.

"Don't." I step ahead. "Please, let it be." My hands cling to his grip but apply no pressure.

His arm tenses, and muscles bulge, if only for a moment. His pulse speeds under my palms. He slows his breath, and his stare is unmoving.

"It means no harm." My voice reaches out. Another moment stretches between us. A gust of wind surges through. I drop my hands and a frail green wells up in the depth of his eyes.

"You win." His blade slides back. "This time." A reluctant clang rings from the sheath.

"That's enough for me," I say. "Didn't you say one step at the time?" He bares his teeth.

"Can't remember." His mouth smothers mine as I throw up a protest, and for once I don't mind.

We walk back and the sun walks between us, as the last of her of honey-dipped rays spread over the fields.

It's been a good day, with many bridges crossed—and still many to go.

Twenty-Five

The days merge in a seamless tapestry of riding and resting. Our convoy conquers the mountains at a steady pace, leaving no men or beast behind. Many who've traveled this path before us have not been so lucky. Their journey ended where the wind wails and the birds of prey circle, and the rocks retreat to depths unknown to any man.

"Nothing to do with luck, sister." Lanying grinned when I asked her about it. "We've got the gods on our side."

I heard she prays to all the gods but puts none above the other. I often wonder if she puts her faith in any of them at all.

The gods are favorable to us again today. Broad flag stones pave our way in smooth green and blue, and our horses' hooves clap in delight. A crisp, fragrant, almost pungent aroma tickles my nostrils. Towering cypress trees lining along both sides of the path throw their cooling shade on our backs.

"Ah, finally." Dendup swipes off his cap with a bow. "At least we'll ride in comfort for a day." He leans back in the saddle.

"A full day?" I crane my neck and peer in an infinite underpass of swaying boughs and speckled bark.

"For sure." His hand flings in the air. "Some old general planted at least a hundred thousand of them, long time ago." He snorts. "Guess he couldn't stand the sun either."

A hundred thousand. My glance drifts up the rough, dark tree trunks, oozing a deep yellow rosin in places where birds pecked their beaks and pot-bellied squirrels dug their tiny claws. *Om Tare.* If there's a hundred thousand as Dendup claims, we'll have shade again tomorrow—for sure.

"Better enjoy it while it lasts." Dendup's cynical tone has found his way back. "There's a famed steep passage coming our way." He reaches in his chuba. His fingers unscrew the top of the flask in the palm of his hand. "One so narrow, they say a single man can keep ten thousand men at bay."

I frown. Another bridge to cross. My body lifts in the saddle. How many more to go?

"Not to worry, sister, from what I've seen, there's not much that will hold you down." He raises his drink to me and I shake my head.

"You're sure?" His teeth flash bright ivory at me.

"No thank you, I'm fine." I shudder. One horrid taste was enough. Besides, I don't need it to strengthen my courage. My hand probes my beads. Like Lanying said, we've got the gods on our side.

Dendup was correct, though. We are granted the shield of cypresses for only one day.

The next morning the trail leads to higher grounds, and the woodland retracts. A barren precipice breaks into two before us, and a winged watchtower looms ahead. Lofty walls stare us down, their smooth stone sanded by the forever-sweeping wind. Jagged cliffs and rugged crags on both sides shoot straight into the sky, like two sharpened swords defending the entry. A precarious pathway leads straight into heaven.

Dendup was right again; this must be the most impenetrable pass in the world.

"Stay in the saddle," Karma says. His stallion paces next to mine.

Guards scramble down and our convoy halts its pace. Words are spoken and bags change hands. We only sit and watch.

Within moments, all is settled, and a high cry roars again. Hooves trample and bodies shuffle. Our convoy lines up in one single stroke and crawls on. The sun has already sunken below the horizon when we saddle our horses off for the night. A few days more to go and we'll rest in Guangyuan.

"You'll love the place." Lanying squeezes in the seat beside me. "It has a thousand Buddhas carved out in the cliffs." She leans aside and her fingertips graze my cheek. "Your battle wounds will have gone by then—nice on time." I flinch.

"Time for what?" I say and wrap my hands around the cup in front of me.

"Well, we've got some visits to pay." Lanying's fingers fold around mine, and she takes a swig from my cup.

"What visits were you thinking of?" Karma joins us. Dendup and Norbu follow in his wake. His voice carries his usual calm, yet there's a tingle of caution mingling through.

"Oh, nothing but a trip to the bathhouse." Lanying's eyes spark a scintillating sapphire above the coarse clay-fired cup. "And to the temple and cliffs, of course." Her lips curl in a smug smile. *I know that look.*

"See you later." She throws up her hands and strides off before the others reach our table.

I glimpse at Karma. *He knows that look too.*

"A bath would be great," I say in my most casual tone. Karma's eyes narrow. Bowls of steaming soup swerve around on our table. *Just in time.* I dig in.

A quiet evening follows, with plenty of drink to unwind for some of us, and early night for all.

With the promise of a day's rest—and a day's drinking for some—the horsemen push our troop forward in a steady pace. Their actions are determined, though never risky. Their focus remains in the now, and never wavers to the lure of the days to come. The god of the mountains speaks to them, and they listen, giving in to her whims and ever-demanding ways. They know any objection will be fruitless, for she's the master they have chosen to serve. All are willing to pay the price, for the freedom she grants is one that's hard gained, but most precious of all. It's the freedom to roam where the mountains reach the sky, and the planes stretch into infinity, and where the soul can take flight amongst the clouds drifting by. These men have chosen to surrender to the wanderer's hard way of life.

"Tomorrow early, sister." Lanying waves across the courtyard. We've reached Guangyuan with only a few beams of the sun to spare.

"Tomorrow." I wave and sling my bag across my chest. My stallion neighs. His velvety nose bumps my shoulder. "No, not you." My fingers ruffle his manes. "You've earned your rest too."

Karma's smile pops up across my horse's back. I duck. He thinks I'm silly for talking like that. With a resolute swing, he hauls my saddle and puts it aside.

"Still think you need a bath?" He marches me through the hallway.

"I don't, but I would like to." My fingers hook the back of his belt. "Want to come with us?" I glance aside. *Did I just say that?* My lips pinch and a flutter twirls in my stomach.

"Hm, I think her behavior's rubbing off on you," he says. *He never mentions her name.*

"In here." An iron latch slams, and he flings our bags in the corner. "And I'm not too sure what to think of it." His hands anchor on his hips, and he dips his chin to meet me. An opaque green glazes his eyes.

"It's only a wash." I cast my eyes down, my hands smoothen my unruly bun. "I didn't have one since..." I bite my tongue. I will not say it. "Just let me rinse the last of it away."

His thumb probes the ridge of my eyebrow, where a fiery reddened stripe stores the memory of broken glass scattered on bone and battered flesh torn open, of a battle that I lost on strength, but won with the heart.

"A wash." He cradles my face. His lips trace the fine line above my eye.

"Only a wash, I promise." I speak the words before I realize—they are what he wants to hear.

"Good, and then I'll take you to see these Buddhas she was on about." His hands press into my cheeks. "I haven't seen them either, and I don't want you to wander around by yourself."

My hands slide around his wrist, and I step back, holding his reach.

"You know I never wander around on my own." I try on a determined tone. "Even though you might not always like the company I keep."

His eyebrows raise, and the corners of his eyes fight a smile.

"You've got that right, love." With a quick flick of the wrist, his fingers grip the lapels of my shirt. He pulls me near. "I'll tell you, you're too naïve when it comes to her dealings."

The furred skin lining of his coat tickles my cheek. My fingers search and find the warmth of his skin. "It's only a wash."

He sighs and surrenders.

"A wash," he states, and his arms close me in. "And then you'll get right back here and wait for me."

My ribs ache, but my heart leaps a little. *A bath.*

"I will, I promise." I draw on my toes, my fingers scrape along the rough skin of his jaw. "Now, you sure you don't want to join us?" I make no attempt to keep my grin at bay.

His hands jolt to my sides, and I squeal as laughter rolls right through me.

"Yes, fine, I get the message." I wrestle his embrace. "I won't ask again, now let's get our food." I lose and he wins.

"I had something quite different in mind." With a decisive tug, he slips my coat open.

My eyes widen in surprise. "I have no idea what you're on about."

"Sure, you do, you started it." A mischievous grin spread across his face. "Inviting me for a bath with your sister."

I gasp. "I was only being polite." My objection sounds so weak, even I have to laugh.

My coat lands on the floor, and his belt lands beside it.

The night falls early for the two of us, and we forgo our food, as some things are more pressing right now; like securing a bath to wash away the stains of a battle past and to prepare for another one, one that is sure to come.

Twenty-Six

Mist covers the courtyard. Morning sun mingles with pearly drops of opal and gray. The fresh scent of last night's rain, one of soaked earth and bruised grass, of budding cherry blossoms and rose buds, drifts in a balmy breeze.

"Got your book?" Lanying's arm slips into mine.

I frown, and my hand drops over my bag. *My book?* The stiff leather hides it, but my fingertips sense the contours of the wrapped pothi pages. I haven't touched it since we left home.

She hisses an order at the two guards lagging behind us. One of them skirts away. Within moments he's back—hooves prance on the cobbles and the thinning haze reveals an agile body. The guard leads a fine stallion on his side.

"The drawing." Lanying's hand squeezes mine. "We need it today."

An iron bolt clangs, the gate swings open. *The drawing.* I halt.

"You mean...?" My nail probes the rough stitching around the clasp. It's in there, etched in black on brown paper, the exact image of Karma's inking; I promised not to show.

She nods and rushes me out onto the street. "I'll tell you later." Her feet fly while mine hobble behind her. The guards' heavy breathing behind me pushes me on.

Wide puddles sink into the cobblestones of the main street. The last of the flimsy fog flees from the back alleys. Two lions rise, their marble coats gleam a veined silver through a frozen creamy white. Fierce and staunch, they secure a red lacquered gate.

"In here." Lanying hushes me through the raised doorway. The scattered chirps of a caged huamei bird greet us from a secluded patio behind. "My friend's away for the season, but he's made sure we're more than welcome in his house."

Pink peony scrubs bloom in large pots at four corners. Red lanterns sway from curved hooks on the sides. A wiry crab apple parades its blushing buds with pride in the middle, and a tranquil fountain flows from behind. *What are we doing here?*

Two girls in flowing robes skirt from the gallery. Lanying flicks her wrist, and they withdraw into the house.

"Our bath's ready." Lanying's smile carries her usual smugness, and there's no use in asking—she won't answer, not yet.

The warm water soaks my skin, and the fragrance of honey and rice eases my mind. My eyes close and the possibility of a bathtub at the stables back home drifts before me. *If only... then again, why not?*

Tea is served, with fruit and sweets on the side.

"You're not showing yet." Lanying pops a date in her mouth. "There's still time." Her jaw chews with vigor.

I sigh. "No, thank you." Her casual tone weighs down on my heart.

A tiny woman who I mistook for a girl fusses around the room with bundles of clothes.

Lanying slips out of the tub and into a large towel. "I brought you something appropriate to wear."

"Where are we going?" I wade to the side and put my chin on the tiled rim. My body breathes deeply, filling my being with the calm of the water.

"We're not going anywhere, sister," Lanying says. "But we do expect visitors to arrive any time soon." Her gaze sifts through the dresses.

"Visitors?" I haul myself out of the bath and snatch a sheet lying around. "What visitors?" Aren't we the visitors here?

Two petite hands put me on a stool and detangle my locks.

"Visitors with valuable information, sister." Lanying twirls in a cloud of silk and crimson. "So let's make sure they'll spill more than they intend."

Male visitors. I jerk my head, a knot catches the comb in my hair. An abashed voice shrieks a shaken apology behind me. "It's fine," I say. Lanying drapes a muted purple dress around my shoulders.

"Hair up," she instructs the woman with a brusque nod, and flurries to the door.

It's not long before hooves clap in the courtyard. Two riders, I count. Lanying hooks her arm in mine.

Two men enter the hallway. Long, stiff robes with short, armored jackets, white faces and a hefty thump in their stride. *Mongols.* My heart slams in anguish against its cage.

"Nordun, meet Altan." Lanying's voice sounds sweet and secure. "The brother of Xia's husband, and a dear brother of mine."

His darkened eyes pierce mine, and his companion grumbles.

Cold sweat veils my forehead. *Be nice.* A faint smile breaks on my lips.

"Let's sit." Lanying leads us to a room where dishes are plenty and liquor flows. The men dig in, and Lanying leads the conversation.

I sit back. Lanying pours some more.

My fingers pick on a plum. She's good, she knows what she's doing. They talk about trade, horses, and the latest news from afar.

They keep gawking my way, and I pretend not to understand. The one she called Altan points his chin at me.

Lanying puts her hand on my arm. "Show him the drawing, sister, we want to be certain."

I rummage through my bag. *I promised.* My palms stain the red cloth as I unwrap it. The pages shift and a small drawing falls aside.

I hand it to the man opposite me. My fingers flutter with fear, and he pretends not to notice.

His gaze flings over the inking, but his eyes widen on my book. I bite my lip. *What now?*

His dark glance meets mine and my heart quivers. His nails scratch the corner of the page.

His words are quiet but clear, and he directs them at me. *He knows I understand.*

"There's a woman from that clan in Xingyuan, on the outskirts." His hand covers the drawing. "She's like you—you'll know when you meet."

My mouth goes dry. *She's like me.* My fingertips tingle. What does he mean? His gaze locks me in.

"We're going to battle soon." He squares his shoulders and leather groans. His hand glides over my book. "You tell me." Again his words are slow and deliberate, and he won't let me go.

My stomach churns. His companion moves closer. The smell of charred meat and sour milk chokes in my throat.

"He wishes you to do a divination, sister." Lanying's smile carries a sweet, yet sharp undertone. "He believes you're good." She purses her lips.

"I can't." My body squirms, my eyes cast down. *A divination for battle.* "I've only just learned."

"Nonsense, sister." Lanying's laughter scoffs, her hand waves in dismissal. "Even they know you're better than any of those monk quacks that go around."

The heavy bodies before me stay unmoved and wait in determined patience. *What to do?*

"Sister." He heaves, and his hand smoothens the crumpled cloth of my book.

I peek up, and my eyes meet his, and there are charcoal clouds billowing in the darkest of night, and savage sparks of a blacksmith's pit sweltering within. My shoulders sink, and something inside of me cracks open. A profound sense of mercy sweeps through the hollows of my heart, persuading me to face the fate of the men sitting before me.

My hands fold into one, and my mind turns within, and I call upon Manjushri, the wisdom Buddha, to guide me. *Om Ah Ra Pa Tsa Na Dhi.* His mantra spins through my thoughts.

My palm opens, and I cast the dice. The polished bones roll on golden red cotton. All hold their breath as the square cut cubes reveal their fortune with the flick of a wrist—twice.

"Tsa Ra." My voice croaks, my fingers flip the pages. I know the meaning by heart but want to be sure.

"That's good, right?" Lanying's voice urges from a distance.

"Very good." I say, and I mean it. "It's the great fiery weapon, the one that conquers all." My words are met with a joyous relief from across the table. Lanying pours more liquor, but the man's eyes are still on me. The darkness in them has turned into the shade of mid-winter, of leaden skies where the ravens fly after the storm has passed.

"Tsa Ra, are the words of Yamantaka," I say, and glimpse at Lanying to make sure my explanation comes out good. "The chief of the wrathful army has shown himself to you." Lanying raises her glass and I swallow my sadness.

"You will be successful." My fingers line the leaves and an unexpected resignation settles within me. "All enemies will be destroyed, and you will be victorious, be it through force."

Cups overflow, and teeth flash in the sunlight. I fold the drawing and wrap the cloth around my book. The transaction is settled to all men's satisfaction. The last of the liquor is drank, and our meeting draws to an end.

With a light tread, the men march out into the courtyard. Lanying hands over the reins to the stallion she brought, but the man refuses. His heels scrape, and he turns to me.

"We are family now, sister," he says in the same subdued manner as he spoke at the table. Still, I draw a step back.

"No need to fear, for we take care of each other," he says, and his eyes mirror the bluish hue of sunlight on the slate cobble stones from within.

My heart wavers and profuse shame flushes my cheeks. The gods have spoken. Who am I to doubt upon whom they bestow their triumph?

"Please, you pray for our victory." He bows ever so slightly. "And we will watch over you."

His stallion neighs, and his hand tug the reins tight. With an effortless move, he mounts his horse and they're off.

"You were great, sister, telling them exactly what they wanted to hear." Lanying slings the reins back to the guard. "It's off to the temple, I guess?"

My eyes burn, my head pounds. The sun is at its highest. My body caves, but my mind knows it can't hide.

"Yes, it is," I say, and walk us into the shade.

I've requested the dice, and the gods have answered. No matter the outcome, now it's my turn to honor their request.

Twenty-Seven

Lanying raises her eyebrows. "Don't you ever do that again, sister."

"Do what?" The divination went well, so what did I do wrong?

"Doubt yourself, of course." Her tone is biting. "Especially in front of others." Her arms fold across her chest. "It doesn't become strong, intelligent women like you and me."

Strong. It's everything I'm not feeling at the moment. The sun drains my body, and the divination occupies my mind.

"Now there's a woman you might take as an example." Lanying nudges her head at the sculpture before us. Walking into the gate of the temple hall, it's the first thing we see.

A rich tone of gold gleams on the intricately carved sandstone towering before us. My eyes don't recognize her—is she a goddess, or merely a queen? A silk nun's robe drapes around her body. Serenity graces her face. A plain collar adorns her wide neck, and the headdress of a Buddha crowns her head. She appears to be in meditation as her hands fold over her knees.

"This is Wu Zetian," Lanying says. "A saint, and the only empress who ever reigned over these lands." She bends her body to the white marbled floor. I do the same.

"And that is her husband, Emperor Gaozong of Tang." Lanying looks up at the sculpture next to the empress. "When he fell ill, Wu Zetian saved his reign."

"An empress." My voice drowns in the vast corridor of the deserted temple. How can this be? For sure she's not a goddess, but a female reigning over these lands? She can't be only human either. I turn to Lanying. A pleasing blue lights in her eyes.

"I'll tell you, sister, it's not only gods and noble men that dominate this earthy existence." She takes my arms and walks me to the side. "Wu Zetian here was not even of royal descent, and still she ruled, long after her husband had passed."

We sit on a slim marble bench. My fingertips trace the veined swirls of rose and red and pause on the worn patches where many have rested before us. The heat of the day shies away.

"Tell me about her," I say. "About Wu Zetian." I lean back. My body's weary, and my mind needs a rest before I can honor my reluctant debt. I've requested the wisdom of Manjushri, and now the proper prayers and practices must be done. *A prayer for force and victory, a prayer for destruction.* My hand sinks in my lap. There's a long day to come.

Lanying closes her eyes. A smile broadens her cheeks. When she opens her eyes again, they're almost translucent, glossy, like the sheer sapphire glass beads that Father once brought home after a long journey, and my mother then treasured in her special box. The kind of blue that you'll only find in a far land, one that reminds you of home.

"Wu Zetian was only a young girl when they came to the palace." Lanying sounds almost humble, not her usual demeanor. "She was one of the many concubines of Emperor Taizong, but soon became his secretary, for she wasn't afraid to show her intelligence—as most women we know." She snorts and our laughter rolls through the hall.

It's true, many of us women hide our minds, even amongst our own. Dechen used to scold us if one of us played dumb in class, pretending not to know the answer to one of her puzzling questions.

"To hide your brilliance, is to deny others a lamp in the dark," she used to say. "Everybody loses if you decide to play the fool and not be true to yourself." The real meaning of her words was lost on me then, but I now understand—it takes courage to shine your light and stand in your truth. I wasn't brave enough back then, for I dreaded being different from others, or worse, have others think I considered myself better. How silly I was.

My fingers twirl the red cord around my wrist. A smile stretches my heart. How lucky to be in the company of precious Buddhist teachers and sisters in solitude, and of sisters in this mundane life who are not afraid to stand in their truth.

I glance aside and Lanying tilts her head.

"Ready for the rest of the story?" she says. "We've only just begun."

I nod. I'm more than ready to hear it all.

"So when the Emperor died, Wu Zetian had to join his other concubines, as they forced them to become nuns." Lanying stresses the last word. *Nuns.* I understand it might seem a restricted way of life to lay women—if fact, I learned it's a wonderful way of life, but only if our karma is right.

"They could never lay with other men after being with the emperor." She pauses and rolls her eyes. "Imagine that—the things men do to control us."

I smirk, and she wrinkles her nose.

"However, the emperor's son Gaozong had his eye on Wu Zetian," Lanying continues. "He was the emperor now and decided for her to become his wife, but as with all powerful, brilliant women, the men at the imperial court turned against her."

We both sigh at the same time—it's all too familiar. I pinch her arm.

"What did they do?" I say, and I can only imagine, for people can be so cruel.

"They claimed the emperor's marriage to his father's former concubine was incest," Lanying says, and purses her lips. "And when that didn't work, they slandered her in the worst conceivable way."

I sit up. A pair of gray robes and shaven heads pass us by.

"They said she strangled her own baby girl to put the blame on another woman who stood in her way," Lanying whispers. *A baby girl.* She shakes her head. "Of course, the emperor wouldn't hear of it, and he made her empress to rule these lands with him, even after his death."

"You think she did it?" My words waver at the thought. *A baby girl.*

"Of course, she didn't." Lanying's answer is clear cut. "Sure, she had to be ruthless, as any ruler has to be." Her voice pitches, her eyes breath a feverish fire, with flaming rings and a burning blue at their core.

"So, they made up these stories, these petty men of the court, claiming Wu Zetian killed two of her own sons." She shrugs at my gasp and wipes her nose with her sleeve. "Now I know little about that, but I'll tell you, if it were true, what weaklings these sons must have been." A certain disdain curls in the corners of her mouth.

I look down at the floor and wiggle my toes. The coolness creeps up on my soles. A mother killing her own daughter, her own sons. I shiver—how can that be true?

"They also scorned her for taking a harem of male concubines," Lanying says, and her deep chuckle lifts the air around us with delight. "She had every right to, for who can deny her the pleasure of doing what all men have done and still do in her place?" She rakes her fingers through her elaborate hairdo. A wave of ebony breaks free and cascades over her shoulders.

"Despite it all, Wu Zetian stood her ground and ruled these lands for over twenty-three years." She jumps up, her feet bounce of the marble. I slide off my seat and wander beside her to the icon of the woman who was a human like us and a fallen goddess for all in her time.

"There have been—and always will be—plenty of women that know how to rule this world." Lanying's hands anchor on her hips and she beholds the woman in an admiring gape. "But it's the men that record history and do an excellent job in hiding the brilliance of women." She cocks her head, and her eyes recede to two perfect halves of an indigo moon.

"They twist and mangle history with their written words," she says, and her shoulders fall. "They ruin and discard the reputation of women rulers until only the scandalous, the nasty bits are remembered." Her nostrils flare. "Like they did with Wu Zetian." Her poignant truth hits my core. An icy draft gushes through. My toes spread on the stone floor, my feet seeking solid ground.

"It's up to women like you and me, sister, to remind our female ancestors for what they truly are—noble, talented women who lived their own lives in a world where men lay down the law." Lanying hooks my arm.

I hold her hand and we walk out with a quiet knowing within, a silent understanding, one that exists only between women—be of all places and times.

"I guess living our own lives as women means we can't afford to get noticed too much." My thoughts scatter in the rays of the midday sun. The stone stairs warm our every step.

"Well, if that the case, I must be lost by now." Lanying shields her eyes with her hand. "But you, my dear sister, you can be saved." She turns to me and with a flick of her wrist, her fingers stroke my cheek and her mouth kisses mine with no shame. I let her, and I smile, for her heart is not lost, she's only hiding behind walls, made by the scared little girl she once was and now can't bear to remember.

"How long do you need?" she says as I unwrap my book from its cloth.

"As long as it takes," I say, for I've never done this one before.

A prayer for force, a prayer for victory.

I close my eyes and my mind seeks inside for my heart and her purest intention, and I let the words flow from my lips.

For the lone warrior whose cry roars on the battlefield, and the ones whose stolen lives he has to repay. For the lost girl whose cry is smothered, and the ones who deem themselves to be gods.

My heart spreads her wings as the words set her free—words of wisdom to withstand the anger, words of compassion to overcome the hatred. My heart says a prayer for all of those grasping at straws.

Twenty-Eight

The last touch of burned bouquet fades into a fragrant cloud of spicy lemon and verbena. White sunlight drenches my skin. Cream splashes on pink and purple—the magnolia trees lining the temple garden are in full bloom.

"Good prayer?" Lanying swings her legs over the lacquered bench.

"Good prayer," I say, and it was. I guided my intentions the best I could, expecting nothing in return.

"Let's go." She waves, and a guard shoots out of the shade. "Something tells me our brothers are waiting, eager for your return." Her rush of silk pushes me on.

A muggy whiff lingers in the market. The heat drowns the empty teacups stacked in a shallow basin. People loiter along the stalls with their shadows on the verge of lengthening. Heads doze off under caps. Birds squish in bamboo cages, and a filthy dog skips away.

"Hmm, too late." Lanying halts, but the guard has already turned the corner. "They're back before us." She squares her shoulders, and her arm slides in mine.

"That must have been some bath, sisters." Dendup's eyes roll around us. "Complete with a change of clothes." He rubs his chin. "It suits the both of you."

Lanying nods and looks past our elder. My toes curl in my boots. *Too long.* We've been gone too long.

"All went well then?" Lanying's eyes scout the courtyard and mine do the same.

"It did." Dendup hauls a bag from his horse. "One thing left before we head out tomorrow. Won't take long." Lanying nods again.

Something unsettling stirs within me. I don't understand what they're talking about, and they don't want me to know.

"You took your time." Two arms close me in from behind and I jump. "All new?" Karma's lips skim my ear.

I turn. "All new."

My eyes set at his chest and stay there. If I face him, he'll see. An awkward silence surges between us.

"Want to tell me?" He chooses his words with care and speaks them with caution.

I peek at Lanying. His thumb strokes my jaw.

"We had a bath, visited some friends, and went to the temple." Lanying's cute smile cuts between us. "We did our part of the preparations, how about you?" She flings her hands at her hips. Dendup steps near.

"You visited friends." Karma states in a restraint manner. His fingers trace the soft fur on my lapels.

"We saw Altan," Lanying says, and shrugs as if it's nothing.

"Altan." Dendup whistles under his breath; his feet shuffle back.

Karma's hand crumples the silk on my shoulder. I look up, and he looks away.

"Altan confirmed what we already suspected." Lanying raises her chin. "I realize you're not thrilled about it, but I wanted to be sure." She shifts her stance and leans back, as if she knows what to expect. Her guard appears beside her; her stallion dances at his leash.

"You've got that right." Karma's voice tinges on the edge of anger, but he doesn't move a muscle. I pick a loose thread from my sleeve. *This is not going well.*

"We're all here for you, brother." Lanying lowers her chin, and her tone dives down with it. "But we all work different ways, so accept it, and move on." She flicks the reins from hand to hand and vaults into the saddle with a flawless spring and a gentle landing.

"I would never put her in danger." Her stallion rears on his hind legs. "Or leave her, unlike some of us."

Her last words splash on the smooth cobbles before us and seep between the cracks and crevices. I watch them stain a dark blue onto gray. Dust clouds up, and she's off.

Dendup hastens away with his packhorse. Karma's stare holds me down.

"You met Altan." His voice lashes a quiet chill against my cheeks. "What did he want?" His eyes pry and mine look away into a pale leaden sky. "What did he ask in return?"

"Nothing." My answer's too hasty. "He asked for nothing." My palate's parched, and my hands crawl up my sleeves.

"Lanying offered him a horse, but he refused to take it," I say, my voice wavering. "He didn't ask us for anything in return."

My mind lays silent. A faint thunder rumbles and charred leather groans. I blink. *We go to battle.* A dark voice swells in the distance.

You tell me. My mouth opens. *The divination.* I want to swallow, but I'm too late. My words spill over, about the conversation at the lacquered table, and the divination he requested when he saw my book.

"You spoke his language, showed him the drawing and did a divination for him." Karma's voice freezes and sweat pearls on my upper lip. *I broke my promise.*

"You do not know who he is." He moves closer. "Do you?" A silver frost veils his eyes.

I wrangle my response from my throat. "I don't, but I couldn't refuse."

"You shouldn't have been there." His knuckles whiten around the pummel of his long knife. "Let's hope for all our sake your divination was right."

His jaw sets and a hard line breaks on his face. Something cracks and sharp slivers pierce the fragile space between us.

My heart drops. I watch it shatter like thin ice at my feet.

"Let's go." Dendup voice calls out and hooves scrape on cobblestones.

An iron latch slams, and none of us look back.

I drag myself through the hallway, a dull throb hammers in the void of my chest. *This is not how we're supposed to be.*

"Looks like you could use a cup, sister." A cheerful greeting sounds from the kitchen. "And I mean proper tea this time."

I glance up and a girl with joyous eyes invites me in. The way she speaks, I can tell she's from my part of the mountains. How come I didn't notice her before?

"Here you are." A cup of frothy milk tea and a wide smile arrive my way.

"Thank you." I sink beside the crackle of the stove and relish the rich flavor of home as the blend of salt and cream nourishes my being. *Home.* My heart drifts to the mountains, where the sky hugs the eternal snow on the lofty peaks, and the flowers in the valley burst into the most bountiful of bloom.

"You're good, sister?" A rag flies past my face and an infectious high giggle follows.

"A bit tired." A swift swipe of my sleeve clears my vision. *She's a jokester like Pema, this girl.*

"Then you can use another one," she says, and a generous pour fills my cup to the brim.

Boots trail through the hallway. The shuffle of a hefty bag tags along.

"I see you too found the best tea around here." Norbu flops down in the seat next to me. A fresh breeze flares the simmering stove, and a warm glow spreads around.

"Well, it's more like she found me." I smile. His presence always lifts my spirit. Another turn of tea finds its way to us.

I glance at the sack thrown in the corner. "They send you around again?"

"Yep, but I don't mind." He sips his tea and makes a face. "You got away early, I heard." He chuckles, and I join him in his delight.

"I did," I say. "That bath did me the world of good." I roll my shoulders and my lungs release a deep breath.

"And the cliffs?" His blade blinks and an overripe orange parts with its skin. "I only saw them from the other side, but those Buddhas are amazing, aren't they?" He hands me a slice. Juice drips, and I lick my fingers.

"Didn't see them." My teeth sink in the bitter sweetness. "We went to the temple after my bath." Another sweet slice slips right behind it—so good.

"You didn't?" Norbu slurps the last piece away. "They're on the other side of the river." He wipes his knife on his shirt. "I'll take you." He jumps up.

A thousand Buddhas. I weigh the last piece of fruit in the palm of my hand.

"We've got plenty of time." Norbu waves away my hesitation. His chuba swings over his shoulder. "It's warm, but just in case." His boots are already at the door.

"Thank you." I hand my cup at the young woman whose tea eased the edge of my afternoon and grab my bag.

A cloudless sky bows over the courtyard. A saffron sun lays her shadows down on the pavement—she still has a long way to travel before she's home. Norbu's right, we've got plenty of time. *A thousand Buddhas.* If only my sisters could see.

The river rages in churning heads of white foam and angry splashes, like a fierce hound guarding its master's priceless possessions, ready to attack. My eyes widen, but it's not the river that frightens me—it's the cliffs before us that capture my breath.

"Incredible." My hand clutches my beads. The entire rock face is sheathed with holy statues and sacred caves, chiseled in the vast crags like a dense honeycomb. *Om Mani.* There's not a thousand but a hundred-fold of a thousand, all buddhas and bodhisattvas shrouded in stone. My head bends, and my being beholds the infinite in a single moment. What a stunning act of devotion and determination this is.

"Amazing, right?" Norbu steps across a ledge separating the caves from the path. "Come." He reaches out, and I take his hand.

My knees wobble, and the slanted eyes of a stoic stone Buddha descend upon me. There're no words, only immense gratitude sweeping through.

Together we walk through the shrines, all telling the tales of adoration, of the suffering of humans and the salvage of saints. We clamber up narrow treads and slide down the slippery gravel. Vines twine along, and Norbu's hand steadies the way.

"If only my sisters could see this." I pull my scarf close. A cloud drifts by, and the sun dips herself in a pond of muddled lemon and lime.

"You miss them." Norbu slips his arms in his chuba. "And your life on the mountain." With a resolute tug, he ties his belt around and we stroll on to where we began.

"Sometimes," I say. There's a sadness in my voice that I didn't see coming.

"I'm sorry to hear that," Norbu says. He glances aside. "Anything I can do?" His words come with care and a genuine smile.

"It's only a feeling, it will pass." I shake my head. "But thank you, you're always good to me." I pause and slide the beads around my wrist. The jade shine twists around the faded red reminder of my sisters' protection wherever they are.

"I wasn't there when you needed me." Norbu hints at the raw patches on my knuckles, where broken glass and gravel grated the skin.

"That was me being foolish." I try to smile. It doesn't work.

"Still, I won't let it happen again." There's a firm determination in his voice, one he rarely shows. "I'm here for you." He reaches out. "You know what I mean." A dark auburn shine seeks my eyes.

"Norbu." I step back. The river roars closer. "Please, don't." I understand what he means, but I don't want him to say it. For once the words are spoken, they will swallow everything we hold dear between us. We'll drift apart, becoming strangers who once called each other close friends.

"I have to, Nordun." He tips his hat back. "If only once, for I want there to be no misunderstanding." His sure, yet sorrowful smile tugs at the tip of my heart. My lungs struggle for air.

"You made your choice," he says. "You choose to love Karma, and I respect that." He tilts his head to me.

I nod. *I made my choice.* Then why does my heart hurt like this?

"But I choose to stay close to you." His thumb hooks at his waistband. "I'll make sure you are safe, something he should have done but obviously can't." He casts his eyes on his boots and plants his heels in the muddy shale between us.

"And if you ever decide to choose otherwise, I'll be here for you." He looks up, and the ground moves between us. "Because I won't leave." His gentle voice whispers yet sounds loud and clear.

The breeze ceases, and the river quells her wild water. All things seem to come to a halt. My heart pounds against my ribcage. A blackbird's call chirrups through the air. Twigs snap and gravel crunches under foot soles.

"That's very generous of you, brother." Karma's solid calm radiates behind me.

I freeze, and Norbu lifts his chin. The sudden silence rings in my ears.

"I took you along because of your father asked me to," Karma says and moves at my side. "I took you along even though I've seen the way you look at her—and I understand, for she's beautiful, in every way." His hand strokes the fur lining on my collar and trails to my belt.

I wince. There's nowhere to hide out here.

"I trusted you as we're brothers, traveling together." An unnerving undertone stirs through the quiet in Karma's voice.

My fingers fray the fuzzy hem of my sleeves. My mind searches but can't decide. *Where is this going?* I glance aside.

"And I still do, but there's one thing you need to understand, brother." Karma shifts to face Norbu head on.

"You don't come between me and my woman." His fingertips touch mine, but he doesn't take my hand. Instead, he leans back on his heels, waiting for his words to sink in.

"It's not like that and you know it." Norbu's stubborn stare makes his stance obvious. "I respect Nordun's choice, but I'll stay close to keep her from harm." His voice hardens, his eyes blaze a fiery red among a burned brown. "Because I doubt if you will when the time comes, brother."

Norbu! Those last words came out like a nasty sneer—not like Norbu at all.

"Well, that time won't come." Karma's heels dig in the gravel. "And I'm here now."

A slight breeze picks up, loose strands drift around my temples.

"Yes, you are," Norbu says, and his eyes dart over to me.

I didn't want it like this.

"I'll see you both later." He draws his hat, and the fire in his eyes disappears. He wanders away, and I stay behind.

My mouth opens, but there's nothing to say. *Not now.* A slow hand tucks my straying hair behind my earlobe.

"Come." Karma's arms envelop me in a desperate embrace.

I vanish into the tight weave of his coat. *Let me stay here.* My body seeks solid ground.

He holds me tight as a storm crashes inside of him, slamming his heart against my ribs. A sob soars from the depth of my being, and a gale force smothers my throat.

"I'm sorry." His lips press on the top of my head.

"Me too." My fingernails anchor in his chest. *I won't let you go.*

Together we weather the eye of the storm until it swells at its height and takes its time to subside.

“I don’t want to be like this,” he says. His heart sighs. The sweet scent of rain-sodden earth and freshly bruised leaves draws around.

“Then don’t.” I come up for air and take a step back. “Don’t ask for promises I can’t keep and don’t hide things from me.” I wipe my nose. “It’s causing nothing but misunderstandings between us since we’ve set off from home.”

Home. My voice sounds raw, my heart quivers. It’s this man that I want to be home with.

“I’m not hiding anything, love,” he replies in that sure tone of his. “I’ve told you everything you have ever asked me.” His fingers lock mine. ”Everything.”

I look into his eyes, and he moves closer to see. *I never asked.* A cold hits my core. My body squirms. I never asked him.

A moment passes, and the realization sinks in. His eyes darken as they see.

“What happened to my cousins?” My lips form the words of the question I’ve been hiding.

Don’t tell me. I close my eyes, for I don’t want to hear.

“The family only ordered the oldest of them, for now.” he says in a flat tone. “I owe them, because of Lhasa.” I look up and he doesn’t look away. “They wouldn’t let you come if I didn’t.”

The pain is like I expected, a kind of blunt and dull. Like a finger poking into a lump of freshly churned butter and leaving a squishy hole inside of it. Not sharp edged or piercing. A bitter taste fills my mouth.

“When?” I hear myself say and my mind looks back at the winter, at our time together at home. A sad gloom creeps between us and he shakes his head.

"Don't." His fingers slide around the back of my belt. "Don't look for faults, for I'm human and faults are easy to find."

I tuck my hands in the pleats of his chuba. "I'm not looking for faults." My fingers seek his warmth. "All I want is honesty between the two of us." A waver gulfs through my stomach. *Do I, really?*

"I don't always tell, because I don't want to hurt you." He lays his lips to my ear and tugs at my belt. "You know how that is." He stalls for a moment. "For you do the same."

A flaming heat shoots up my cheeks. My chest caves into his. There's no denying. *The betrayal foreseen.* I didn't tell him, for I too want him to be safe.

"You already saw, didn't you?" I draw a shallow breath. "The divination and what more it said." I gather my courage to face him. A mellow smile curves his lips.

"I did." A dark emerald turns in his eyes. "But that's not what I mean." His hand lifts my chin. My shoulders sag and a fierce shame blurs my vision.

"Then you know I'm with child," I say, and the ground falls beneath me.

"I've been waiting for you to tell me." His arms scoop me up and sit me down on the ledge. "There's nothing more I want in this life than to father a child with you, so why keep this from me for so long?" His cheek presses against mine, and there's a gentleness beneath his roughened skin, something soft and tender, waiting with patience for a kindred spirit to share in his gentle ways.

Why? I duck my head, for I was mistaken, hiding something as precious as a child from its father. Now I sit with a gaping void in my chest and a heart filled with regret.

"Oh, love, she's beautiful, our little girl." His breath meets mine, and in his eyes bursts the green of spring, of sunlit boughs and soft moss, and of velvety buds that tell of the warmer season to come.

"You saw her?" I take his fingers as they wipe the streaks from my face.

"I did, the night she came to us, just before Losar," he says, and the words rush from his lips. "When the last of winter snow fell, and you said I was crazy to come, but everything inside of me screamed—I had to see you." A light glow blushes on his cheeks. "It had been only a few days, but my heart knew. It had been much too long."

"I remember." My mind recalls that night when he came riding. "The snow fell so thick; it snapped the mighty oak in the yard like it was only a twig." His eyebrow raises and I grin. And for a moment we're both back, right there in the kitchen—that was a good night.

"Now why would you hide something so beautiful on me?" He shifts beside me.

"I'm afraid." I lay my head against his shoulder. It's the truth, and I don't know why, but we're here and we're good. All is well.

"I'll promise you." His lips press a kiss in the palm of my hands. "We'll be home before winter—together."

My fingertips linger along his jaw. *You can't make that promise.* But my thumb strokes his mouth. His words are all I want to hear.

The dusk fades the shadows, and the air becomes fresh and restful. A pair of crickets raise their raspy evening song against the smooth hymn of a lone lark. We cross the raging river and hold each other near.

"Please go easy on Norbu," I plead.

A gate screeches open. We've reached the inn, and our companions are near.

"Oh, I will, I can't blame him for wanting you." Karma's face gleams with rare pride. "Besides, I admire his honesty." The open door welcomes us with wafts of laughter and the stale stench of liquor. "There are few decent men like him out there."

We step over the threshold, and Karma hauls me right into the kitchen where the drink flows, and our friends await us.

"Tonight we celebrate." Karma raises his cup. "And I might even get drunk."

I glance at Dendup, and we both agree—it's about time that he did.

Twenty-Nine

Nausea weaves through my stomach and lashes a cold tide down my back. The rich taste of home that settled my being only yesterday now lurches in a sour, burning sensation against the back of my throat.

"Maybe just some boiling water?" I shiver and hand my cup to the woman who filled it only a moment ago with enthusiasm. "Sorry, sister." My hands tremble and I rumble through my bag.

"Too spiced then?" Warm lips press on my clammy forehead. "The food yesterday?" Karma's cheeky smile meets my lips. His long hair hangs loose, his shirt lays half-open, and the scent of him and me and the long night behind us lingers around.

"I tell you; she's going to be a fierce one, that little girl of ours." He slings his chuba on the seat beside me. There's not a trace on him of the copious amount of drink he consumed yesterday. Instead, there's the deep glow of gratitude in his eyes, and a rare pride shines through.

My teeth grind the sliver of dried root in my mouth. "I'm sure she will." I savor his delight. His smile has never left since I told him, but a tinge of shame remains in me. He asked me yesterday why I kept this precious gift from him for so long. I told him I was afraid. It was the truth then, but now I know—I wasn't afraid. I was selfish and let fear turn my thoughts to what I stood to lose.

Fear weaved her tales of false assumptions in me, telling me how Karma would send me back to the stables to be safe. Or even worse, how he would abandon his mother's call and come home with me before we reached her. It would come to stand in our way, drive us apart. His longing would never stop. It would haunt him forever—as it haunted me too.

So I did the worst thing one can ever do—I closed the doors to my heart. I did everything my grandmother warned me not to. "When you're uncertain about what to do, just open your heart and love," she told me in class, and outside. "Keep it open, even if fear or doubts creep in, wanting to shut that door."

Never have my grandmother's words been more true. I got confused, believing I could protect my heart by raising my walls. How wrong I was. "Trying to shield ourselves in this way ends up being what harms us the most, for a closed heart causes suffering—onto ourselves and onto others. The open heart only offers an immense joy."

Dechen's truth rings in my ears and I meet the loving eyes of the one I hold most dear. He presses a kiss in the palm of my hands.

"I got you something." He digs the sheepskin lining of his coat. A tanned roll of somewhat-crumpled paper comes out.

A scroll. My heart skips a beat as I unfold a row of characters, black ink scratched on a single bruised sheet. What writing is this? My fingers trace the lines of a foreign script, each of five characters going down, one after another. Every line is crowned with a delicately drawn Buddha, wrapped in a red robe and resting on lotus petals painted in bright blue.

"I was told it's a book of names of the Buddha," Karma says. "I got it from a man in Ya'an but didn't have time to get it translated." His fingers skim the edges of the scroll. "Anyway, I thought you could figure it out yourself, as you're the educated one of us." His shoulder nudges mine.

"It's gorgeous." My eyes devour the writing before me. *The names of the Buddha.* My mind tumbles over the bows and curls intertwining in characters.

"I know how much you miss the monastery, your dharma studies." Karma's hand envelops mine. "And now life's changing even more for you—for us." I pull my gaze from the page and glance aside.

"I figured you didn't tell me sooner, because you were afraid you had to give it all up." His tender touch traces along my wrist. "But you don't have to, love, for there are plenty of women out there who are great practitioners and wonderful mothers."

A great practitioner. My fingers latch onto his as my mind wrestles off the gripping remorse. *If he only knew.* I've been judging him, criticizing him for keeping secrets, while all the while it was me hiding things from him. What I thought to be a fault in him was nothing but a reflection of my own distraught emotions. He didn't hide—I was the one believing my perception of him to be real. All those years in the monastery, and I still let my mind play tricks on me. A slow sip of hot water soaks the bitter root around my gums. Will I ever learn?

"You're capable of so much more than you can ever imagine." Karma lifts the scroll from my hands and folds it away in my bag. "And while humility is good, I'm expecting nothing but greatness of you." He leans in, and his hair tickles my cheek. "You'll be a shining example for our little girl."

He gulps down his tea and swipes his mouth. “Ready for the day?”

I’m not. My mind’s still in awe of his words. “Almost.” I take another sip and swirl my cup. “Need a moment to let this settle.” All is good. I stretch my fingers, the skin on my knuckles blushes in pearly pink.

“Karma.” My mind perks up, but my voice is cautious. “Who’s Altan?”

The Mongol’s dark eyes pry into my mind, the faint smell of wet fur whiffs in my nose.

“Your sister can tell you.” Karma’s jaw sets as his chin points to the door. “She seems to know him very well—so I’ve been told.”

I turn and there she is. Crimson brocade billows on a breeze of sweet jasmine and heady, rich musk as Lanying strides through the door. Silver fox fur weaves from her collar down the fringes of her coat. With a wicked smile, she tosses her long locks over her shoulders. This woman knows how to make an entrance, whether or not she intends it.

“Sister, I told you, he’s a brother of Xia’s husband.” She squishes beside me. “And a bahadur in the Khan’s army, most convenient.” White enamel blinks. “I’m starving.” She sinks her teeth into an apple.

“And he’s ruthless.” Karma’s sharp tone bites between them. He fastens the buckle on his belt.

“Well, he’s not much different from you then, is he?” Lanying hisses and smoothens the pearly trim along her sleeves.

Iron scrapes on leather, and with a swift slide, Karma’s long knife finds its place in the folds of his chuba. He turns away, his lips tight.

The stove crackles, and steam rouses up from the kettles. A sigh escapes. I doubt if these two will ever find peace.

"So, you told him." Lanying's tongue clacks near my ear. "Now he thinks he owns you." She runs her hand down my back and leans in to look over my shoulder.

"Just remember, brother, you got away with it in Lhasa." She slides aside to face Karma straight on. "But if you ever break her heart again, I swear I'll break both your legs." She gets up, and her voice rises with her. Her feet swing over the seat, but her eyes remain fixed on him.

Karma's mouth twists in a moody sneer. "I'll never be forgiven, will I?"

"You've got that right." A bright Norbu comes bouncing in.

Lanying raises her eyebrows, and without another word she sneaks out of the door.

"Don't you start on me too, brother." Karma shakes his head and gathers our bags. "I guess I can't win today." He slaps Norbu on the shoulder and leaves me with a hushed wink.

You've got to pick your battles wisely, Karma told me not too long ago. Well, he does.

Norbu wraps his hands around a fresh cup of tea. He takes his place at the simmering stove. "I'm happy for you, Nordun," he says, and his eyes turn a timid hazel among a honeyed brown. "I am, if this is what you want."

My pulse speeds up. What can I say?

"Thank you," my voice whispers. "It is what I want."

My mind speaks, yet my heart holds this man sitting before me so dear. How can I explain something that I don't understand? Something that should not be there?

He tilts his head and catches my blurry gaze. I blink, but there's nowhere to hide. A mellow sun peeps through the window. A rag flies by. Another cup of tea finds a thirsty throat.

"I meant what I said, I won't leave." Norbu's tone is resolute, there's no hesitation. He leaps to his feet and hauls me up. "I'm with you, sister—all the way."

Together we step out into the crowded courtyard. Another day awaits me in the company of my love and my good friends. What more can I want?

Thirty

The rain is our constant companion on our path through the mountains, falling from a sky in velvet and white. The blossoms and broad foliage form a fresh green canopy but give meager shelter as we make our way through virgin forest and weathered rock sheaths, over shallow bridges spanning raging rivers, and plank roads wedged in windswept cliffs. Our trail consists of muddy water in motion and shifting soil beneath our feet.

There's nothing to enjoy about this refreshing downpour of springtime. Each drop soaks through my coat, through my skin, stealing the heat from my body a bit at the time, for days at an end. I curl my fingers in the soggy fur of my sleeves and slide my beads while holding on to the reins. Yet somehow there's a strange comfort to be found in this rain and its predictability—it's part of life and therefore bound to change. As with everything on this earth, it will eventually cease to exist.

"Sure, now she shows herself." Dendup glares at the silvery sun. "At the end of the day."

We've made it before dark to Hanzhong. Our caravan crowds the rolling field around the inn. We're intact and secure. The sky draws her curtains of pearly gray to reveal the last light of the day. I slide back my hood and lift my face to the sun. Little droplets of sweet rain run with the salty sweat on my skin. My horse neighs, as it wants to spur me on. All are ready to retreat.

"There're many things I can get used to, even the coldest of days." Dendup lines his horse with mine. "But I've had it with this damn drizzle." He shakes himself like a big dog after a storm.

"Not to worry, brother." Norbu's eager hands reach out. "I bet there's a warm welcome waiting for you inside, for us all." He gathers the reins and, as on any other evening, takes care of our horses while we carry the bags inside.

"We're here." Karma swings his drenched chuba over the rough beam. Mine follows with a dull thud. They'll be dry by tomorrow.

"So is she." My hands under the silk of his shirt, I shiver.

His skin emits a mild heat on my mine and his heart thumps an incessant drum through my veins. He's been quiet these last few days, my love, but he's been never more alive in the midst of the night. We share his dreams of deer hooves skirting on barren boulders, winds sweeping over endless grasslands, and of eagles' wings soaring into an eternal blue sky. Her call has never sounded so clear—his mother's here, and we're close.

"Come on, you lovebirds." Dendup's frown peeps from the doorway. "The food smells decent enough."

I laugh. *Lovebirds.* That used to set fire to my cheeks.

Dendup's right—the food is decent enough, as it is in any inn we've been. Served in enormous bowls, there's plenty to go around, satisfying every hungry mouth. Big jugs of strong liquor follow, and soon the cups spill over, lifting the spirits of all.

"Here's to a fruitful journey," Dendup says and grins. "But most of all, a speedy return to the mountains we know." He gulps his cup in one go, and bids for another.

"Ah, brother, don't tell me you're not enjoying the ride." Lanying sweeps in and squeezes herself at his side. "We've been making a decent profit on the way, that always eases the days in the saddle." She throws a smug smile over his shoulder. "Besides, I'm sure those lovely ladies over there are more than willing to make your nights pleasant as well."

Dendup snorts and leans in. "Let's not forget the real reason of our visit to these sodden lands, sister." He pretends to ignore Lanying's remark, but his eyes peek at the "lovely ladies," as she's called them. No doubt he's taking his pick for the night.

"Time to tell us all what you know." He drags his glance back to the table. "And most of all, what makes you so sure that she's here."

Lanying eyes the jug, and Norbu pours another round. I rest my head on Karma's chest. *How to explain?*

"My contacts told me." Lanying's fingers rim her cup, and her eyes are on me. "And they are reliable, as they've always spoken true to me." She takes a sip and lets it settle before she slides her hand ever so subtle onto Dendup's arm.

"But first you tell me, brother, all you remember from the day they brought Karma home." Lanying's tone lowers. "Sure, you remember more than you tell?"

I hold my breath. I didn't mention it. How does she know he's been silent about it all these years? My ribs squeeze around my heart. Dendup straightens his back. *Here we go.*

Instead of the expected outburst, Dendup lowers his head. "I know little, only heard the rumors of another man they left in the river to die."

Lanying veers up. “See, I knew it.” Her eyes narrow on Dendup, but he doesn’t flinch. He sets his sight on his cup. Is that remorse I see shining through?

Relief soars through my lungs. *All is well.*

“Tell us again,” Karma says, and shifts in his seat. “About what you saw with your own eyes long ago.” His fingers tangle in my hair as if he seeks distraction from what he’s about to hear, even though he’s the one who asked.

“As I told you, I saw little, I was just a young lad.” Dendup’s gaze flutters over the table. “I saw you as they brought you with them, dressed in rags, on a horse that wasn’t ours.” He lifts his cup, but stalls in mid-air. “They burned your clothes, and scrubbed you in the river, and Grandfather took you in.” He shrugs. “You were fine, but three of our best men, our strongest men, died within the turn of the moon.” His cup lands, still filled to the brim, and reluctance spills over the table.

“I remember them well.” He rubs his furry brows. “They were the men that brought you with them, and all of them died.”

“All but Grandfather.” Karma speaks with confidence, yet there’s no consolation in his words. He bears a terrible burden—the death of three good men of the tribe.

“All but Grandfather,” Dendup echoes. “And that’s all I saw; the rest is just here-say.” He waves his hand, and Lanying lets go of his arm.

A faint tinkling rings in my ears. *The tiger bells.* A shiver shoots up my spine. Karma told me Grandfather found two tiny silver bells sown in the hem of his worn shirt. He took them out before he discarded the rag in the fire. They must have protected them from whatever Karma brought with him.

Karma’s fingers stroke the nape of my neck, to let me know—my thoughts are his.

"But what I do remember, is that nobody came looking." Dendup draws his hands over the table. "Nobody came looking for you, like good families do when their son is lost." His eyes flash at Karma. "You better watch yourself now that you're looking for them." A glimpse of care and despair shades his face.

"For once we settle, brother, for once we agree," Lanying says, and she pinches her nose.

Lanying's agreeing with Dendup? *Where is this going?* I veer up and lean in.

"We have to proceed with utmost discretion, like our elder says." Lanying glints at Karma. "We don't know what's left of your family, or what their intentions are." She swirls her cup between her fingers, and contemplates a sip, giving Karma time to respond.

"What's your plan?" Karma says, as always unmoved. He hides it well, but every muscle tenses behind my back, and I feel the blood pound through his veins.

"It's not appropriate for men to approach a woman of standing," Lanying says. "Especially not a high-ranking Mongol as she appears to be."

"High-ranking?" Dendup snaps and all heads on our table bob up. Even Karma's chest surges behind me.

"Yes, high-ranking, so even more reasons to proceed with caution, as you already suggested, brother." Lanying's mouth curves in a somewhat sly smile. "Therefore, I've secured an introduction from my trusted contacts for Nordun and me to visit her." She raises her cup to her lips and takes another slow sip.

"An introduction?" I hear myself say. Sure, I carried a few sealed letters from Xia to her. It must be one of them—she never let anything on.

"Yes, an introduction from a sister," she says. "We should go tomorrow, the two of us, if we all agree." She tilts her head to the side and casts a convinced look around the table. "We'll take two of my most trusted guards with us, as our elder said—we have to be sure."

I cringe. I never saw this coming. Lanying's a master in getting her way. Now she pretends to side with our respected elder, only to use his words to her advantage. Again, she's a step ahead of us all, forging a future of possibilities. She never seems to rest her mind in the moment. How exhausting that must be.

"I don't know," Dendup mutters, and he gazes at Karma, who doesn't utter a word. Surely both men see what Lanying's doing, though, for they often scold her clever ways.

"If any of you have other ideas, I'm more than open to it." Lanying waves her hand. "I do however think a friendly visit amongst sisters is the best way to assess the situation." She pouts. "We'll find out what this woman and her family are up to, and if it's safe for Karma to go."

Safe. My nails scratch the carved edge of the table. My mind spurs ahead. She's his mother. Why wouldn't he be safe? *Nobody escapes the army, sister.* I blink. Xia's words have been on my mind. Surely that cannot be true.

"Take your best guard and Norbu," Karma says. *What?* I jolt my head as Karma turns to Norbu. "If you're willing, of course."

"You don't have to ask, brother." Norbu's answer is swift and sure. "I'll make sure they stay safe." He beams a bright smile at me, but my mind stuns at Karma's approval.

"Good, that's settled then." Lanying raises her cup. "Like our elder said, let's toast to a profitable journey and a speedy return." She tosses me a wicked wink. "And put your trust in your sisters."

I can't believe it. She did it again.

It's late when Karma wraps the blanket around us, but only the two of us have retreated to the room.

"Promise me, you won't follow us tomorrow." I put my lips to Karma's ears. "Tell me you'll stay in and wait for me." Our cheeks caress, and my teeth sink into his lip.

"I will," he says and sighs. "I'll wait."

His answer doesn't come with conviction, but it's the only answer I can expect.

This time it's me who asks him to make a promise—a promise I know is almost impossible to keep.

Thirty-One

"You could have told me, you know." I hook my hand at Lanying's arm. "About the introduction." Pebbles grind under our boots as we cross the sun-drenched courtyard.

"I could have, but then we would not be walking here, sister." Lanying cocks her head to the side. "As you can't hide anything from Karma." She walks on, shielding her eyes with her hand.

"That's a sure thing." Norbu chuckles. "He would never let you go without him."

I frown as I have to admit—they're both right.

An iron bolt screeches, and we're out of the gate. A sliver of suspicion gnaws at the edge of my mind. Karma assured me over tea he would wait at the inn. He let me go this morning—too easy.

"Come on, sister, no time to lose." Lanying's decisive stride guides the way—or rather her trusted guard, the stocky man who saved my life and always averts his eyes whenever I try to meet him—leads our way. He maneuvers us through a maze of winding alleys, up along the main street where the vendors stall their goods for all to admire. A dazzling array of vibrant colors catches my eye as we fly by. The most delicious fragrances of tart lemon and sweet jasmine, ripe melon and spicy cardamom, and magnolias in full bloom seduce my feet to slow down and linger awhile.

Lanying won't have any of it. Securing her arm in mine, she keeps me from straying, steering me past the middle of town, down the south side, where a white-plastered pavilion spreads its gray glazed curved roof up on a rolling hill overlooking the river.

"Where are we going?" I halt. "I thought you said she lived on the outskirts of town." My fingers forge on her forearm. Lanying clacks her tongue. The guard stops, and Norbu tips back his hat.

"True, but I have it in good confidence, that she takes a walk here every morning." Lanying waves at the hill ahead. "It's the best location to admire the river—and for us, the best opportunity to see what's she's about."

"What are you saying?" I peer at Lanying, and then at Norbu. He shrugs. He hasn't got a clue either.

"Oh, come on now." Lanying anchors her hands at her hips. A silver sheath blinks through the folds of her coat. "We would be fools to charge into the lioness' den unprepared—that's not how battles are won, sister." She narrows her eyes.

"First, we observe—with patience—to get the advantage of knowing her ways, before she gets to know us." She raises her chin, and my heart sinks at the bottom of my boots.

"She's not the enemy." I sigh. How does one ever find peace while loaded with such blatant distrust? My heart goes out to my sister.

"Well, we don't know that, do we?" Her edged voice flings a sharp suspicion in my face.

"Give us a moment." She flings a blazing blue glare at the men and pulls me aside.

"Listen, sister." Her breath scorches against my cheeks. "Rumor has it she killed her own son." I gasp and my heels dig in the gravel.

My heart quivers. "She didn't."

"Altan told me." Lanying hisses. "And he's not the only saying so."

I shake my head. "I didn't hear him say that." My fingers grip the tassels swaying on her coat. For sure, she could never... *Focus.* My nails catch a loose thread.

"He did." She presses her lips to my ear. "She's supposed to be a spirit healer." Her words drift from a distance.

"Still." My voice falters, but my mind stands assured. "She didn't kill him, as he's very much alive." I turn my face to the sweltering sky. My chest expands. *She didn't.* Relief fills my lungs.

"We don't know what her intentions are." Lanying's fingers lock mine. "Let's find out before we do anything else."

I meet her eyes, and look into a tranquil ocean, with hues of blue and buttery currents lit by the sun.

"What mother would kill her own son?" I whisper, and her gaze lightens in a shade of silver and gray, brilliant and bright, like a raging sea before the first rays of midnight touch on its waves.

"A mother who holds her son to be more precious than her own life." Lanying's voice is almost fragile. My breath stalls as her sudden sorrow skirts over my skin.

"Let me tell you, sister, for there are women out there who sacrifice themselves for the sake of their children," she says. Her fingers wring around my wrists, trying to hold on to something that isn't there. "Women who want to spare their sons and daughters the cruel fate they are doomed to live in this present existence." Her voice cracks and catches in her throat.

An icy cold shatters my core.

"Oh, Lanying." My lips freeze, for there are no words to describe the force of the unbearable sadness that thunders upon us. A wave crashes through, devouring us both, and leaving nothing but a gaping abyss in the place where hope and joy used to live.

"Don't." She swallows and a taut veil of stubborn acceptance folds over her delicate face. "Don't you say it, for there's not a day that goes by I don't think about the terrible choice I had to make." She lifts her chin. "But there's yet a day to come I regret that decision." A hint of triumph soars in her voice, but it's drowned in the desperation that shines through the milky gleam brimming in her eyes.

She smoothens the crumpled brocade of my sleeves and rests her forehead against mine. My hands fold around her cheeks, a seething fire that melts the hardest of ice. A single tear drops as she lets mercy in, and the world holds her breath while she's at peace. It's only for a split moment though, but I suspect it's the most time she's ever dared to forgive herself for her deeds.

"Let's go," I say, and now it's me who's pushing her on. She smiles, a genuine thanks for not asking any further, or ever returning to this moment that she confided in me.

A pair of blue wings tumbles above us, and the warbling song of a swallow twitters through the air. Cherry bays line the wide slumped stairs we climb. Norbu and the quiet watchman follow in our trail.

"This is grand." Norbu speeds up, his legs conquering two steps at a time.

"It used to be the palace of emperors." Lanying halts at the top of the stairs. "Now it's the pleasure ground for all who can afford to stroll around during the day."

I walk on. The pavilion displays itself with pride on lacquered pillars, lavishly gilded and carved on all four sides. Red silken lanterns swing on every beam, and the serrated green of osmanthus trees dots the sloping grounds. Low benches hide their seats in the shades of the swaying cypress. This is for sure a pleasure ground, and many stroll around. Some with their heads bowed, probably lost in thoughts, while others look up to the sun. Most of them face the company they're keeping, weaving a little, chatting as they go.

"How will we find her?" My eyes wander over the immense gardens. So many people. Where to begin?

"I suggest we circle around." She nods at Norbu and the guard. "Mingle in the mass and keep our heads down at a safe distance."

A smile breaks across my face. "You might have considered another dress if you wanted to blend in." I nudge at the fiery blush of cerise that blooms on the intricate weave of her coat.

"What's wrong with a splash of color?" She rolls her eyes and her arm draws around my middle. I freeze, my body numb to her touch.

"What?"

It's her. My ribs tighten, and my heart hammers against my chest.

There she is, making her way towards us. She's frail, but moves with that quiet confidence I know so well.

She's in pain. I search and see. Her long robe flows, and her feet tread with caution. Yes, the pain is clear in the crease of her brow.

She comes closer, and I still can't move.

"You've come," she says, and her words sound like his.

I bow my head to her trembling hands. "You called me."

Our hearts meet, and the sun shines upon us. The whirl of restless green and golden in her eyes settles in the shallows of newly found hope.

She cradles my face. “I’ve waited a lifetime.”

“Your waiting is over, Mother,” I whisper. “I have brought you your son.”

Thirty-Two

The sun sets over the western peaks as we gallop out of the gate. We ride in a single file with two guards leading our way and two guards closing our line, courtesy of Lanying and her ever present suspicion. Upon meeting Karma's mother this morning, she stepped in without hesitation and grilled the poor woman until my toes curled numb in my boots. So much for needing an introduction to a high-ranking lady—as usual, Lanying ignored all décor.

Karma's mother showed great patience—he must get it from her. She answered all Lanying demanded, and more. Yet Lanying's distrust isn't satisfied, and she instructed her guards to stay with us at all times.

"It's her," I said to Karma when we came back to the inn this morning. He was waiting in the kitchen, as he promised, with Dendup at his side. A large jug was wedged between them. Even the strongest men need fortification sometimes—nevertheless the look in his eyes blinked as sharp as his blade.

"Tell me." He pulled me beside him, and I told him all. About the pavilion, how his mother came up to me, and most of all about the hope in her eyes. He listened and held my hand,

and asked for nothing more than I gave him. Then he reached out, poured another round, and raised his glass to Lanying.

"Thank you," he said, and looked her straight in the eye. "We could not have done this without you, Lanying." His voice pitched at the sound of her name.

She stared back at him without blinking an eye, her cup stalled above the table.

"I didn't do it for you." She spoke slow for her manner, and her gaze moved over to me. "Just get my sister back home safe before winter." The soft blue blinking in her eyes tugged at my heartstrings. How skilled she is in hiding her heart—and her true motivation for reuniting a mother with her son.

"Still, I'm grateful," Karma said, and him speaking these words means more to me than he'll ever know. For gratitude feels like a small word, but the intention behind it is infinite. It's the place where weary hearts find safe harbor and broken trust heals again. Maybe not all is lost between those two. I still have hope.

Lanying slammed her empty cup on the table and marched to the door. "To make arrangements, as we have to stay vigilant," she said, and left it that way. She didn't return until the shadows stretched over the courtyard. Still, we would have waited for her.

The house is like any other in its surrounding. Gray stucco walls, a red gate with rosebushes blooming in the corners. A golden glow shines from the corridor, all lamps are lit on the inside. Servants line in single file as our horses scramble inside the crowded yard; there's so many waiting at the door. She's standing tall on the threshold; white and blue silken flow from her sleeves, the traditional offering to receive her long-lost son.

No introduction is needed. She opens her arms; he bows his head, and in a split moment, all that separated mother and son falls away. They walk inside and we follow. Somehow it all feels like a dream to me. A dream that I'm aware of while dreaming; a dream and I'm not really here.

It's not until we sit at the table, and he takes my hand that I awake.

"It's her," he says, and the emeralds in his eyes shine like when I first met them.

"It's her," I say, and my heart is at peace.

The welcome is lavish, as expected. Rich and copious dishes fill the low tables and cups overflow with red and white spirits.

"Please, eat, drink." Attendants appear at the orders of Karma's mother. Our company digs in; it's been a while since we were served like this. I take a sip of my drink, and catch Lanying staring. I tilt my head at her. She arches her eyebrows and lifts her chin. *Om Tare.* It's clear she's at the end of her patience, and I fear her courteousness might leave her soon too.

"Mother." Karma speaks to his quiet way. "Thank you again for receiving us all in such a generous manner."

She smiles and with a slight nod, the servants retreat. The clatter of cups ceases. A sure and uncertain expectation rises in the room.

"You've come a long way, my friends." Karma's mother puts her hand on his arm. "I can not express my gratitude enough, as you brought me my son." She bows her head to Dendup. "Alive and well." Her eyes go around the table and meet us, one by one.

"I understand from my son, there are no secrets between us," she says. "So please let me tell you of what happened, even though I don't know all." She sits back on the cushions, her hands clasped in her lap.

The silence in the room fades to absolute stillness, with only the flickering of the lamps moving the air.

I glance at Lanying. Her elbows angle on the table. A cagey gaze pierces right through me. *Just in time.*

Karma takes his mother's hand. "Please, take your time, Mother." These words, that gentle touch—his thoughtfulness stirs a happy sigh through my soul.

"Your father and I, we were born on the great plains, near the Kathan Tuul river." Karma's mother begins to talk, and something above us whispers—of lost homes and far-away lands, of love and misunderstandings, of what once was, and never is forgotten, of a tale engraved in a mother's heart.

"We came together with the army, following our great Khan, for your father was an excellent warrior, fighting many battles." She pauses, and a long-gone sadness surfaces on her face. "He entered the great blue Sky when you were only a little boy."

My mind follows her words closely. *The great blue sky.* So the man left in the river was not Karma's father. A somewhat unfitting relief scurries through my thoughts.

"Your father's brother wanted you near, as his wives had not given him a son at the time." She hesitates. "He sent his men for you to join him in Shangdu, so I had to let you go, even though my dreams warned me not to." She rests her hand on Karma's forearm. "You never arrived, nor did the guards. Father's brother searched all over for you, even revenged the families of the guards, but to no avail." She turns to Dendup and lowers her head. "Please tell me, how did you find him?" Her hands tremble, but her voice is crystal clear.

"Our men found him near Chengdu." Dendup clears his throat and takes a quick sip. "There was one man with him, but he'd fallen ill." His knuckles whiten around his cup. "They left him to die in the river."

If shame were to find a quiet moment, it couldn't have been more deafening than right now. Lanying's blue stare crosses mine and my hands draw in my sleeves. *They left him to die.* Imagine if it had been Karma's father.

"Chengdu." She shakes her head. "That's the other side from where you were supposed to go." She lowers her voice. "No wonder we couldn't find you."

Karma nods but doesn't speak. He only holds her close.

Lanying veers up and seizes her opportunity. "But how could this happen?" Her words fly over the table. "You must have some idea?"

"We never found out." Karma's mother sighs, and her gaze draws into the distance. "But someone must have bribed the guards." She leans into Karma. "But I always knew you were alive."

A door creaks open. Feet shuffle in. Another round of food and drinks is set on our table. Lamps are topped up to brighten the room, and the air lightens with a more relaxed conversation. Karma's mother speaks on without hesitation. Surely, she has her own questions, but she's patient, and most likely feels that some of us are not.

"It was my wish to stay here, to wait for your return." She passes a delicate silver platter with sugared fruits on it around. "Your father's brother respected my wish, so no children came after you and your sister."

"Sister?" Karma's eyes widen. *A sister.* My heart delights.

"Yes, you have a twin sister," she says, and the fine lines around her mouth soften. "She's back home on the grasslands with the rest of our tribe." The golden threads in her eyes glisten among the green. "You share the gift, you know—she hears, and you see."

The gift. A quiver runs up my spine, for I know what she means. It's the gift of being called by the spirits, to travel to the other sides and back. He never told me in so many words, but he has the gift too.

Hooves scrape in a distant courtyard, and the crescendo of a nightingale meanders through the night. Dendup raises his glass to a joyous reunion, and all of us join in.

"I can't make the journey home anymore, even if I wish so." Karma's mother spreads her hand on her chest. "If they could only see you now." Her voice fades, and her fingers fold along the collar of her robe. A lump thickens in my throat, and Karma draws me near.

A door opens with a bang, iron clashing on timber. Wicks flicker and shadows appear.

"It can't be." A woman in purple and gold breezes in on the midnight cold. "I came as soon as I heard." She shoots to the front and lunges at Karma.

"Tuya, it's him," Karma's mother says, and the woman stands still.

"I need to see it." She yanks the fabric up Karma's forearm, and she stares at the inkling without batting an eyelid—not even once.

"It can't be." She stumbles and cradles his face between her hands. Her dark eyes glister with fever as they search in a frenzy. At last, they settle. "It's you." Tears streak her cheeks.

"You have to forgive my sister," Karma's mother whispers. "You two were so close before; she was going to raise you since she's your father's brother's first wife."

Karma shifts, and she sits beside him. Servants speed to pour our cups again and again. The conversation strikes up, but not where it left off. It's like Tuya's arrival brought a wavering among our company. A weary restraint stiffens inside of me.

"Your husband, he's not with you?" Lanying asks, and her tone is most genteel.

"No, he's in Shangdu, in service of our Khan, as is our son." Tuya smiles. "Of course, we'll send word to him as soon as possible." She twirls her cup under her fingers.

"I see." Lanying narrows her eyes. "You must miss them then." Her hands spread on the table, and she draws back in her seat.

"I take care of my sister," Tuya says. "She hasn't been well, but please, you all stay the night." She dips her chin, and her fingers smoothen the sable fur on mother's collar. "We'll talk more tomorrow, but for now it's better she rests."

"I'm fine, really." Karma's mother puts up a weak protest. Her face has paled, and a vague blue rims around her eyes. Tuya's right, she doesn't seem well.

"It's been a long day for you, Mother." Karma bows his head, and her hands touch his cheeks. "We'll come back tomorrow, and we will have all day."

The night has fallen, and a midnight blue broadens the starlit sky. A silver moon lightens our path and lets us travel with ease back to the inn.

"You found her." Karma's lips gaze my forehead. He draws me into the tender hollow of his body.

"She found me." I lay my head in the crook of his neck and rest my fingers on the edge of his jaw. "She found me just in time."

Thirty-Three

The queasiness in my stomach ebbs and flows like a cold tide, lashing the peppery sweetness of the steeped root right back in my mouth. Sweat stains my palms and my beads slip from my fingers. *Om Tare*. Lanying said it would get better soon, and I can only hope.

"Sickness is a chance to deepen our practice," my grandmother used to say. "It's a chance to take on the karma of the illness of others so that they are free from their suffering."

At the time it seemed like a grand idea to me, taking illness as part of the Buddhist path to serve all sentient beings like a genuine Boddhisatva. Silly me—what did I know? I've never felt sick, not like this. I rest my head in my hands.

My body sighs. The stove murmurs. A bird flutters its chirrup from the windowsill. The timid sun fills the kitchen with rosy pinks and sandy yellows, welcoming the new day with grace. My fingers trace the pungent steam swirling about my cup. *This too will pass.* This is what I know. I sip in solace and wait.

At least we don't have to travel any further. We've found Karma's mother—she's here, and not in the far lands of Mongolia. I should be pleased, and I am, but a vague disquiet waves on the edges of my mind. It's been there ever since Father said it out loud: *I doubt if he'll come back once he finds his blood relatives.* My fear of that is ready to spur from its hiding place and wreak havoc in my mind. I twirl the beads, and the jade blurs a cloudy green in front of me. Mornings are always the worst for doubts creeping up, especially when my mind's not filled with prayer yet. *Not now.*

We didn't speak, not once, about what we would do when we found her, but Karma gave me his promise to come home with me before the winter.

A fierce shame flushes my being. *Stop it.* Can I be any more selfish? His mother, so frail and patient—she waited a lifetime for him, her only son. And here I am, thinking about my own needs, my own desires to have my love close.

I wring the cup. How ignorant of me. This is not genuine love—this is me being greedy, wanting to possess him in order to make myself feel secure. I see it clearly, yet the emotion is so strong. I blink, but the tears won't retreat. Another wave of nausea passes through. This is not me. It's being with child that makes me so clingy. *It has to be.* I put my head down. Sangmo had it too, I remember, shedding tears on every occasion.

My body shudders at the last of the medicine. If only this bitter brew would settle my shaky mind, too.

"Well, that was interesting." A puff of sable fur lands beside me. Lanying. I never heard her coming. "Last night, I mean." Her hand leaves a cool touch on my forehead. "Need some more water?"

I shake my head. "It was." I swallow the last piece of soaked root. "Can't believe we found her."

Her hand wipes the sweat off my brow. "She doesn't look good," she says, and orders another boiled water.

"She doesn't," I say, and glance aside. "I wonder what ails her."

Lanying sucks in her cheeks. "No use denying it, sister," she says. "You feel it too." Her eyes shine a feverish blue.

I shrug. "I don't know," I say. "She seems genuine. "*She does, right?*

"Something's off." Lanying's feet shuffle, sand grits on the floor. "You want to know what I'm thinking?"

I don't. But my mind peaks with interest. "What?" My eyes settle on her mucky boots. I wonder where she went last night.

"I think she knows damn well who took Karma a long time ago." She rolls her shoulders. "She's just afraid to tell."

Betrayal. A wary whisper weaves through my thoughts.

"Where's Karma, anyway?" She digs into her coat. "Here, good." Her hand holds a few candied nuts.

"His mother sent for him early." My tongue wraps around the brown glazed kernels. "He wanted to wait for me, but I told him to go." A gooey syrup dissolves in my mouth and I shudder—too sweet.

"The fool!" Lanying veers up. "I warned him not to go by himself." A nut gives in with a loud crack under her bite. "Well, at least he's guarded." She jumps to her feet. "I ordered Jié not to let him out of his sight."

Jié, the faithful guard. "No need to worry then." I stretch my limbs. As if Karma needs a guard.

"Worry about what?" Norbu leans in from the doorway. "Good morning to you two." He smiles right at me, half of his shirt wet from a wash. "Dendup won't be up for a while." He jumps to the stove and wrings his hands at its smoldering heat.

"Well then." Lanying raises her eyebrow. "What are we waiting for? Let's go."

She barges out of the door.

I rise with reluctance and let my feet find solid ground. Seems like the medicine has worked its wonders again.

"Take your time." Norbu's hand scoops my bag. "I'll get the horses ready." He shoots out of the door. My hand steadies on the table. How blessed am I with my friends?

The sun blazes her beams, and our horses trot out of the gate. It always amazes me how fast spring gains her strength over the last remains of winter. Then again, the moon has turned twice since the day we left. By now the flower buds peep on the meadows, and the yaks roam the higher slopes at home. Time travels fast out here on the road.

Karma's mother stands tall at the doorstep. A relaxed smile rests on her face, and my heart delights.

"Finally, there you are." Her arms reach out, and several servants skid from the corners to take our horses and bags. "Karma's not with you?"

Her embrace is warm and welcoming, but my body stiffens at her words.

"You sent for him, Mother," I say. "He didn't arrive yet?" My voice dips.

"No, but I didn't send for him." She sounds far away.

Promise me you won't leave him. Sangmo's desperate plea soars in my ears. I blink. My head spins. *No matter what.* I promised her.

"I'm sure he'll come soon." Lanying's hand clutches at my forearm. "Let's go in, I'll send my men for him." Her arm locks around my middle and pushes me on.

"Yes, please." Tuya appears from the corridor. "We're happy to see you all again." Her robe flutters in front of me, a dark purple hemmed with golden brown. Black spots shoot from the shadows. My feet stumble over the threshold, and Norbu catches me in time.

"I'm sorry," I mumble. Cold sweat lashes down my back. "I'm fine now."

My words are ignored. Norbu won't let me go until I'm planted in a pile of fluffy pillows with a cup of fresh lemon water in my hand.

"To travel in your condition." Mother shakes her head. "I'm sorry you had to come so far, my child." She tilts her chin and in her eyes glows the same hue of green, that luscious color of the early spring tide when Karma first spoke of our little girl. *She knows.*

"You're with child?" Tuya's tone brings a sense of surprise. "That is wonderful." A servant rushes and pours more tea. A plate of fresh fruit slides our way.

"It is." Lanying slides beside me. "And Karma's over the moon." She puts her hand over mine and beams a bright smile around. "Also pleased to see you doing better, Mother." My fingers tense under hers. What is she up to?

"Thank you." Mother sinks back in her seat. "I always feel better in the morning, and now." She pauses. Her hand spreads across her chest. "I can't tell you how much it means to me you brought my son." Her face softens and the warmth of her love flushes her high cheekbones with the blush of a rose.

"All those years I called out, but he didn't hear." Her eyes haze over with weary acceptance. "His heart locked tight when they tore him away, but I never gave up hope." A humble charm lights her face. She's genuine—my heart knows it well.

"And then you came to him, and as he held you close, I knew you would hear my call," she says. "For your heart holds no walls, my child, it holds only love." Her hands reach across the table, and I hold them to never let go. She lost him once, this mother's heart, and I don't want her to lose him ever again.

Iron crashes on timber and hasty hooves bolt in the courtyard. A horse neighs and my heart leaps. It's Karma—I'd recognize the sound of his stallion anywhere.

The murmur of men comes our way.

"I told you my guards would find him." Lanying leans back in her seat. All eyes set on the door.

Foots shuffle and halt at the threshold. A stilted silence enters the room. Nobody moves. The door opens ajar.

A man staggers in. It's Jié, the quiet guard, and he doesn't look up. He only stands there, his gaze on the floor.

My eyes search, but I don't see Karma. A dull throb drums in my ears.

"You lost him, you idiot!" Lanying leaps up. "I told you to stay close!" She lashes out and I flinch.

Her hands grip her sword.

"Don't!" Norbu shoots from his seat. "He's hurt." The guard sags to his knees, and Norbu's just in time to haul him up.

"Where is he?" Lanying rips the helmet from the guard's head and blood stains the floor.

"I'm sorry." The man groans. "There were too many—we couldn't hold them off."

I open my mouth, but there's only a whisper.

Betrayal. It was shown to me by the gods.

Om Tare. Why didn't I listen?

Thirty-Four

The guard's face pales to a ghastly ashen. His lips move, but there's only a panted murmur. The ground shifts from underneath me, and my feet take flight, wanting to run.

"Where is he?" Lanying shrieks, and the man stumbles back. His body's hunched like a limp dog waiting for his master to strike.

Shadows pass in a slow motion and the sun hits my eyes in a blur of crimson and coral. It's Karma's stallion. My knees hit the cobblestones. I reach out, and warm blood runs from my hands, coiling thick and strong, down my sleeves.

It can't be him. My hands search, and my eyes follow the man hanging over the saddle. I grab the collar of his blood-soaked coat and twist his lifeless body around. Another gush of glittering red spills from the ripped flesh at his throat. A heavy sob hollows from my heart.

It's not him.

It's not my love laying here in my arms. It's the man who called on us early this morning and rode out with Karma.

"They came out of nowhere, and took this man out, fast." Jié's broken voice sinks behind me. "They came for Karma, but we wounded them well."

"Who?" I say. "And where's Karma?" My stiff hands stain the auburn gleam of blood on the slate-blue surrounding us. All is still, even our breath.

"Army men." The guard's body shifts beside me. "There were six of them, and they took him away."

Six of them. My body caves even further as the guard's words strike another blow to my mind. *Nobody escapes the army, sister.* Xia told me so, but I chose to ignore her.

"I tried, but I couldn't." Jié speaks, and I hear him. "He ordered me to go back and keep you safe."

Keep me safe. That's what I should have done. I should have listened and kept him safe.

The sun throws lanky silhouettes around us, of people and horses, and of voices that hiss of death and despair.

My heart shudders as my fingers probe the violence on the ravaged face in my lap. Prayer fills me for this precious life gone, ripped away in anger, in ignorance, in greed. *Om Mani.* What a terrible death many of us have to endure. Blood clots in red-brown and cakes under my nails. I should have kept him safe. Then this man might have lived.

"Here, let me." Norbu throws a blanket over the man's body, and another life is gone. He wraps the wool tight and carries it away.

"Please, my child." Karma's mother calls from above. The blue slate stone seesaws under my knees.

The gate swings open. Hooves scrape and dust clouds in front of me.

Boots land with a sharp rap on the ground and Dendup's roar thunders around. "What the hell happened here?" He flings his arms around me and hauls me up. My legs won't hold me.

"I'll tell you what happened here, brother." Lanying lunges with a vengeance from the back. "While you slept off your perpetual intoxication, somebody in this household took care of Karma—again."

Offended cries recoil from the servants in the corridor. My ribcage bruises under Dendup's stubborn restraint.

"What do you mean?" His muscles ripple around me. "Where's Norbu?" A thick vein rolls in his neck.

"He's taking care of a dead body." Lanying's eyes veil with a frosty blue. Her stare pries in every corner. "He clearly knew too much, so they slit his throat." Her spit lands right at our feet, and I watch it seep through the cracks.

"Sister, are you hurt?" Dendup releases the pressure around me.

My lungs heave a breath of stale air, and I clench my teeth. I know the drill by now, and the bile retreats to my throat.

"I'm good." I quiver. "But this man needs help."

Jié shakes his head, but a servant speeds at Karma's mother's hand to take him away.

"There's no time to lose." Dendup fastens his belt. "We have to find Karma."

Lanying points her chin to the corridor where a dozen pair of eyes watch us. "Not here." She ushers us in.

"Tell me." Dendup sags in a seat. He pulls me beside him and won't let me go.

"What's to tell?" Lanying's voice breathes fire. "Karma's mother sent a servant for him, and now he's missing—one day after showing up here—again."

I cringe at that last word. *Again.*

A man's dead and my love is gone. There's no need to be rude.

"Lanying, please," Mother whispers. "I didn't send for him. Besides, this man has served our family well for many years." Her voice trembles. "It makes no sense."

"This is a gross insult. My sister has nothing to do with it," Tuya hisses from across the table. "Not then, and not now."

"Really." Lanying's tone says it all; she's ready to attack. "That's not what I heard."

Don't! I want to scream. My head ducks to avoid the awful allegation that is sure to come.

Lanying snorts. "We all heard the rumor that your sister killed her own son."

There it is. The accusation soars over the table, slicing through the precarious trust we've built among us. My heart shrinks and I can't bear to face her—she who waited for him for so long.

"Says who?" Tuya pinches her lips and retreats in her seat.

"Says your own kinfolk." Lanying leans in. Looks like she's ready to jump. "Even my husband Altan, who serves with yours in the Keshig under our Khan."

Husband. I stare at her. A brash smile arches on her lips. Husband. Did I hear that right? I turn to Dendup. He seems unfazed.

"Altan." Tuya backs down even further. "You—the wife of a Mongol?"

"One of his many wives, according to your custom." A triumphant twinkle shimmers in Lanying's eyes. "But for sure his favorite, as you can all imagine." Amusement creases in the corners of her mouth, and she does not conceal her glee.

"Now, all this talk, it's rubbish." Dendup's fist strikes the table. "As Karma is very much alive." He turns to Karma's mother and lowers his voice. "My apologies, sister, but we have to go, no time to lose."

A door opens, and Norbu steps in. The guard, all cleaned up, stumbles behind him.

"We're ready." Norbu draws his hat. "Well, that is I am, for this man here needs rest." He turns to Jié and orders him to the inn, but the humble guard refuses.

"I can't," he says, and takes his position at the door. "I promised to keep your sister safe until further orders." He widens his stance and lowers his head, a guard in wait at his post.

"Suits me fine." Lanying barks at the guard's bowed head. "You're useless, anyway." She turns on her heels. A chilling draft gushes through the room.

"He's at the servant's quarters." Norbu kneels at my side. "Just thought you wanted to know."

"Thank you." I squeeze his hand before Dendup drags him away.

The sun shines her high rays through the windows. I shiver at her cold. Death and despair. *Om Tare.* Dried blood flakes on my skin.

"I can't believe this is happening." I look up. Mother's blush has waned to a pearly pallid. "Please, Mother, won't you rest?"

Tuya rushes out. "I'll get some tea." Her footsteps fade into the long corridor. I nod, and the guard closes the door.

I drape a blanket around her bony shoulders. "Mother, will you tell me what ails you?" I lay her head to rest in the crook of my neck.

"It's my time, child," she says. "I've known it for long." A shallow sigh moves her chest. "I've been holding on tight, waiting for him to come."

A golden sun steps forth from the tall window and wraps us in her warm and brilliant rays. I close my eyes, and the sweet-tempered scent of blooming mountain meadows, and of churned earth under the summer sun floats all around. My heart trembles. *It's him.* My love, I know him well.

"He'll be back soon," I say. "Please hold on a little longer, for he so much wants you to meet her." I rest her hands in my lap. "Our little girl."

The door creaks, and a woman enters. Her face is puffy, and her cheeks streaked in red. She holds a tray, and her hands shake.

"Come." Mother sits up in her seat. The woman sets the cups and scoots out of the room.

"I'm sorry." I steep the tea. "My friend, she can be quite blunt." A faint green tinges our cups.

"She loves you more than anything else," Mother says. "Anyone can see." She smiles at the surprise on my face. Her words are not what I expected.

"You never doubted me, but many do." She sips her cup and her stare sets in the distance. "Even my own family won't allow me to return to our grasslands." She turns the intricate golden band on her wrist. "If only they knew."

Lanying was right—there were rumors. *Altan.* His charcoal eyes pierce my mind. *Her husband.* Why didn't she tell me? A sense of suspicion stirs through my thoughts.

"My husband's brother spared my life." Mother sets her cup on the table, and I pour the water over once again. "I wanted to send him a message this morning, but Tuya said to wait." Her eyes haze in gray and green. "Now what do I say?"

I stir the tea and wait for it to settle. "Mother, who knew Karma was here?" A strange calm comes over me. My mind turns to Xia and the Dao, her mysterious way of nature taking its course.

"Only me and my sister, and our servants, of course." She takes a moment to consider. "They've all been with me for many years, and I can't think of anybody else."

Her answer is what I expected. There's nothing we can do, not at this moment—nothing but letting things unfold.

We drink our tea in silence, and she retreats to rest.

"Please, will you take me?" I ask to Jié standing in patience at the door.

For there is something I can do, but don't want to in front of all.

He doesn't hesitate and guides me to the back where darkness surrounds us, and a soul dwells in despair. Ripped away from this human life, it now has to find its way alone. With no human body left, it roams through the death bardos, blind and ignorant, for a time unknown to man.

I lift my face to the tiny window and the beads slide through my fingers. *Om Mani Padme Hung.* A faint breeze plays with the loose strands of my hair, a smooth gaze against my cheeks. A fleeting thought drifts by—one of a precious yet transient life that was given, and now passes in time, into the infinite cycle of living and dying once again.

It's been a long time since I prayed for the death, but my heart still carries the words. Gratitude surges through my being, for none has changed. Somewhere out there is a soul in need, and wherever he may be, may my humble prayer guide him, from my own fragile mind here on this earth to his in the in-between.

My being relishes in the stillness. *Om Mani Padme Hung.* How good it is to be of solace again.

Thirty-Five

Dusk comes sooner than expected. The sun gilds the frayed edges of the sky in golden and gray. Mother and I retreat to the front, to the fire that rumbles while we wait.

As the nightfall welcomes the shadows to our room, the darkness crowds my being with uninvited guests of anguish and unease. Thoughts of what lies ahead, and of what is unknown, cloud my mind, twisting the gravest possibilities into steadfast beliefs.

"Mother, why don't you tell me of your home," I say, for I need to divert my restive mind. Who knows how long it will be before they return?

So she tells me of the vast grasslands where the animals roam, and her people live in tents of felt and skin, of the desert and dunes that sing their song at midnight, and of the deep blue lakes and crystal frosted mountain peaks that reach into the infinite. She tells of her one true love that passed on but never left her, of her daughter far away, and of children born she never met. But most of all, she recalls the memories of the boy she once lost and now has returned—and of how life comes full circle, if you only dare to hold on to the hope that it will.

She tells me all, and there's much more to tell, but horses' hooves speed through the gate, halting in the courtyard. Boots thud like hollow ghosts haunting the deserted hallways in the middle of night. Silk swishes through the door, and leather belts unhinge—our sister and brothers have returned.

"They have spotted a large group, riding toward Chang'an." Lanying plants her feet near the fire. "Army men with captives on their way." She wrings her hand to the heat, and as always tells it straight.

"Captives?" I jump up for Dendup to take my place. "What captives?"

Dendup drops on the seat, his chuba flings around his sunken shoulders.

"Men who are taken to join the army." He hides his eyes under his cap. "They bring them up to the camps for training." His hand explores the fur lining of his chuba, and he pulls out a tiny flask.

The army. My feet freeze to the ground. The hearth hisses and sparks fly—a servant rakes up the heat. Dendup tips his empty flask and groans.

"Or sell the men off in Chang'an." Lanying tosses her coat in a corner. A silver sheath dangles from her hip.

"Sell them off?" I say. Her words try to scramble their understanding between my restless thoughts. *Focus.* Servants swirl around, and trays bang on the table. "Sell them for what?" Norbu's hand touches mine.

"For slaves, Nordun," he whispers. "Slaves to whoever offers the most."

Slaves. The heat from the hearth scorches my cheeks. "But Karma's a free man." I stammer. "He's a free man." I'm sure.

"Nobody's a free man out here, sister." Dendup pulls me to his side. The stench of his liquor chokes my throat. His looped gaze stares me in the face, and I see my blatant naivety reflected in his blurry eyes.

Of course. We've ventured into foreign territories, in lands where our bonds of blood and privileges bear no meaning. Only a fool would not understand.

"Anyway, we're leaving early tomorrow." Dendup's voice resounds his determination.

"We'll take a part of the caravan, only my fastest men and horses." Lanying paces from the hearth to the door and back. "There's no time to lose."

"Let me send our best men with you." Tuya appears from a corner. I never saw her enter the room.

"I don't think so." Lanying's response is as swift and sharp as the way she swings her sword. "They'll only be holding us back." She draws a deep breath, and there's more on her tongue, but she holds it in, and I'm thankful—again.

"You all stay here for the night." Mother's eyes plead, and with the generous servings of food and drink, our company is quick to agree.

It's past midnight as we retreat to our rooms where the darkness awaits. I secure the window—a dim moon hides behind a veil of smoky ash and smothered soot. My body sags into the mat, weary of the day that is behind, but my mind's alive, and filled with fear of the night to come. I curl myself into the loneliness of the empty space beside me. *Om Tare.* Please, let sleep come fast.

A slight gust of air drafts from the door and the latch clinks from the hinge. Timber creaks under tiptoes, and a leather belt drops on the floor.

"Move over, sister." Lanying's slender body flutters beside me. "I always forget how cold the nights are without a lover at my side." She wraps the blanket snug, and I shiver as she rubs her icy hands in mine.

"For sure, you must miss your husband on nights like this." I pinch her arm, and she wiggles by my side. "You didn't tell me about Altan?"

Her cold breath puffs at my cheeks. "Hmm, Altan." She sighs. "Ours is one of convenience, as most marriages are." She pauses and pulls herself closer. "I needed protection and he... well, let's just say he needs somebody who appreciates the darker side of him, and dares to serve his fantasies—if you know what I mean."

A fierce heat sears from my neck all the way up to my cheeks. Even the tips of my ears are on fire. *I don't want to know what she means.*

"We've got an understanding, him and me." She chuckles. "He takes good care of me, and I treat him the way he likes me to."

"Yes, I get it," I say, and I dig my head in the blanket. "No need for further explanation."

She giggles again, and I have no doubt her mischievous grin flashes over me.

"I sent word to him this afternoon," she whispers. "He might be able to help."

I come up for air. "You trust him?" She shivers and I rub her back.

"It might seem weird, but I do," she says. "He even knows Karma's uncle—they served in the same unit for a while." She blows her breath on her hands, and I can almost hear her think.

"Tell me," I say. "No need to hold back." Now I shiver. *Do I want to know?*

"Now here's the interesting part." She pulls my hands under her chin. "When Altan told me of Karma's mother killing her son, he said the rumor was spread by one of the uncle's wives, the one who was to raise the son."

Altan. The savage warrior with the charcoal clouds billowing in the dark of his eyes. I squeeze her hands and listen close, but my mind's eye wanders off.

"Later he mentioned it was the mother's own sister that said it." Lanying speeds ahead and my thoughts slip back to Altan and that afternoon. *We are family now.*

"At the time I thought I had misunderstood him, but then Tuya appeared—a wife and the sister." Lanying halts for a moment as if she senses I need to catch up with what she's talking about.

"I'm here," I say, and I am.

"So, I put the two together." Lanying takes a quick breath. "Tuya is the one that spread the rumor, the same rumor she denied so blatantly in front of us this afternoon." Her voice pitches in a whisper, and she squeezes my hands until it hurts.

"Why would she do that?" I spread my fingers under hers. "To her own sister?" Sure, anyone can see Karma's mother could never... I turn my mind away.

"Beats me." Lanying shrugs. "But somebody in this house knows more, might be a servant, who knows?" She clacks her tongue. "And I'm going to find out who did this to Karma, but first we'll get him back."

She lays her head down on my chest. "You're good?" Her hand draws down my middle.

"I am," I say and rest my arms around her shoulders. I am fine—for now.

"Remember that night we shared in Lhasa?" She snickers at the memory, and I delight in the joy of her laughter.

"It's not that cold here, sister," I say, and I mean it. "And not that lonely either."

Thirty-Six

More than half a moon's turn—that's how long it will take us to get to Chang'an. Lanying told me last night. *Half a moon's turn*. Her words march on the muffled beat of a drum resounding somewhere deep in the house. Bells rattle and roll in the distance, waving their tinkle through my ears. It feels like a world away and I don't want to open my eyes. There's a new day ahead.

Half a moon's turn. My hands search for my beads. I should prepare.

A thick cloud of weisang billows in the courtyard. Mother stands at the doorway and my feet are unwilling to leave. She dips a finger in the bowl of milk she holds and flicks it toward the sky. White drips descend with the words of a prayer. "May the mercy of Eternal Tengri and the blessings of heaven and earth be upon you." My heart weeps and at the same time, it rejoices at her blessing. Altan was right after all—she and me, we are alike.

The crimson sky hazes into ginger and orange as our short caravan crawls in a single line out of town. My body sways at the gentle trot of horse hooves, but my mind won't wake, not yet. I need more time. Morning tides are never easy, never kind on my feeble mind. This morning smothers me in a bleak blanket of loss and loneliness, with edges of frayed and frazzled despair.

This too will pass. I will not give in.

We climb with the sun, touching the ridges of lush hills and barren cliffs. Timber planks hold on to the fringes of the crags, and twist and turn themselves along the threshold of heaven and earth. Somehow the long days on these rickety roads have eased my anxiety into a wonder. Balconies bending on shaky poles, braving the wind and the rivers raging beneath us—how daring and determined the brave men who laid down this path before us. For certain, there can't be another place like this? Though, what have I seen of this world?

My stallion twirls his ears at the touch of my hand on his neck. A muggy breeze brings the sweet scent of soaked grass after rain. My mind unfolds itself from its taut blanket of anguish and a deep yawn flees from my weary chest.

The days stretch into silent rides with few places to rest. We are lucky though—at every nightfall there's an inn or at least decent shelter in sight. I guess it's not luck, but rather the deliberate pacing of the seasoned horsemen leading our group. Karma was right; Lanying knows what she's doing. She's got the best men working for her, even I can see.

At every inn, and every time we come across others coming from where we are going, Lanying gathers word about groups traveling ahead. Sometimes there's confirmation of army men speeding toward Chang'an. Other times there are only hesitant looks and cautious hints, and none that can say for sure. It's in those times that I find myself blessed with Norbu's gentle ways, Lanying's dogged determination, and Dendup's somewhat awkward, yet endearing care for me.

"Sister, come, sit." Dendup draws a seat for me near the low table. "You've got to eat to keep your strength." His one hand slides a bowl of some steaming brew to me, his other draws a jug nearby. "One more day to go to Chang'an."

I look at him, and he turns away. He's useless in hiding his worry. I let him finish his jug, but when Norbu jumps up to order another, I take my chance to ask. "Dendup, please tell me." I put my hand on his arm. "How come men don't leave the army?"

It's been on my mind, but I didn't want to know until we were close.

"Oh, sister." Dendup's eyes search for Norbu to arrive. "The Khan's army is organized in most clever ways. They put the men in what they call Arbans—groups of ten. These groups are bound for life, or should I say death." He reaches for another cup and Norbu is swift to pour. I fish a fatty bone from my soup.

"If one of the ten escapes, his nine remaining comrades are executed without fail." His words drown in his liquor. "As you can imagine, nobody even tries." I push my bowl aside.

"Whether it's in the army or some other way, all Mongols have to serve their Khan." Norbu sits down and peels an orange in the palm of his hand. "A man with Karma's fighting skills and ability to speak all these languages—they'll be keen to have him anywhere."

His fingers tear the juicy flesh in parts. "Here." He puts the slices in front of me and tells me to eat.

I chew a small part, zesty yet sweet, and relish Norbu's gentle smile.

"There's no escape for Karma, especially once his uncle knows his whereabouts." Dendup grunts and clears his cup in one go. "That man will march him straight to the battlefields. If we don't find our brother before his uncle does, we'll never get him home." A tiny spark lights in his smoldering stare, and I hold my breath for the full-blown rant to burst through.

"Dammit, I told him this would happen." Dendup's fist hits the table. *There it is.* "But he just wouldn't listen." He roars and a few cups clatter. "The ignorant fool."

I duck, for there must be more to come.

"And where were you when Karma got captured, and my man tried his best all alone, being so worried as you claim to be?" Lanying's voice is a sneer over the table. "I'm sure the family won't be too happy to hear your brother got away while you were sleeping—again." She sets herself beside me and snatches a part of orange from my plate.

Again. Like the time in Lhasa, she means, when Karma left us all without a word of warning. Only I knew he had to go, for I let him hear his mother's call.

"You think I would come all the way out here if I didn't care for my brother?" Dendup's crossed eyes leer at Lanying.

I shift back in my seat. *Here we go again.*

"Oh, sure you care." Lanying leans in and hisses at him. "For family's orders to fulfill and keep precious cargo safe."

Dendup huffs and lurches over the table—or rather attempts to, as Norbu is fast to pull him back in his seat. A jug tumbles and spills whatever was left over the earth-beaten floor.

"Stop bickering, the two of you." Norbu's firm arms keeps Dendup down. "Save your mutual grievances for another day; now is not the time."

Lanying clacks her tongue and lifts her chin at Norbu, no doubt to lash out with another sneer.

I shake my head at her, and my plea is heard. Lanying waves her hand and another jug hits the table.

I finish the last of my tea and call it a night. A quiet Jié guides me to the room, as he has never been far from my side since Karma left.

Where are you, my love? Darkness surrounds me. My body sinks into the thin mat, and my heart shatters into a thousand pieces, spilling all over my cheeks.

Nobody escapes the army. The words ring in my ears. Never did it occur to me that my love might be in danger like this. *He must have known.* For sure he must have known—and considered the risk of it all, anyway. Father must have known too, but he never let it on, not once.

My body tenses, my stomach churns, and nausea sloshes at the back of my throat. I fold my fingers around the raveled corner of my mat. My mind lashes out at me with the most malicious thoughts of death and despair. I need something to hold on to as I slip away.

Samsara. This is what it is; vicious thoughts spin around and around, and my mind's grasping at straws. *Samsara.* I see it crystal clear. My love is gone, and my mind abhors at the void inside of me, at the reality of no escape and no place to hide. *Focus.* My hand clutches my beads, a cool touch on my skin.

Samsara. I see it clear, the fear that wreaks havoc in my very being. There's no use denying it, for there's no escape from it all. I have to face it as it is, or it festers into something dark within me, something that devours me, or drains me for the rest of my life.

Samsara. My grandmother taught me well. "Remember the Buddha," she used to say. "He looked fear right in the eye and let it be."

But things in the monastery were all so different. I was a child and had nothing to fear but the darkness of my room in the midst of the night. Whenever the dreams came to haunt me, Dechen would tell me the Buddha's tale again, and again.

"Remember the Buddha's encounter with Mara," she said. "The demon kept coming to plague the Buddha with many temptations. So one day the Buddha said, "I see you, Mara. I know you're a trickster. I see what you're trying to do." And then he invited Mara to sit down with him and offered him tea."

I used to laugh at the thought of the Buddha having tea with a demon, instead of running from it, or chasing it away. It helped as my nightmares would vanish like snow melting at the sight of the sun.

Little did I understand that Mara, the demon, was the image of our own desires, of everything we think we need to make us happy, but don't possess.

Mara is that false sense of security that we turn to when we find ourself in a situation we can't control, in a reality we can't escape. We all run to something different to sooth us when we get uncomfortable, and my mind seeks shelter in imaginary tales of impossible eventualities and the sure uncertainties that lay ahead.

Focus. My love is gone, I feel afraid, and there is escape. My mind spins stories to make me feel secure, and I know these tales are not true. *Focus.*

My lungs fill with air and I sit with the fear, and all the tales that whirl around in the midst of this storm of emotions. I sit with it, and I have all night, and I'll just let them be.

I rest my head on my knees and my scarf releases the scent of spring rain on blushing pedals and freshly bruised leaves, and of a warming breeze that sweeps over meadows and mountain tops, and carries the sweet hope of a summer that's far away but sure to come.

My body softens and curls in the mat. My stomach takes another turn. *Our little one is getting stronger every day.*

I search my bag for the new pouch with dried roots that settle my insides so well. The bittersweet sliver soaks on my palate, and my mind considers a rest.

It will take a while for me to weather the storm.

That's fine with me—I've got all night and I'm human, after all.

Thirty-Seven

The midday sun stands proud in a silver white sky. Its bright yellow glow blotches the crumbled stucco walls of the inn. A slanted gate creaks and swings on its rusty hinges. Dust and gravel scuts on worn flagstones as our horses' hooves clatter inside.

"They say Chang'an used to be the grandest city once." Lanying slides from her stallion. "Now it's nothing but a filthy trade town."

A row of faded red lanterns dangles in the shade of the chipped clay-tiled roof. A rosebush wilts in the corner, its petals brown and limp. Splintered shutters shield the lengthy windows, and there's not a sound but for our boots shuffling and our beasts trampling around.

"What's this place?" Dendup scratches his head. His cap slides aside. "Seems deserted to me."

Lanying point her chin at the open doorway. "Just head in, and you'll find out."

Dendup hops into the hallway and within no time returns, sporting the biggest smirk I've seen on him in many days.

"They've got proper food." He beams. "And decent chang too." He hurries back inside, and we follow to a kitchen where a fire burns with the comfort of home, and a simple soup is ladled in wooden bowls, served with hunks of fresh bread and salted butter on the side.

"So, what's next?" Norbu slurps his soup. "How do we know Karma's here, anyway?" He tilts his head at Dendup, who's still engrossed in his thukpa.

"If he's here, we'll find him." Lanying chews the last of the bread. "I'll go to speak to some people." She pushes her empty bowl aside. "Come with me, you'll like the place." Her hand trawls down my back.

"Let me wash up for a moment." I scoot out of the kitchen into the yard. Stale water bubbles from a shallow basin and cools my heated cheeks. My insides hurl another wave of bile against the back of my throat. The soup was excellent, but I ate too fast. I sneak a sliver of dried root in my mouth and slide my scarf over my head.

"We'll walk." Lanying hooks her arm through mine and nudges at Jié to follow. "It's close."

With her determined trot, she steers me through alleys where the foreign tongues of zealous traders banter and animals crowd in every corner.

Smoke swirls from moldering cinder in copper pots, and the heavy aroma of fried dough and roasted nuts puffs from tiny windows. Tea is served with chatter from open doors, and bundles of spices and dried fruits heap along roughed timber thresholds. Roars of animals and beasts resound from raised gates. A shutter slams as we pass.

"In here." Lanying pushes us through a narrow-arched doorway, hidden in plain sight. Broad-leaved bushes and sprawling pine trees throw a cooling canopy over a rectangle courtyard. The latch locks behind us and an instant silence descends.

"I thought you would like the temple here." Lanying points at a row of glazed roof tiles that shimmer on flared eaves ahead. "It's different, but the people are good." She flicks her wrist at Jié. "Just keep your head covered, I'll see you there."

A temple. My heart delights and my eyes seek the familiar. Chiseled stone columns and smooth polished timber pillars stand together, an intricate pattern of swirling characters dances towards the sky. The doors are wide open, but there's no swish of robes or footsteps pacing the floor. There's not a soul inside.

For a moment I'm lost, for there's nothing my eyes recognize. No statues and no thangkas to pay homage to. No prayer wheel to turn, incense to burn, or butter lamps to light. There are only thick wool carpets lining in rows to the front of a barren room.

I close my eyes to the honeyed sun shafts that peep through the etchings in the window screens. My knees sink into the knotted rug, my icy hands clasp in my lap. The stillness stretches itself within me, full and complete. My mind soaks in my needy prayer.

I can't hear you anymore, my love.

Where are you and most of all, are you safe?

A shiver traces along my spine, and a shadow passes by.

"Sister, you don't look well." A soothing voice kneels nearby. "Please come and have some water." A gentle touch presses into my shoulder from behind.

I raise myself and follow a woman veiled in gray. She leads me to the back of the temple where a small fountain splashes and spurts.

"Please." She beckons me to take a seat under the drooping branches of a weeping willow tree. She watches me as the fresh water quenches my thirst.

"That's better." She nods at me. "Now tell me where you're from."

Her blue eyes shine as I tell her of the mountains and the meadows of my homelands, and the eternal snow on peaks that rise into the sky.

She reaches out and lays her hand on mine as she says she too is far from home, but her home is made of golden sand, and dunes that disappear into a vast horizon, and a million stars that light the blue velvet sky stretching in the midnight-heavens, reaching as far as one can see.

"What is it you're seeking here, sister." She looks over my shoulder at Jié, watching us from a distance.

"My loved one," I say, and she wipes my cheeks with the tip of her veil.

"Please tell me, even though I can't help." She bows her head. "For sometimes it helps to speak out loud, to set free what bothers us the most."

Her fingers trace the beads around my wrist, and my heart spills what it can't hold anymore. It speaks of the love I found when I dared to leave the home I knew so well and ventured into the unknown. It whispers of a heart that was closed but learned to open, and a deep trust gained and almost lost, of a mother who waited a lifetime for her son to return, and a baby girl yet to be received, and of friends that are so different yet so dear to me.

"And now all is silent." My voice fades into a blur. "And I'm afraid I'm losing faith." A profound sob escapes from my chest, for I didn't mean to speak those words, that last confession. Heated shame flushes my face. *I'm losing faith.* Me, the one who once vowed to dedicate herself to the benefit of all.

I'm losing faith. Me. I close my eyes. Could I proclaim anything worse?

Her fingers stroke the inside of my wrist, where my beads twirl a vibrant emerald green along the ginger golden fur of my sleeve. Her eyes meet mine and a daring blue flashes through.

"You know, sister," she says. "Sometimes the faith that leaves us unprepared for suffering might be a faith that deserves to be lost." Her caution makes my heart quiver. A bead of sweat trickles down my neck.

"When our faith is shaken to its very core, that's when we have the chance to examine what we believe." She pauses a moment, and I shiver. "And if necessary, replace it with a faith that can strengthen us, even in the most challenging times of our life."

A faint breeze murmurs in the willows. She too has lost love or faith, or both, being far from home. My mouth runs dry, and I swallow hard.

"And sometimes we only need to realize there's more than meets our human eye," she says, and the hopeful blue in her eyes hazes to a melancholic gray. "And it's only Allah that knows all, or in your faith, the karma that is created, that is at play." Her pupils widen into a full moon that draws over a sure sea of green and teal.

My fingers lock into hers. She does not hold my faith, still she knows of it well.

"It's in these times we need to deepen the shallows of our faith." She raises our hands to her chest. "With the trust that all will work out—for it's the work of the divine."

A lone dove perches on the edge of the fountain. I blink, and in her smile is all the love that she has to give.

"So ask the divine to strengthen your heart." She presses my palms on her cheeks. "And trust in the good of it all, as the outcome—however we may wish—is not in our hands."

A silver shade moves across the sun. The cotton of her simple dress rustles.

"Don't forget, I'm Fatima." She glides from the bench. "Please ask for me next time you come."

She leaves without looking back, her veil trailing behind.

All is still, but for the low call of a dove taking flight. *Trust in the good of it all.* My heart is willing to believe. My trembling hands slide my beads.

"Sister." Jié steps nearby. He's been standing there all along. "I think we go." He turns towards the rapid footsteps tapping our way.

"I've found him." Triumph echoes in Lanying's words. "I heard where Karma is."

She lifts her chin, but it's too late, and my heart plummets to the floor.

For she holds a frightening worry in her eyes, one that even she can't hide.

Thirty-Eight

"Please," I whisper, and my insides scream. "Take me to him." Lanying picks up her pace, and I grab her sleeve.

"No way, sister," she hisses. "You don't want to go there." My feet stumble to keep up with her.

"I need to see him." I heave and halt. My stomach throws up a protest again.

"You can't." She throws her arm around my middle and holds me up. "Not where he is." Her sleeve swipes across my forehead. She presses my cheek in the fur that hems the lapels of her coat.

"Then at least show me," I say. "Show me where they keep him." My fingers crawl into the smooth silver lining underneath her coat.

Her chest rises with reluctance, and her stance hardens under my palms.

"Please." I slide my fingertips along her jawline, and her body softens with a shallow sigh.

The shadows throw themselves upon us as our feet sprint down winding alleys towards the outskirts of the town. A harsh gale grinds the shale on worn flagstones, and colors fade to dust. A wooden gate towers in cruddy mud raised walls, and deep cries holler from behind.

"Wait here." Lanying's gaze scoots to the score of watchmen lingering in front of the gate. She marches off, her shoulders straight. Her crimson coat weaves like a proud banner behind her. It takes a while, and bodies move back and forth, but she disappears, and the gate stands ajar.

"What is she doing?" I reach for Jié. This can't be true. She's gone to see herself.

I leap, but Jié is faster, and his firm stare holds me down.

"No, sister," he says. "We wait." His tone is humbled yet certain—but I can't stand by and wait.

My mind paces in circles, my boots toss up sand. What if he's not in there; what if she doesn't come back?

It's not too long before she slips out the gate.

"He's here," she says and looks over my shoulder. "I didn't see him, but at least he's here." Her eyes avoid me, but her arm hooks through mine. "I'll tell you later." I waver but don't dare to ask.

Clouds of pink and gray blossom and wheeze a raw bite through the air. The sun has not left the day yet as we arrive late at the inn. Bags and packs crowd the courtyard, where weary men tie up unruly beasts. Norbu slumps the last of the bags in a corner while Dendup stoops on a low bench in the kitchen. Red rims their sunken eyes; they had a long day too.

"Karma's kept in there." Lanying shifts beside me at the table. "He'll be going up north soon to join the army." She pauses as the men dig in the thukpa that arrives.

The army. A spicy brew fogs in front of me, and the pepper scent stings my nose.

"They don't seem to know about his uncle." Lanying slurps her noodles. "So, I guess Karma didn't talk at all." She pokes my shoulder and urges me to eat.

"Later." I push my bowl aside and sip some water. Norbu pulls an orange from his coat. He peels the zesty skin, and I chew the juicy slices he hands me.

Dendup eases back and draws his cap. "There's no way we can get him out of there." An sure hesitation sets around.

"We might have to wait until they move him." Norbu springs up hope, but Lanying shakes her head.

"Even then." She sucks in her cheeks. "Let me think and see what I can do."

I smile at her. She's trying hard, but I don't find solace in her words—not tonight. A vague ache gnaws its way through my insides. *Om Tare.* Prayer, that's what I need.

"It's been a long day," I say. "I'm off to bed." I haul myself up at the edge of the table. A sharp pain snakes through my backside.

"I've got a few things to do." Lanying's gaze flies across the table. "Keep an eye on her."

She walks me to my room. Her hands stroke a cool touch, and her voice soothes a comfort against my cheek. She wraps my blanket tight. The door closes. All goes quiet. My body folds and searches for the warmth of him, for the tender hollow that is not there.

Let sleep come soon, I pray to the dark. Feet shuffle on the outside, and I drift off.

I'm leaving now. She's here again, my little girl. Her voice is with me ever since we left Xingyuan. She says she needs to leave, and that it's her time to go. She told me before, and now she's far away.

"Will you not hold on for a little longer?" I whisper. "He's here, and we're almost there."

I think she doesn't hear me.

The ache inside of me digs deeper. It shatters my core. A burning pain unfolds its soaring wings through my body. It hurts. My breath falls in ragged, shallow gasps. It hurts, it hurts so bad.

I'm leaving now. No, please don't go. We've only just met, and I already hold you dear.

The mat shifts from under me, and tidal waves come crashing in.

It's my time. How can it be? You've just arrived. I plead to the darkness moving in. Where are you?

I have to go. Please, my little one, just give me time to love you. I want to hold you so near.

Sour sweat soaks through my coat. My tears flow, salty and feverish.

I try. I try so hard, but it hurts, and she has to go. That's what she says.

A door slams open, and the light streams in, and there are voices calling for me.

Please, come back. My body lifts, and I call out to her, but she wanders away.

I'm going now. Please, take me with you, wherever you go.

There is pain, and it's more violent than I could ever imagine, more savage than my memories will ever allow me to relive.

And the heavens roar and rip wide open, and all the stars come tumbling down. And with it comes the dreadful dark on which she slips away. For it was her time, she had to leave.

All becomes silent, and the tide washes over me.

She was with me, but now she is gone.

There's the pain, and it ebbs from within me, fleeing fast, but the memory of her finds its stronghold within me.

A raging moon sets over the twilight, and familiar voices cry out.

I'm still here, but she's not.

"I thought we lost you, sister." Lanying's eyes appear in an empty sky, and it's her voice that whispers. "We almost did." Her arms hold me near.

"What happened?" My mouth is dry. My body is drenched. There's a harrowing hollow pounding its way through my insides.

She's gone. The memory of her will never leave me.

"You fell ill." Lanying lays me down. "Norbu brought you to us just in time."

I raise my head in an unfamiliar room. I look at her, and she looks at me.

"She's gone." I close my eyes and take another dive into the dark. She's left me, my baby girl. *Please, I want her back.*

"I know." Lanying cradles my hands and holds on to me, without saying another word. But I taste the tears she cried beneath what the rest of us can see, beneath all the eyes miss yet the heart sees all too clear. And in an instant, the darkness turns into the light as she shows me the purest of her love.

Together we sit.

We sit and she waits as I'm struggling to find some courage to resurface amidst the wreckage left by a little life that wasn't meant to be.

"We think you've been poisoned." She speaks slow as she pulls me back, very gently, into this world. "Sister, what did you eat?"

Poisoned. What does she mean? My eyes widen into hers.

"Same as you," I stammer. "But I didn't take a drink, only water at the inn."

Poisoned. How can that be? My mind lays silent. My body aches for my little girl. *Focus.*

"And I drank some water at the temple," I say. "And I had an orange that Norbu gave me, that's all." Is it? I'm not sure.

"I had some of that orange." Norbu's head peeps from the doorway. "And I'm fine."

I wince. He must have been standing there all along. My hands crawl, the blanket draws under my chin.

"So that can't be it." Lanying shifts to the bedside, and Norbu takes a seat at the end.

"I've been feeling off since yesterday," I say. "I thought more medicine would help." My eyes close, and a veil of despair covers my being.

Please come back to me. I wish all would go away.

"I gave you that." Lanying tucks my blanket close, and her hands bring a shiver to my skin.

"I finished it, so I took what Tuya gave me." I hear myself, but I don't want to speak. "It's in my bag. It tastes the same."

Please come back to me. My body curls, and a void inside me screams.

I come up for air, and heavy boots hurry in the hallway. Jié is quick to slow them down. Dendup barges in the door.

"I'm sorry, sister." He brings a breath of liquor to the bedside. His shirt is half-open, and his chuba dangles around.

I stare at him. He averts his eyes. I search, but he's not here.

Where are you, my love? I need you near.

"And where were you?" Lanying's lash at Dendup is unforgiven. "Nowhere to be found—again." Her fingers hook onto his dangling belt. "You're useless—as always." She lugs the leather, and her heels rise from the floor. She's ready to jump at his throat.

"And you're unnecessary cruel—again." Norbu lunges and grabs Lanying's wrist. Dendup stumbles back. Lanying jerks at Norbu's arm and fences him off.

"Get out, now, both of you." Norbu drags Dendup to the threshold. "Do us all a favor and have it out with each other—outside, once and for all."

Stunned faces fall upon him as Norbu works them both out of room—Dendup as well as Lanying. Jié steps out after them and secures the door.

Norbu sits down beside me, and I take his hand.

"Thank you," I say, but he shakes his head in denial.

"You better thank Jié, as he came to get me." His hands warm my fingers. "He heard you ailing but didn't dare enter your room alone." His eyes cast down on my blanket. "He knew the nuns here are good at treating diseases, so he carried you here, and I came along."

A lone desolation sets on his shoulders, and he hunches. "I'm sorry, Nordun, there was nothing I could do."

The first rays of the sun fall through the frame of the window, but they can't touch me now. The night has gone before and left a void that is too deep. It is too quiet inside of me, and for a moment I wonder if the light will ever reach again where it once shone so brightly.

"Will you please stay with me?" I say, for my body is broken. There's nothing left of me, even my tears refuse to spill.

Norbu lies beside me with no hesitation, and he opens his arms to me with a love that is undemanding, a love that only gives, and expects nothing in return.

He holds me, and his embrace keeps me safe in the night that's been too brutal and lasts far too long.

Thirty-Nine

Night has come, and I awake. I don't know for how long I've slept, or how many moons have turned. There's a space beside me in the bed that still holds Norbu's warmth.

I slide my legs over the edge, and my feet find a wooden floor. I tiptoe across the room in a thin cotton dress that is not mine. A dull ache cloaks my body.

The door stands ajar and Jié sits asleep beside the threshold. He must have been here all this time.

"Sister, come." A pair of loving arms receive me, and caring hands guide me through an unlit hallway. She says her name is Lien, and she sits me down next to a stove that simmers in a kitchen. A wool blanket wraps around me. I nod and smile at her, but I'm not sure if I'm really here.

Her tea tastes like the sweet grass of summer, and my insides relish in the invigorating touch of lemon and green. A window shutter rattles in the wind. I squint and there are shreds of the dark night that batter my mind with devastation, loss, and death. *She's gone.* I'm here, but I don't want to be.

Lien sits beside me and holds a bowl. "He said you like oranges." She hands me a slice of the fruit and my tears flow for Norbu; he's been too good.

"Eat, you need it." Her sleeve dries my cheeks. "Your body suffered great loss."

I eat, and she slides her beads in the rhythm I know so well. Together we sit, and I wake up to a dream that I fear to be real.

"Thank you, sister," I say, and Lien pours me another cup of tea.

"Some bread?" She offers, and I accept. The fresh crust crumbles on my lips.

"Tell me, sister," I say, for I can't hold it in. "How can I live with my loss, live with the loss of something that was never mine?"

I did it before, that time Karma left. I sat in the eye of the storm, waiting for the pain, for the loss, for it all to pass through. No holding on. This time is different. The pain is too savage to harbor, and I can't bear to sit with it while living this life.

"It feels like I'm standing on the burial ground." I swallow. "Where the vultures come to feed on me, picking my bones, and devouring my mind." The tea soaks the crumbs sticking around my gums. Lien's beads take a pause, and she eases back in her seat.

"Yes, you are, for we all stand on the burial ground." She reaches for her cup. "We're always surrounded by death and impermanence, but we never really see." The fine lines around her mouth deepen as she sips her tea. "It's only when death touches us that we experience this life is not ours to hold, but sacred and transient, passing in time into the eternal cycle of this living."

Passing. My baby girl has left before I got to hold her.

"The loss and pain you go through, expand far beyond what our bodies, and especially our minds, think we can endure." Lien puts her hand on my arm. "Yet, we can't hide, as there is no escape." She tilts her head to me and holds me in her gaze. "We can only move forward by acknowledging it and not turning away."

The empty cup weights down my hand. It will slip if I don't hold on tight.

"But how can I be with something that rips me apart, and at the same time let it be?" I blink and my flingers claw around the fine porcelain.

Lien smiles and points her chin towards the stove. "Try touching that scalding hot stove. What happens when you do? You will pull away as soon as the heat gets near, for you know the stove will scorch your skin."

I glance aside. *My little girl has left.* My mind smolders on the ashes that blaze a terrifying shade of red. My nails scratch the cup. If I squeeze any tighter, I'm sure it will crack.

"You don't rest your fingers on the stove and think, let's be with the pain." Lien's chuckle sounds like she's mocking me. I'm sure she's not, but I still cringe.

"In the same way you don't burn yourself on the emotion of your loss, on that pain that you think will tear you apart." She takes the cup out of my twisted fingers and puts it on the table. Then she opens my hand in hers. Pink calluses run their way across her palm.

"You stay present and touch your pain, but only very briefly at first," she says and holds our fingertips near the torching glow of the stove. The heat is there, and it gets nearer. I want to let it burn, but she retracts our hands and puts them in my lap.

"Don't try to endure it for too long, but only for a moment." she says. "Then rest and do it again and again—look and feel, moment by moment, and notice what's happening to you."

My fingers spread and I see the faded scar that lines the palm where hardened leather once tore my skin. *Home.* The soothing scent of the mountain meadows lingers by.

"Moment by moment, only then you are able to sit with the excruciating pain you thought would tear you apart." Her fingers stroke my hand. "It's there, and it hurts, but you can be with it, for it's only in moments, and in moments the pain will pass—if you only dare to stay."

She cradles my fingers and sets them free. I spread them again. *Moment by moment.* Sweat glitters along the faint pink mark that once was a gaping wound.

"Please don't let the pain scare you." She clacks her tongue and straightens her back. "Let it wake you, for this burial ground is our home, and everything's always changing, always passing, moment by moment, even the pain."

It will pass. My heart spills the agonizing yearning for home, for the stables nestling in the lower valley, for Father, and for Sangmo, and for my little, stubborn pony with his jolly whinny tickling in my ears.

If I only stay. My little girl has left me. I clench my fist.

Lien gets up and swings the kettle. The last drops settle in our cups.

"And remember sister, since nothing lasts forever, every day is a chance to start anew." She pokes at the stove where the smoldering ashes spark a hint of orange and amber until the golden glow flares to a blazing red.

Nothing lasts forever. My little girl is gone. A harrowing ache rages inside of me. How can I start anew with nothing left?

As calmly as she brought me here, she leads me back to the room where Jié sleeps beside the threshold and the door remains ajar.

I lay my body back on the mat and close my eyes to the darkness. *Moment by moment.* My mind plunges into the suffocating void she left after her departing. All is still, and I don't ever want to come up again for air.

But as always, a new morning comes and I awake. I should have known.

The dull ache has settled in my body, and a strange stillness resides within. A birdsong flutters from the open window, but I don't recognize its tune. My toes scrape the wooden floor. My face searches for the sun.

Inside of me gapes a horrifying black, but the sky shines in shades of golden. A pearly veil of mist drapes herself around the sun, and a branch sways near the window. Blossoms cloth like the ivory cream on fresh milk and churned yogurt, between leaves of lush green and edges of shimmering silver. A warming breeze carries their subtle scent. I lift my head to savor their sweetness, and all the while I hold my heartbreak near.

How can it be that while we observe our pain and loss, we can still see so much beauty in this world? How can it be that heart that feels so small, can bear this vastness of suffering while it also holds this enormous hope of love and joy? My fingers trace the windowsill. A tiny ladybug blots in red before me. It spreads its wings and takes its flight. All is still, and I can't escape.

It's not long before the door opens further. I know it's her by the clicking of her heels.

"Sister." Lanying's arms envelop me. "I knew you would pull through."

Her fingers comb through my tangled locks and peel off the flimsy cotton clinging to my limbs.

"Wake up, sister," she whispers in my ear. "Get dressed." The clothes she brought match her gown of embroidered purple, woven gold, and silver fur.

"I have a plan that I think might work," she says. "But I need you to come." The blue in her eyes is as strong as the ocean waves I have heard of, but have never seen myself.

A tiny beam of sunlight bursts through cracks in the broken window of my mind.

"I'm awake." I say, and duck my head in the dress she holds, even though I'm not so sure, but my love is out there, and I hold him more dear than I hold myself.

Every day is a chance to start anew.

It's what Lien told me yesterday. So today I will try.

I will and stay.

Forty

Lien stands in the doorway of the kitchen. Her round face lights up the dim hallway like the first full moon that rises over the peaks in the bleak of midwinter.

"May we meet under better circumstances next time, sister." I bow my head and her embrace brings tears to my face—again.

My knees buckle for a moment as I step into the day. A bright sun glares over a well-kept courtyard where pink planted blushes dot among the gray of raked pebbles. Our horses are scraping their hooves while Dendup, Norbu, and Jié stand at their sides.

"It's good to see you." Norbu hands me the reins of my stallion. I take his hand in mine and swallow hard.

"Thank you." I look up to meet him, and his eyes radiate a soothing brown, like the forest floor in fall, where wilting flowers find their peace to rest after the fierce bloom of a fading summer, and budding seeds find their fertile ground to burst forth into the promise of a new spring. It's too early, but I hope that one day soon he'll let me be the treasured friend to him, like the one he is to me.

"Let's go." Lanying's voice urges me on. We ride the road towards the enormous walls that hold my love locked. *What is the plan?*

I peek at Dendup, but he gazes in the distance. Norbu shakes his head. I spur on my stallion and steer it next to Lanying. I'm not asking, for she won't tell me, anyway.

"Stay on your horses," Lanying orders as we reach the towering gate where men, attired in scorched leather, march us in. Norbu and Jié stay behind.

Iron smashes on wood, and my stallion balks on all fours. A rancid reek of terror and violence conquers my nostrils. My lungs shrivel and my heart plummets in my chest.

Shadows loom and sinister eyes pry from the middle where screaming captives cram in a holding pen and blood dries in the sand. Watchtowers rise from all four corners, and arrows point their heads. I cast my eyes down, but my mind keeps searching—my love. He must be here.

A musty draft gushes through the vacant corridor, and our footsteps echo as we pass.

"Head high," Lanying hisses, and she tugs my sleeve. My heels scrape an apology in haste on the earth-beaten floor.

Another door opens. The stink of charred fat whiffs from the threshold. Lanying wavers for a moment, but rolls her shoulders back and marches inside.

Three men draw around a low table where blackened meat is heaped on plates and sour milk cloths in broad-eared beakers. They don't don the foul-smelling leather and hard hammered iron that protects the Mongolian warriors. Instead, their sturdy frames are clad in short, embroidered robes with rich fur curling along their thick necks.

The threesome makes no effort to greet us, but their relaxed conversation dwindles and their leery looks squint across the table.

I stifle. *What now?* My hands draw to hide up my sleeves.

Lanying jumps ahead and cuts straight to the chase. "Where's my man?" Her tone is almost brutal. "I hope for your sake he's still alive." Her eyes flare into a nasty blue.

I step beside her, and my knees nearly buckle. Dendup's boots drag from behind, and pace from Lanying's left to my right.

My mind shrieks. *I can't believe this.* We marched straight into the lion's den, claiming Karma. Surely this can't be her plan?

The men before us speak in curt phrases. A slight hesitation weaves through their snaking tongues. The man in the middle raises his hand in sure dismissal. Heavy set muscles bulge beneath his baggy, silken sleeves. The man on the left grunts and shakes his head. A fist slams in agitation on the table. A jug clatters aside. The man on the right sighs and rises to his feet. I shudder and step away as he leaves the room.

There's only the dull thud of a finger tapping on the tabletop, and the glassy stares of the men in front of us. I'm reluctant to swallow, but I have to. My throat cracks as I do.

Boots trudge their way through the hallway. Some pass our door, but none of them halt.

I glance at Lanying. *What are we doing?* Her lips curve, but there's not a hint in her eyes.

A brief, brutish scuffle resounds at the threshold. The door slams open, and I dare to look. My eyes haze. *It's my love.* My heart flaps its wings like a wild bird caged in my chest.

He walks past me without looking. My legs want to give in, but the strength of Lanying's gaze on me holds me up.

Lanying lets out a huff. "Finally." She shifts her stance, feet wide apart.

"This man is no Mongol, he's of a different tribe." She addresses the men with an uncanny calm. "He might have been born among Mongols, but his kin left him on the roadside to die." Disdain sets in her tone.

All eyes turn to Karma, who keeps his stare to the floor. My eyes haven't left him and the shadows of the beatings ghosting in purple and blue on his face. The gash above his eyebrow bears traces of freshly thickened blood, and I don't want to imagine what his ripped shirt conceals.

Lanying's hand reaches out to Dendup, who shuffles at her side. "This good man and his tribe raised him—he's one of theirs now, it's the law."

The law. Doubts stir my mind. I see what Lanying's doing, but surely her argument won't hold ground in these foreign lands?

The man on the left lets out a vicious bark. Furious words burst forth from his swollen chest. Lanying lifts her chin at him as her sole response. The man in the middle hops in his seat. Sparks fly among the three of them, and a heated discussion ignites over the table.

"I agree with you on this." Lanying's hand swats the suffocating air. "All men should be in service of our great Khan, so you understand my husband was not overjoyed—to put it mildly—when he learned you snatched our worker from us, and made me come all this way to get him back." She arches her eyebrows. "Right?"

Her worker? Where is this going? My hands burn in my sleeves.

Lanying speaks in the same calm manner, but her voice pitches as she proceeds. "My husband does not have time for this nonsense, as he's too busy taking orders from our great Khan, serving in the Kheshig."

With a jerk, she pulls a bundle of letters from her bag. Hefty seals clank on the lacquer as she tosses them on the table.

Greedy hands reveal the lengthy scribbled pages marked with red stamps on the side.

"As you can see, these men are already in service." Her sneer silences the mutter of the men. "For they have put themselves under my husband's command as workers while we trade with the Ortoq permission of our great Khan."

Three pair of suspicious eyes set on the letters, and the paper rustles under probing fingers. Sputters of disbelief and disapproval splatter from contorted mouths.

Registered workers! My eyes widen on the letters. *Of course, Chengdu!*

My thoughts go back to our stay at Lanying's residence and how she insisted Dendup and Karma would register at the officials as workers under her command. How it bothered our elder to take orders from a woman. I bite my lip.

Om Tare, how clever of her. Registered workers under her authority. Is that enough?

"You're a wife of Altan?" The man in the middle croaks and rubs his forehead. A greased stain stays behind.

"General Altan?" The one on the right squints at Lanying.

"Well, unless there's another General Altan they praise to be as great as the one who has consented to being my husband." Lanying lowers her voice and flicks her wrist at the papers that crinkle in the hands of the men.

"Now why would these men surrender themselves willingly to your service?" The man on the left spits his aversion at Dendup's feet. His eyes seethe with revulsion.

My mind gulps at his blatant display of contempt. Lanying flashes her teeth and Dendup's fists clench at his sides.

"Just look at them." Lanying takes a lengthy pause to curl her lips. "All these idlers from those forsaken mountains drink while rolling the dice." She lets out an exaggerated sigh. "Anyone knows how fools like them are swift to rake up a bill."

She rummages in the papers and pulls out a scribbled piece she flips on top of the stack. "Here you are, their eager consent to servitude to my husband for release of their debt."

Consent to servitude. Dendup's rasping breath halts at Lanying's bold statement. Karma doesn't move and keeps his head to the ground.

Release of debt. I blink and my mind staggers at the words. My cheeks flush. *Can it be?* Those papers, the ones that Dendup and Karma signed, they're not papers to work under Lanying's command, but they're papers that consent to servitude. *Slaves!* Lanying made them her slaves.

My head spins and the timber floor rocks in slow motion—back and forth—underneath my feet. My eyes fix on the papers. For sure, they can't be real?

Servitude. They would never have agreed to that, but then again, they can't read. My insides knot. They must not have known what they signed. Will it work?

Lanying doesn't wait for the men to answer or agree. She grabs the papers in one go from under their noses. "I guess we're done then." She stands tall and thrusts her head in the air.

Done? Surely, this can't be.

Silk swishes in a sure victory beside me. "Come on, then." Lanying turns on her heels and barks her commends as she boots out of the room.

Done! My heart rattles against my ribcage, with all its strength, frantic to get out. Dendup's fingers grip my elbow and push me on.

Shadows pass, and our feet flee from the corridor towards where the harsh light glares a dirty gray on shale.

"Heads up, and ride behind me," Lanying sneers, and I lift my chin.

I can't believe it—this woman! My mind is reeling to catch up. Hooves trample in dust.

Strong arms haul me in the front of my saddle and pull me close to a body that feels hard, and rigid, and seems to bear no memory of mine. My stallion leaps, and the gate crashes behind us. Muffled cries chase us on into a bleak leaden sky.

My heart quivers. Where have you gone, my love?

"I'm here," he says, weary, but sure as ever. He presses me into the tender hollow of him and the sweet scent of the mountains, and of the blooming meadows in summer, and the sun floats along.

He's here, and so are we—together, but will we ever find each other again?

Forty-One

He's here. Cups clank in a jubilant toast over the table as Karma tells of how he was ambushed, and how Jié fought at his side. The matron pushes full plates around and we listen, and all the while Karma's hand holds on to mine.

"They claimed I was a Mongol deserter," he says, and his teeth tear a strip of meat from the bone. "Trying to escape the service to the Khan." The fat drips down his chin, but he doesn't bother to wipe it, and I don't want to let go of his hand.

"It was Tuya that told them that story—I heard them mention her name." He gulps down what's left in his cup.

Tuya. My mouth goes dry. *Betrayal.* The void inside of me screams.

Lanying swipes the jug. "I told you so." Her eyes meet mine in a stark stare over the table.

"Makes no sense to me." I shake my head at her. *Please don't tell.* A dull ache throbs in my temples.

"Who knows what makes sense to that woman?" Lanying shrugs. "She could have a million reasons to thwart family ties—revenge or spite, could even be plain jealousy." She nods at Karma. "You heard your mother—your uncle favored you as his son."

Karma eases back and draws my hand in his lap.

My fingertips graze the bruised skin on his knuckles. He tries, but I won't let him catch my eye. *Not yet.* He'll know straight away.

"Why didn't you tell them about your uncle?" Dendup's eyes twinkle over his cup. "I mean, him being a General must count for something."

His wide grin hasn't left him since we rode out of that horrid place.

"Don't be a fool." Lanying sneers. "That man would have marched him straight into the Kheshig." Dendup retracts, and Norbu tops up his drink.

"Probably, so Lanying, thank you." Karma veers up and raises his glass. "For everything you did, I owe you my life—that's for sure."

Lanying's face freezes over. "I didn't do it for you." She's quick to reply, and her frigid tone matches her crystal-cerulean stare.

"I know." Karma says, his voice low yet beholden. "But you saved my life, and for that I am most grateful." He nudges at Dendup, who hastens his turn to toast.

"It's true, sister, thank you." Dendup's beady eyes peek out from over his drink. "We couldn't have done this without you." Drops of clear liquor drizzle from both sides of his mustache and he swipes his weathered lips with the back of his hand.

Lanying wrinkles her nose and empties her cup in one swig. It lands with a bang on the table. Norbu fills it again.

"Now those letters you had us sign." Dendup grins, and his eyes cross each other for a split moment. "I know they saved us, but I can't remember signing anything like that for the life of me." He squints Lanying's way again. "Those damned stamps and seals, they can't be real?"

Lanying's nostrils flare up ever so slightly, and a triumphant glee twitches in the left corner of her mouth.

It's clear we don't ask, for she won't tell—but I can't help but wonder. It must have been Altan that helped her, or Xia. I remember I carried some papers for her to Lanying. For sure they can't be real?

"You better hold on to those." Norbu stacks the empty cups next to our table. "You never know when you need them." He slides a plate of fresh fruit Lanying's way with a generous smile.

"Hmm, you're right about that." Lanying's fingers pick at a juicy fig without interest. "I hate to say it, but it's better you all go back soon." She pauses before she bares her teeth and sinks them in the brown fleshy fruit. "Even though I hate to see you leave, sister."

I reach over the table. My hand folds over hers. Sun-warmed currents wave through the blue of her eyes, and mine haze with gratitude. How I wish her weary heart could see all the goodness it holds, and the terrible beauty of her.

With a wistful frown, she turns to Dendup. "Let me take care of your goods." She clears her throat. "I'll send the profits your way."

Dendup's hands sway over the table. "You keep them sister, and the profits—I swear."

Karma's swift to add, "Even that's not enough to repay you for all you've done."

"Like I said." Lanying's stare stiffens in front of them. "I didn't do it for any of you, but for my sister."

Dendup's fist clasps the jug, his knuckles whiten. Karma's muscles knot in a rigid rope around my ribs.

I watch their silent battle unfolding before me. There's something reluctant yet sincere about their wish to connect with each other, and something heartbreaking about their obstinate yet helpless efforts to conceal that wish.

Oh, how we humans struggle with each other, and most of all with ourselves.

Karma's grip tightens around me, and I can't breathe.

"Take me to the room," he whispers. "I want you to myself."

My legs barely hold me as I find my way through the hall, to the room where he lays me next to him on the mat. My body curls in the tender hollow of his, and an immense longing for him, for us, unfolds within me.

A low sun caresses the windowsill, and I savor the salt that crusts his torn lips. His fingertips trace the edge of my jaw, but I duck my head. I don't want him to see in me what I've been hiding for him, but most of all from myself—even though he already knows. I felt it in the touch of his hands on my body; he's seen our little girl has left.

"Tell me, my love." He plants his lips to my ear. "You don't have to face me, but please, tell me all."

I don't want to. I bury my face in the crook of his neck. I don't want to tell. All I want is for us to be back. Back the way we were last winter, when the snow covered the fields and he waited for me at the ngakpa's house in the late afternoon, when we spent our evenings basking the heat of the kitchen stove, eating thenthuk and sharing stories with Father, when Sangmo's baby kept us from sleeping and it didn't matter for we had all night. I want us back before death carved a gaping abyss into my body. Back before she left us and I found us both bruised and battered.

"Breathe with me," he says. My body spreads on his chest, and he lets it rise and fall into a steady rhythm. "Trust me, for my love will hold the two of us." His heartbeat pulsates underneath me, and I find my anchor for the storm we know is yet to come.

I want us back—and so I tell all. About the man who returned on his horse with his throat slashed wide open, and his mother's stories of her home far away, of the journey that seemed without end, and of the night that arrived, and our little girl told me it was her time. I tell him about how Jié hurried, and how Norbu held me to last through the savage onslaught of the night in which the stars fell from the heavens and she slipped away.

And all the while Karma's hands twist in my locks, and he doesn't say a word, but his tears soak my skin and his grief ebbs in tidal waves through the shallows of my heart.

Our little girl. *If he only knew.* A roar rips through the vault in my chest and spills the bitter remorse I kept locked up for too long.

"She had to go, but it was me who abandoned her." I heave at the horrid truth of my confession. "It was me who wasn't strong enough to hold her through the darkness of that night. I let my selfish sorrow waste my fickle mind and had no prayer left in me to guide her through the in-between." She must have been so scared, our little girl, wandering those wasted lands of the bardos. Ever since she left, I've spent my time in the twilight, searching for her soul, lost and all alone out there.

His breath halts, and with his, so does mine, until it falls and rises again in a gentle motion.

"Love, look at me." He lifts my face to the sun and widens his eyes.

I blink through my haze and then I see—the new leaves of green that burst from swollen buds, and tall sun-strengthened grass ripples with long heads of gilded seeds under trees that don their brightest verdant hues.

"Look closer," he says, and a golden glow fills the air. Amidst the shreds of mist surrounding me, there's a field of crimson clover, where a newborn dappled fawn wiggles on her lanky legs. Behind her, a nimble deer struts in the woodland, with the proud confidence and gentle grace of ancient spirits whispering in her soul. She turns her head as if to say, "I see you" and the light streaks through the boughs in brilliant and shadowy beams.

"She wasn't alone, our little girl." Karma's words drift on the loamy breeze of a sweet summer at the wide-open plains.

She wasn't alone. It was his mother who guided our little girl, keeping her safe all this time.

He holds my gaze until the deer find their home together in the dense green of the forest before me and fade like an airy dream into the infinite blue yonder above. *Can this be true?*

His bruised lips brush a gentle smile upon mine, and my heart weeps in wonder for this world in which everything comes apart and becomes again, and for this life in which we can hold suffering near to joy if we only dare to stay and look—moment by moment. If we only dare to hold on for another while.

"I need to feel you," I say. My fingers find the beads I tied around his neck a year ago—three for the road and two for our home.

"We're here," he says. "And I'll hold the two of us." His fingers thread through my hair and nestle in my neck.

I rest my lips where the marks bloom in black and blue, like petals unfolding beneath his fevered skin, and relish the ripe scent of the mountain meadows in summer bloom and the salty breeze that rustles through the pine trees swaying in the evening sun.

We're back, not the way we were last winter, but we're here and somehow we've become us again—all anew.

Forty-Two

A bluish light beams through the pillared alley where our tiptoes leave trails of shimmering marks in the dew. White shreds of incense dance over the wide beak of a bronze caldron, and tinkling chimes sprinkle their delicate tones on the chant of prayer buzzing around.

I lower my body and press my forehead in the morning chill that stains the flag stones. It's early, but we're already done.

We were here before sunrise, Karma and me, to do the offering and prayers for the ones that left us before we got to know them, for his mother and our little girl. They're gone, and even though they've most likely arrived again, there's also the shattered fragments of him and me left that need to mend. So we pray.

My grandmother taught me well—nothing is permanent, and we cause our own suffering by holding on to anything lost—and I am most thankful for her guidance. Yet, I'm only human, and right now grief is tearing me apart. For I can't bear to let go of the part of me and him, of our love we never got to hold—not yet.

They stand together—the understanding of impermanence and the intense pain of our loss—and they exist side by side in the very being of me.

Om Tare. My body surrenders once again in gratitude and in mourning, paying homage to that which is larger than I can ever see, and pleading for the wisdom to guide me through this day.

"Take your time," Karma says. "I'll wait for you at the gate." Together we step into the early morning that rouses a brilliance of colors from their sleepy shades. A tincture of dawn still lingers on, like the water beads that dangle from the burgeoning blossoms and twinkle like newborn stars in the sunrise.

"Let's walk, sister." Lanying's arm hooks in mine and there's so much I want to ask her. About the pile of stamped papers that saved Karma's life, and about the ones that helped her, and if she's in trouble now. There's so much I want to ask, but she just shakes her head.

"I'll be fine." It's all she says about it. "I'm going down south for a while, for it pleases that wicked husband of mine." A playful grin pouts on her lips.

Altan. I shiver at the thought of the man with the savage sparks of a blacksmith's pit in his eyes. My mind lays quiet. *Ask it, you chicken.* Is this the right time? My lungs gulp a sharp breath. I guess it never is.

"Is Altan the reason you're not with Karma?" The instant I ask, I recoil with regret. I'm prying into her life while I shouldn't. If she wanted me to know, she would have told me so.

"He's not." Her answer is swift and sure. Her arm unhooks from mine, but instead of letting go, she drags me near. "I told you before, sister," she hisses. "I don't do love—it leaves you weak and vulnerable." Her voice is wrapped in an ominous tone, one that doesn't suit the Lanying I've gotten to know.

"I don't believe you," I say, and she spins her heels to face me.

"But you really should." Her breath skims along my cheeks, leaving a hint of fresh mint and raw honey in a wistful sigh.

"I'm like the dark, sister," she whispers, but makes sure I hear. "And men relish the dark, for like the smoothest silk, it shelters the sight of all that's forbidden, yet it perfects the touch and heightens the pleasure to all who dare to lay themselves down beside her." Her delicate fingers fold along the fur hem of my coat. "Let me tell you, sister, men love descending into the dark, even though it destroys them in the end."

She looks at me, and my heart quivers. In her eyes glistens the black of a twilight in which all hopes and dreams have faded for the morning to come, and all is silent and unseen—a moonless night.

"Karma—he sensed it soon enough, he got out on time." She averts her blustery gaze. "Not many of them do." My knees wobble, but she pulls me on.

She swings her legs over a low bench, and I sit down beside her. The pines spread their canopy of swaying green upon us. Sunlight plays its game of hide and seek beneath the branches, and casts its shadows all over our face.

"You're the light, sister." She slides a loose strand of hair behind my ear and all the while the gloom in her eyes eludes mine. "You're the light men are forever seeking to bask in—and women, too."

She looks away, and a breeze moves the stillness through the branches. A splash ripples in the pristine pond in front of us. Below its surface darts the silver of fish, and on it rests the pure white of lotus flowers in a cradle of humble green. There's not a cloud drifting above, but a faint thunder rumbles at the edges of my mind.

I glance at her. Will I, or will I not? She probably won't hear me out, but I'll try it, anyway.

"You know, you don't have to stay at the dark side," I say. "If you want to, you can easily turn to the light—like the lotus blooming out of the mud." The corner of her mouth twitches ever so slightly into her blushing cheek.

"You don't want to hear this." I say as she averts her eyes again. "But I'm going to say it anyway, as we all come to our struggles in this life." I shift and cross my leg on the bench to face her. "We all feel stuck in the dark most of the time, but we can choose to stay present with the suffering, and meanwhile learn from our loss, discover our own strength within the discomfort, and see the beauty in all that lives beside the pain."

Her face hardens into a mask of indifference, her shield against the glaring truth that she keeps herself trapped in what once was her prison, by revisiting her pain time and time again. Because that's exactly what she does. Instead of mastering her mind, she lets in the vicious thoughts that violate her, like that malicious family of hers once did, dragging her back to the prison that once was her home, the place where doors are bolted, and windows are barred, and tender hearts harden, growing cold.

"We all have a choice to rise above, sister." My voice sounds thinner than I want to. "And so do you." I push on.

"Well, if that's so, I choose not to escape the dirt and grime I was born in." Her response is too hasty. Her gaze flies across the pond.

"I've gotten to like the dark, and the sure relief that comes with it, if only temporary." She tosses her long locks and twists her body on the bench. "I don't have the patience to sit with pain—I like my satisfying escape to the midst of the night." She cocks her head into her neck and draws in her distant stare.

"Sure, I see what is possible, for I see you, but I made my choice long time ago." She turns to me and in her eyes weaves a mix of sad gray and uncertain blue. "I came here flawed and I'll leave here flawed—and in the meantime—I'll seek my pleasure in my pain, right here in the mud." She sucks in her cheeks and tries on a smile. It doesn't work, and she knows it well.

"You're a fool, sister, to think we come flawed, for we are not." I shake my head and the tears burn behind my eyelids. *Not now.* "We all are innate goodness, if we only dare to trust."

A burning shame scorches my cheeks, for I too let secrets and suspicion take me over. Instead of trusting Karma's goodness, I doubted his actions, and him, the one I love, while all I had to do was ask him. It almost ruined us, and it certainly caused me my peace of mind. How easy it is to forget my own errors. I fumble with my beads. *Om Tare.* Please give me the clarity to not make that mistake again.

"No need to deny the past or our own foolish actions, for it's part of our life, like the mud is part of the lotus to blossom." My fingers twist the string of jade around my wrist. "But that was then, this is now, and you can choose to be wiser."

I listen to my own words, and I'm not sure anymore if they're meant for her or for me, but it's my heart that speaks, and its intentions are pure.

"Every moment is a new possibility to choose something different." My hand reaches out to her, but her heart stays unmoved. "And you—you have the strength to rise above the dark—if you only dare to do so."

She stares at me, but also in the distance. "You've got some nerve, sister, calling me out like that after all that I've done for you." Her tone brings a chill to my bones. Still, I won't let go, for I love her, and she needs to know.

"Yes, I do have the nerve." I lift my chin to her disdain. "Because my love for you is too deep to give up on you." I clasp her rigid fingertips as to bridge across our lifetimes, and she blinks. Frosted white sparkles as fine as any crystal, and it twinkles in her eyes.

For a moment there is only the two of us—spirited away from all there is. Her fingers curl over mine, and it's like the smooth velvet that wraps around the silk of budding petals, cooler than expected, but a tender cocoon to all that's too fragile yet to bloom.

I would pry them open to let her eyes feast on the terrible beauty that lies inside of her. But nature sets its own pace, and she's not ready—not yet. It will take time, and a lot more love for her to trust and to burst into full bloom. It's seeded in the very being of her, the understanding that she can, if she only dares to meet the sun.

And if she does, I hope I'll be there with her to witness the wonder of it all.

"We've come a long way, sister." She bows and rests her forehead on mine. "But you're getting way ahead of me now." Her black eyelashes frame a translucent blue. "I'm not sure I'll ever end up where you're going—or if I even want to." The sigh that leaves her lips is slow, soft and gentle, as if her heart relaxes in the middle of us.

"We've had quite an adventure." She sniffs and slides her sleeve across her face, as swift as one can do.

"When spring comes, I'll meet you at your stables." She jumps up and her scarlet brocade flutters around like a peacock showing off its feathers to the daybreak after a long night in the barn.

"Then I'd better burn the weisang right after Losar," I say. A chuckle escapes me. I'm always amazed at the speed at which she's able to turn things around.

"You better, sister, it's never too early to appease those gods of yours." A bold grin soars over her face. "For every time we meet, it seems you've got yourself in some kind of trouble—not that I mind."

She hauls me up and together we stroll to the gate, to a farewell we both don't want to voice.

Forty-Three

"All set?" Lanying tugs at my collar. I nod. The bright morning sun mists my eyes. Stubborn tails swish at buzzing flies, and ardent hooves trample on worn flagstone—our horses are ready to go.

Dendup pours a last round to the men who've come to see us off—they're taking their time to toast a fortunate journey home. All set as far as I can see.

"Don't forget to pass by Xia." Lanying presses my arm. "She'll have the papers drawn up by now." A satisfied tone eases her tight grip. "We'll do some decent trade together, sister, no more trampling along the muddy back roads with your kinfolk—if you know what I mean."

I know what she means by now, about joining the Ortogh, the association that grants permission to do the lucrative long-distance trade. "It's getting too risky to deal without it, sister," Xia had warned me. "No amount of yak skin's worth the skin of your family members." I sure became a lot wiser over tea that afternoon in Ya'an.

"That reminds me." Lanying slips two envelopes in my bag. "Here, these will get you through, in case questions are asked."

My mouth opens, but her hand swats the air in front of me.

"Don't mention it." She shakes her head. "It's the best I can do now that you're wandering the roads in the company of these fools." She points her chin at the drinking party before us, where another last drink overflows the clinking cups under rowdy laughter. Karma's hand wraps around my middle, and a fresh breeze blows around.

"Lanying, I might chance my arm here," Karma says, "But there's another favor I would like to ask of you."

I glance aside. He calls her by her name now. My heart delights, even if the two of them still have a long way to go.

"It's about Jié." Karma gestures the guard behind him to join us. "He's saved Nordun's life—twice—and I want to repay him." His fingers spread and radiate a mellow warmth along my ribs.

Jié. Quiet, loyal Jié. A surge of gratitude expands my chest. All eyes turn to the humble man, who is swift to cast his eyes at the ragged toes of his boots. His bold frame rocks back and forth, his heels crunch in the sand.

"I know he's your most trusted man, serving you for the longest time," Karma says, as calm as ever, but then he takes a sharp breath. "But you name your price, and I will make it happen—no matter what."

Price? My eyes widen at the shy watchman standing before us.

Jié ducks his head at Karma's words, and I wince. My heart sinks for this gentle man who thinks he needs to lower himself for us. Of course, how come I did not notice before? Jié is not only Lanying's servant, he's in her bondage—he's in servitude too.

A hard line draws around Lanying's lips, but then it relaxes, and something moves in the depth of her eyes. She tilts her head and I see—it's a shimmer of the purest blue, a blue that is neither dark nor light but sits in that sweet spot in the middle, reassuring yet exciting at the same time.

"No need to pay," she says, and her eyes won't let me go. "Jié is a free man by my words." She wrinkles her nose. "He can choose wherever he wants to go."

She blinks, and the sun touches in golden threads upon us. *Lanying.* I whisper her name.

"Jié." Lanying reaches out to him, and the watchman stumbles back.

"Thank you," he says, and keeps his head bent to the ground. "But I will stay here and serve you." His toes draw in the gravel. "I was born into service, so you see, I have nowhere to go." He looks up, and unfeigned bewilderment stares us right in our face.

My body squirms, and Karma's muscles harden around my ribs; his arm cages me in. I close my eyes and let the heartache pass as it trudges through my whole being. This modest man, like his master, doesn't know how to be free, and I can't bear to witness any more broken lives for today.

"Then come with us, Jié, to our home in the mountains." Karma eases me into his rising chest. "It would be an honor for Nordun and me to call you our brother, and have you at our family's side." The rapid beats of his heart rush their way through my ribcage.

Our home. He said our home. My hand hugs Karma's hand, and my eyes reach out to Jié.

Our home. My heart feels so full it's about to burst.

"I would take the offer if I were you." Lanying nods at Jié. "You better saddle up or I might change my mind." She throws a wink at me and turns away. All I can do is beam a smile.

"Here you are, brother." Norbu sneaks from behind and hands a stunned Jié the reins of his saddled horse.

"I beat you to it this time—you're all set," he says. "I'll leave it to you to pack up our respected elder." He waves his hand at a jolly Dendup, reveling in what seems an endless toast, and slaps Jié's back under a heartfelt hoot. "And I'm so glad I'm not you."

Jié has a protesting Dendup up in the saddle before I can mount my horse. The crowd roars in laughter, and I delight at the joy sparking in Jié's almond eyes.

"See you next spring, sister." Lanying's hand spurs on my stallion, and neither of us dares to look back.

Hooves clap on loose gravel, and my heart breaks a little for leaving my sister, but this time I savor the pain. For this time, my heart breaks at the right place, leaving a smooth crack for more love to flow in and out, and for my heart to heal bigger than it was before.

My grandmother told me we should always keep our heart open, undefended, and allow it to be touched by pain so we can wake up to the vastness of unconditional love. I wish that one day I can practice her truth, but that day is not here, not yet.

In the meantime, I'll wait and practice with patience, for that day will surely come.

Forty-Four

Evening claims victory over the daytime by glowing the sky with the honeyed tones of ripe melons and sliced peaches. Brittle strands of grass crunch beneath our horses' hooves. White foam breezes from their mouths as we conquer the last hill of the day.

"Well done." I run my fingers through the slick sweat on my stallion's neck. We've been pushing hard to get to the home nestled in the valley before us, the one we left so many moons ago.

It was a frosty late winter morning when we set out on our journey. "Too early. Better wait a few more days," Father had said, but the gods had spoken. Besides, if we'd waited, we wouldn't make it home before the snow's onset—and the rawness in the wind tells us that will be any day now.

We would have arrived earlier, but we stayed on in Hanzhong as Karma had to handle his mother's estate. Tuya had gone when we arrived—apparently, she left right after we set off to find Karma. Only the loyal servants remained at the house. They had taken good care of Karma's mother's remains, arranging all offerings and prayers to Tengri, their Eternal Heaven.

Karma released the servants from their duty and wished them well, but like our trusted Jié, most of them had nowhere to go. They choose to remain at the house, hoping one day Karma's uncle will return. *Om Tare.* Please pray for them, as they are like caged birds with the door wide open—they've never known the feeling of flying and are too afraid to even try.

I wonder if Karma's uncle even knows about Karma's return—he never showed, nor did he send word. Karma's sure they'll meet.

"The time's not right," he said when I asked, and this sometimes happens in our life. We drift apart and come together again, either by chance or after lifetimes of searching—whenever our karma agrees. And when we meet, one fleeting moment can be enough to sustain us, for it reminds us to be thankful for all that ever was.

I see it in Karma—the gratitude for that one evening when he was his mother's son again helps him to bear the enormity of her recent loss. He's a brave man, my love, for when the night comes and the dark gets too much for either of us, he hands me his heart and together we heal.

The eager brays of our horses roll down the hill; their long manes rise and fall in slow motion as we descend. My heart beats faster than the rapid chop of their hooves. My mind spurts ahead—who will be there to open the gate, and who will come to welcome us home?

We ride down the lane where the last of the leaves curl in brown and black on the branches. When we left, these trees were nothing but bare skeletons. In the meantime, they've sprung buds of green and abundance, blossomed into pink and purple and bore their fruits—they lived a whole life during our absence, and so did we.

Now we're back, the three of us riding into the gate, returning with a new brother on our side, our humble Jié. We saw Norbu off at Sonam's homestead two days ago after a grand reception—no expenses were spared to welcome us at his home. It was good to see the reddish color return on Sonam's face, and the brazen jokes spun back in his manner.

What delighted me the most, however, was the heartfelt way Sonam's arms opened to his son, and how Norbu accepted the unspoken apology, with no waver, no questions asked. Sometimes absence endears what we took for granted before, and distance moves our hearts closer to the ones we were set to leave behind.

And sometimes time moves our hearts in different directions, like I hope time will do for Norbu and me. When we left, Karma made Norbu promise he would visit us soon, but I know he won't. Our hearts are dear to each other, but his heart holds a love that's deeper than mine. I wish for him to find somebody who will share in his love, for he has so much to give.

"He's home." Karma's voice calls me back to the moment. He points at the gate where the shadows reveal a man standing tall, and white silk that flutters in the wind.

"Father," I whisper, and my horse takes a sprint, as if trying to match the gigantic leap of my heart.

"We've made it, Father," I call out. "The gods of the mountains had mercy on us."

It's true—the gods were at our sides when we traversed the rickety planks, slippery stone paths, and mighty mountain peaks, and defied the torrential rains that drenched our skin and the early morning cold that crept into our bones. The gods were at our side keeping the preying robbers and wild animals at bay, and Lanying's papers answered the questions foreign tongues asked in the inns where we sheltered from the night.

Father's arms catch me, and a cloud of silken wraps around us. The gods have brought us home at last.

"I never doubted they wouldn't, my child." That's all Father can say before Sangmo comes flying. A little girl's chubby cheek presses against mine. Her fluffy locks tickle my nose, and my heart spills as her scent of warm milk and sweet rice touches my very being.

"Look at you now." Sangmo's sleeve streaks my face with flour and butter. "You're silly, no crying, you're home."

We both keep each other near as we walk our way to the house. Her little girl's arms cradle around me, and I can't let her go.

Servants hurry at Sangmo's directions, and the kitchen fills with the spicy aromas of cooked meat and a hearty brew. Chang flows in abundance, and the laughter of men drowns out the merry clanking of cups. The little girl finds her sleep in my lap, and Karma's hand rest around my middle to let me know he's near.

Of course, it's Dendup who does most of the talking, and to be honest, nobody can do a better job. He tells with verve about the roads reaching to the heavens, and the profits of trade along the way, and how we found Karma's mother with the help of "our brilliant sister" in Hanzhong.

Dendup almost makes it sound like our journey was one without great effort, but Father is no fool. He never takes his eyes off Karma and me while Dendup waffles on.

Sweat pricks my neck as Dendup's tales come to a close, omitting all of our adventures in Chang'an and beyond. I guess he knows it's not for him to tell.

Father pours another round, and a quiet unease spills over the kitchen. There's only the whistling wheeze from the tiny girl on my lap and the hushed hiss of the stove.

Karma shifts to the front of his seat, but his hand keeps me near. He drags his cup from left to right and looks up at Father. "I think it's my time to tell," he says, and his voice sounds so calm when he recalls of the morning his mother's messenger came, and Jié risked his life for him at the ambush, and how Lanying's clever preparations saved his life.

"I would not be here if it wasn't for the determination of my brothers and sister, and for the courage of my love." He turns aside and his thumb caresses my cheek.

"I know you don't want to tell now." There's a tremble in Karma's tone for only my heart to feel. "But I want your father to hear it from me—and how sorry I am I couldn't be there for you." He pauses and his eyes hold me, warm and strong. "So, will you let me tell, my love?"

I nod, and he tells of the night the stars fell from the heaven and his mother brought our little girl home. And how he wasn't there when he should have been, and how Jié saved my life—once again. My breath shallows as the memory scrapes its sharp claws along my ribs.

"I am sorry, Palden-la." Karma clenches our hands in a fist. "I kept my promise. I brought your daughter home, but I couldn't keep her from harm." And my heart holds onto his as my fingers crush under his grip.

Father tilts his head, and a shadow falls over his face. "There is nothing you could have done to prevent it, for this happens often, even at home." He rubs his chin and rests his gaze on Karma. "I know by now you will go to the ends of this world for my daughter." A darkness shifts in his eyes.

My mind stirs in wonder. Father is right—Karma would do anything for me, but why then his unsettling look?

"While you were away, I heard off the orders the family gave you last winter, and how you resisted them, even at the point of their blades." Father lifts his chin and shakes his head at Dendup. "Three lives—I'm sorry but seems to me they were out to get you killed this time around."

Three lives. My mind staggers. An icy shiver rushes down my spine. Three lives—how can this be? He told me he took "only" one.

"They wouldn't let me be with Nordun otherwise," Karma says, and my fingers go numb under his hand. "I bargained them down to one." His gaze shoots over at Dendup. "For now."

A shrill silence pierces the space between us like an arrow soaring from a bow that's strung too high. Karma's hand loosens around mine, but my heart locks around his—I'll never let him go.

"I think it's time we let the family know you're done enough for them now," Father says and orders the servant to pour another round. "I'm sure by now they understand that even though family isn't always in the blood, it certainly isn't found in the blood spilled at the cost of another family that is so near." He directs his words to Dendup and speaks them with great care.

Karma treads his fingers through mine, and my heart breathes with relief. *Om Tare.* No more mindless killings, no more wasting of precious human lives.

"Family is the ones who want you in their lives, and treasure you for what you are, no matter what." A deep glow of genuine happiness lights Father's eyes. "So, let me welcome you, my son, and let me tell you, it's good to have you home." He reaches out across the table to Karma, who meets him half-way to seize his hand.

My heart feels like it's about to burst out of my ribcage, taking flight to embrace the incredible man before me, the one I'm so fortunate to call my father in this life.

"Let's not forget to welcome our brother." Father raises his cup to Jié beside him with a smile that spreads to every part of his face. "Thank you for saving my daughter's life once again. We are most honored to have you in our family and our home."

Modest as always, Jié bows his head, but Sangmo's quick to set him straight.

"Head up, brother," she calls him out. "You're among family now, and here we only shake hands or share hugs." Her arms fling around his broad shoulders, and Jié's rugged face flushes with the brightest of crimson I've ever seen on a man.

"You've got that right, sister." Father puts down his glass and slaps the shy man on his shoulder. "You're family now, and here we look each other in the eye."

Another toast clinks in the air and joy surges around our table.

I close my eyes and let the happiness soak my skin and sink into my bones.

Karma's breath tickles my ear. "You're good?"

I smile. "How could I not?"

I open my eyes and look into his, and it's all a blur, and somehow, it's all truly clear.

We've come together by choice and are strengthened by love—we're family now.

Nordun's—and Karma's—story continues
Into Faraway Lands, set for release in Summer 2023.
Sign up to receive sneak peeks of Nordun's new adventures & special offers at www.elleslohuis.com / scan the QR Code

Author's Note

Even at the start of drafting *A Pilgrim's Heart,* I knew—Nordun's journey will not end in Lhasa; her story is far from over.

I had intended to write only *The Horse Master's Daughter,* a tale as a gift to Nordun, my Tibetan niece. But somehow Nordun ended up with Karma, her budding love and the special gift of hearing his mother's call... now how could I ignore that?! To me it was obvious, Nordun would help Karma in his search for his Mongolian mother, and more travel and adventures were already spinning in my mind as I wrote *A Pilgrim's Heart.*

After Lhasa, the next stop would be Mongolia, at least so I thought it would be. Researching the journey from Tibet into Mongolia along the Silk Road at the times of the Yuan dynasty, when Tibet and China were part of the Mongolian empire under Qubilai Qa'an I realized there were too many exciting opportunities as regards people and places in China alone to pass by.

So I adjusted the speed at which I myself, as a writer, set out to travel, and let the scenery, and of course Nordun and her company dictate the pace of the story. As it turned out, finding Karma's mother in Xingyuan (present day Hanzhong) is only the beginning of Nordun Mongolian adventure. Yes, Nordun's – and Karma's – story continues *Into Faraway Lands*, set to be released at the end of 2023.

Facts and Fiction in the Nordun's Way Series

Echoes of Home is set in Tibet and China, at the time of the Mongol Empire and its Qa'ans. For more details about this historical setting, the debates around historical accuracy, and how I came to the choice of this place and period in time (which I've explained lengthily in the author's notes of *The Horse Master's Daughter*), please read the 'behind the scenes' section at my website www.elleslohuis.com

As a historian, I always want to do justice to the times and the people inhabiting the times. For all my books I do extensive desk research and consult experts in the field, for *Echoes of Home* the same too. Besides desk research, I also wanted to do in-depth field research. It was—and still is—my intention to make the journey from modern day Drango (Luhuo), home of Nordun's stables in Tibet to Chang'an (near present day Xi'an) in China myself, but due to visa restrictions it was—and still to date is—not possible for me to go the road Nordun and her company travelled.

Fortunately, I spent three magical months in Kham with my Tibetan in-laws and their friends who have gone these roads many times. They've shared first-hand tales and travel anecdotes with me.

I always come across amazing artifacts, places and people doing research, like a beautiful $9^{th}/10^{th}$ century scroll called 'Book of Buddha's Names' with a small panted Buddha at the start of each line. This scroll was discovered in one of the Dunhuang Caves in China, and when I set my eyes on it, I was sure Nordun would have loved it, too. So I made Karma give it to her on their journey together. Visit my website www.elleslohuis.com to see the gorgeous scroll and how I've placed the many artifacts, places, and people I discovered during my research in the *Nordun's Way* series. You can also download a copy of the beautiful hand-drawn map of Nordun's travels I've commissioned there.

Not much is known about the exact villages/settlements and their names in Tibet at that time. Therefore, I have taken the liberty of incorporating some villages/cities that exist in Tibet at the present time.

This brings me to a last note on facts and fiction—transliteration. For readability, I've used the (phonetic) Romanized transcription whenever Tibetan terms, personal names, or place names are mentioned, and I've transcribed the Chinese terms, personal names, and place names in pinyin.

Elles Lohuis
Almelo, 2023

The Horse Master's Daughter

Nordun's Way Book One

"An exciting story full of surprises and rich drama, with an unforgettable main character in the fiery Nordun. If you like skillful world building, evocative atmosphere, and strong characters, you will thrill to The Horse Master's Daughter."- Nancy Bilyeau, bestelling author of *The Blue* and *The Fugutive Colours.*

Tibet, 1285 – Hidden away in her grandmother's monastery after her mother's tragic death, Nordun's life has been shrouded in secrets. Born into a family of royal horse masters, she was divined to become the first ever female horse master—but that destiny was never shared with her.

Now, returning home for her father's blessing to take her monastic vows, friends and foes challenge Nordun to the impossible—to claim her heritage to the stables.

The last thing Nordun wants is to tame a feral horse... but if she refuses, her cherished childhood home will be lost.

Desperately unprepared and armed with only her compassionate heart, Nordun ventures into the far and rugged unknown.

Will she fulfill the ancient divination and turn the tables on her family's fate, or return to her sisters in solitude to serve all sentient beings as has been her aspiration for most of her life?

Join Nordun on her reluctant quest through the turbulent times of thirteenth-century Tibet with its royal clans, Mongolian invaders, smugglers and Silk Road traders, to the places where demons lurk, and through the trials which afflict every family and human life—courage and cowardice, love and lust, loyalty and treachery, and cruel endings which do not always sprout into the new beginnings we desire them to be.

The Horse Master's Daughter is Book One in the historical fiction series Nordun's Way, a heartfelt heroine's journey, sprinkled with nuggets of timeless Buddhist wisdom, and can be read as a stand-alone novel.

A Pilgrim's Heart

Nordun's Way Book Two

"Heart-wrenching at times – yet with an ending that is so beautifully moving, I did have a few tears in my eyes.... Adventure, romance, tension and a noble quest –all delivered with fabulous storytelling and beautiful writing." - Amazon Review

Tibet 1285. After a reluctant but ultimately successful quest to save her childhood home from her cruel uncle, Nordun is ready to forgive him for his sins, despite knowing he murdered her mother long ago.

Her family, however, is set on revenge — they've ordered Karma, the man Nordun is falling for, to hunt her uncle down and kill him.

Desperate to avoid more bloodshed, and determined to stand by her Buddhist beliefs, Nordun joins Karma on his journey under the false pretense of going on a pilgrimage to Lhasa, the place her uncle is hiding.

As they cross raging rivers, traverse vast grasslands, and conquer the mighty mountain ranges of the Cho-La, Nordun realizes the man she loves is indeed a kindred spirit—but he is also a merciless warrior, who believes compassion has no place in a family blood feud.

When faced with the inevitable, will Nordun risk losing her love, and her life, to save the man who killed her mother?

We follow Nordun on her crusade across the rooftop of the world, to the lands of Gods, where the fickle fate of men is in the hands of the ones who reign through force and fear, and the unshakable faith of a woman in the innate goodness of humankind proves to be the very thing that can set a man free.

A Pilgrim's Heart is Book Two in the historical fiction series Nordun's Way, a heartfelt heroine's journey, sprinkled with nuggets of timeless Buddhist wisdom, and can be read as a stand-alone novel.

Acknowledgements

A warm thank you to my extended family in Tibet. For welcoming me into your home and into your hearts, and showing me the true meaning of family beyond boundaries.

Thank you to Dawn Ius, rock-star writing coach and editor extraordinaire. For giving me the room to roam, and reigning me in – on time - with 'The Rules'.

Thank you to Kirsten, my bff. For cocktails and coffee, and sea and sun, and never, ever letting me off the hook.

Thank you to Janneke, my fairy godmother. Yes, it's only ever a work of the heart.

And most of all, thank you to Tsewang, my husband. For being at my side, all the way - how blessed I am.

About Author

Elles Lohuis is a historical fiction author based in The Netherlands. A voracious reader and ever inquisitive explorer of far-away lands and foreign cultures, she holds an MA in History, an MA in Business, and a PhD in Social Sciences.

Elles writes books that enthrall, engage, and enrich you, to sweep you away to distant places and times gone by, opening a window to a world and its people that nowadays seems wonderous, foreign, and fascinating - but was once typically ours.

At the moment, Elles is back on base to complete her first historical fiction series *Nordun's Way*, a heartfelt heroine's journey, sprinkled with nuggets of timeless Buddhist wisdom.

Connect with Elles and receive more sneak peeks of her writings, research, travel, new releases, and special offers at www.elleslohuis.com or scan the QR Code

And download your copy of the hand-drawn map of Nordun's travels, specially commissioned for the *Nordun's Way* series Books One, Two and Three.

Glossary

Ani / ani-la: Tibetan term for nun.

Bardo: Tibetan Buddhist term for the intermediate state or gap experienced between death and the next rebirth. Tibetan Buddhists believe this bardo can take up to 49 days; so prayers and other ceremonies are performed every day for 49 days after death.

The term bardo also refers to the gap or space experienced between any two states in which the old reality is lost and a new reality has not formed yet.

Bodhisattva: enlightenment-being who has vowed to dedicate his/her life to the sake of all beings.

Butter tea: traditional Tibetan drink made by boiling strong tea and adding milk, yak butter, and some salt. Traditionally Tibetan people have Tibetan butter tea and tsampa (roasted barley flour) together for breakfast.

Chuba: ankle-length, crossover robe that is adjusted at the waist with a long sash and pulled up to different degrees according to sex, rank, or region.

Dakini: a "sky dweller" or "sky dancer," the most sacred aspect of the feminine principle in Tibetan Buddhism, embodying both humanity and divinity in feminine form. The dakini appears during transitions: moments between worlds, between life and death, in visions between sleep and waking, in cemeteries and charnel grounds.

Divination: Mo, or dice divination, is an ancient predictive technique that is part of the Tibetan culture. The Tibetans consult *Mo* whenever making important decisions about their health, their family, property, personal matters, spiritual practice, friends and relationships, business, and travel. The answers of a divination come in the form of statements, advice, and instructions regarding practices or prayers suggested.

While there are different forms of Mo divination, the form in this book uses two six-sided dice with Tibetan letters on it as described in the book *Mo: The Tibetan Divination System* (2000) by Jamgon Mipham (published by Snowlion).

Dri: Female yak

Dzomo: A female crossbred between a Tibetan yak and a domestic cow.

Gen / Gen-la: Tibetan word for teacher.

Karma dakini: a specific dakini appearing to the Buddhist practitioner to mirror one's delusions, energize one's meditation practice, and activates one's realization.

Khata: traditional ceremonial scarf made of silk. The khata symbolizes purity and compassion and is presented on many ceremonial occasions, including temple visits, births, weddings, and the arrival or departure of guests. Most khatas are white, symbolizing purity, auspiciousness, and prosperity. There are also khatas in other colors: blue referring to the sky, green symbolizing water, red representing the space of protective deities, and yellow signifies the earth.

Khatvanga staff: ritual instrument held in the crook of the left arm of advanced Tantric Buddhist practitioners during ceremonies. The staff symbolizes the triumph of wisdom over illusion.

Kora: transliteration of the Tibetan word "Skor ra," meaning "circumambulation" or "revolution." The kora is performed by the pilgrim walking around the sacred site in the circumambulation in a clockwise direction, according to the traditions of Tibetan Buddhism. By circumambulating with the correct motivation, a person can purify their negative karma and can generate the seeds of enlightenment.

-la: the suffix "la" is a term of respect which can be affixed to the end of a title, as in "ani-la," or "gen-la," or can be affixed to the end of a personal name, as in "Ghedun-la."

Lama: Tibetan term used for a respected monk or high teacher.

Mala: a string of 108 prayer beads, one for each of the delusions (or worries) that afflict human life.

Mani stones: stone plates or rocks that are carved with the Tibetan Buddhism six-word mantra *Om Mani Padme Hum* or other mantras. Mani stones, or Jewel stones, as they are called, dot the entire Tibetan landscape. They are placed near monasteries, beside villages, along roadsides, along rivers and along long walls.

Mantra: phrases of words and syllables recited as an aid to concentration on a beneficial state of mind, in order to protect the mind from negative states. Mantras are spoken aloud or sounded internally in one's thoughts, and can be repeated continuously for some time or just sounded once. In the Buddhist practice, specific mantras like the Tara mantra (*Om Tare Tu Tare Ture Soha*) or the mantra of Avalokiteshvara, the bodhisattva of compassion (*Om Mani Padme Hung)* can be used to bring the mind greater compassion, better clarity or deeper understanding.

Momos: a type of steamed dumpling with a meat or vegetable filling.

Om Mani: first syllables of the mantra of Avalokiteshvara, the bodhisattva of compassion (*Om Mani Padme Hung),* often recited to focus and to protect the mind from negative states.

Om Tare: first syllables of the Tara mantra (*Om Tare Tu Tare Ture Soha*), often recited to focus and to protect the mind from negative states.

Prostration: placing your body flat on the ground, face down, in a submissive position. Prostrations are often performed before meditation or teachings, and believed to be a means of purifying one's body, speech and mind.

Sentient beings: term used in Buddhism to refer to the totality of living, conscious beings.

Sky burial: technically not a burial but a death ritual which entails taking the body to a designated site in the mountains, the charnel grounds, where it is left to feed vultures.

The custom is known as "jhator" in Tibetan, which means "giving alms to the bird." The Buddhists in Tibet believe that the soul is immortal and death is only the beginning of a new life. Instead of letting the body vanish naturally, it is better for almsgiving to another kind of life and liberates the soul from the body, enabling it to gain entry into rebirth.

Tara: female Bodhisattva, known as the "Mother of Liberation," and representing the virtues of success in work and achievements.

Thangka: Tibetan silk painting with embroidery, depicting a Buddhist deity, famous scene, or mandala.

Tsampa: ground-up, roasted barley flour. Traditionally, the tsampa is mixed with tea and a little butter from yak's milk.

Thenthuk: hand-pulled noodle soup whereby the dough is not modelled into noodles, but is flattened.

Weisang: ritual of burning branches of pine, cypress, and juniper trees to pray for blessings and offering gifts to gods. Weisang is done on many occasions, such as celebration of birth, wedding and harvest, warding off attacks by enemies, ensuring safety on a road trip, fending off illnesses, eliminating any evil, purify the air and attracting good luck.

Yak: long-haired, short-legged domesticated cattle. It that was probably domesticated in Tibet and introduced wherever there are people at elevations of 4,000–6,000 meters (14,000–20,000 feet) in the Himalayas - China, Central Asia, Mongolia and Nepal.

Made in the USA
Middletown, DE
23 August 2023

37188945R00194